FALLING FOR THE MARQUESS

The Strongs of Shadowcrest
Book Three

Alexa Aston

ARE YOU SIGNED UP FOR DRAGONBLADE'S BLOG?

You'll get the latest news and information on exclusive giveaways, exclusive excerpts, coming releases, sales, free books, cover reveals and more.

Check out our complete list of authors, too!

No spam, no junk. That's a promise!

Sign Up Here

www.dragonbladepublishing.com

Dearest Reader;

Thank you for your support of a small press. At Dragonblade Publishing, we strive to bring you the highest quality Historical Romance from some of the best authors in the business. Without your support, there is no 'us', so we sincerely hope you adore these stories and find some new favorite authors along the way.

Happy Reading!

CEO, Dragonblade Publishing

Additional Dragonblade books by Author Alexa Aston

The Strongs of Shadowcrest Series
The Duke's Unexpected Love (Book 1)
The Perks of Loving a Viscount (Book 2)
Falling for the Marquess (Book 3)
The Captain and the Duchess (Book 4)

Suddenly a Duke Series
Portrait of the Duke (Book 1)
Music for the Duke (Book 2)
Polishing the Duke (Book 3)
Designs on the Duke (Book 4)
Fashioning the Duke (Book 5)
Love Blooms with the Duke (Book 6)
Training the Duke (Book 7)
Investigating the Duke (Book 8)

Second Sons of London Series
Educated By The Earl (Book 1)
Debating With The Duke (Book 2)
Empowered By The Earl (Book 3)
Made for the Marquess (Book 4)
Dubious about the Duke (Book 5)
Valued by the Viscount (Book 6)
Meant for the Marquess (Book 7)

Dukes Done Wrong Series
Discouraging the Duke (Book 1)
Deflecting the Duke (Book 2)
Disrupting the Duke (Book 3)
Delighting the Duke (Book 4)
Destiny with a Duke (Book 5)

Dukes of Distinction Series
Duke of Renown (Book 1)
Duke of Charm (Book 2)
Duke of Disrepute (Book 3)
Duke of Arrogance (Book 4)
Duke of Honor (Book 5)
The Duke That I Want (Book 6)

The St. Clairs Series
Devoted to the Duke (Book 1)
Midnight with the Marquess (Book 2)
Embracing the Earl (Book 3)
Defending the Duke (Book 4)
Suddenly a St. Clair (Book 5)
Starlight Night (Novella)
The Twelve Days of Love (Novella)

Soldiers & Soulmates Series
To Heal an Earl (Book 1)
To Tame a Rogue (Book 2)
To Trust a Duke (Book 3)
To Save a Love (Book 4)
To Win a Widow (Book 5)
Yuletide at Gillingham (Novella)

King's Cousins Series
The Pawn (Book 1)
The Heir (Book 2)
The Bastard (Book 3)

Medieval Runaway Wives
Song of the Heart (Book 1)
A Promise of Tomorrow (Book 2)
Destined for Love (Book 3)

Knights of Honor Series
Word of Honor (Book 1)
Marked by Honor (Book 2)
Code of Honor (Book 3)

Journey to Honor (Book 4)
Heart of Honor (Book 5)
Bold in Honor (Book 6)
Love and Honor (Book 7)
Gift of Honor (Book 8)
Path to Honor (Book 9)
Return to Honor (Book 10)

The Lyon's Den Series
The Lyon's Lady Love

Pirates of Britannia Series
God of the Seas

De Wolfe Pack: The Series
Rise of de Wolfe

The de Wolfes of Esterley Castle
Diana
Derek
Thea

Also from Alexa Aston
The Bridge to Love (Novella)
One Magic Night

PROLOGUE

Battle of Talavera—Spain—28 July 1809

CAPTAIN AUGUST HOLT quickly gazed from left to right, his mind whirling at breakneck speed.

The British and Portuguese joint forces were in trouble. The allies had taken up a defensive position just east of Talavera and had already repulsed two attacks from the enemy at Medellin, one late yesterday evening and again at dawn this morning. The lull afterward had given both sides time to recuperate, and now the French had declared a full assault.

Sherbrooke's infantry was in disarray as Wellesley tried to plug the gap. August knew the numbers thanks to the officer's meeting he had been present at only a few hours ago in Wellesley's tent. The French had ten thousand men now advancing against the three thousand soldiers of the British-Portuguese alliance. It would be a bloodbath, regardless of which side won.

And August would go down fighting for king and crown.

He gave the signal, leading his men in a charge, shouting encouragement, his voice already hoarse from the previous engagements and trying to be heard over the dueling cannons from each side. If Ruffin's division could make headway, then Wellington's 48th Foot could plug the hole left by Sherbrooke's unsuccessful attack. August would do everything in his power to aid the British commander's efforts.

He had a pistol in his right hand and a saber in his left as he raced along the battlefield, leaping over the bodies of fallen comrades. A few horses surged forward from behind him, all but one passing him. That one mount shrieked, being struck by fire. August tried to bolt to his left as the horse fell, but he didn't get far enough away, and the beast knocked him to the ground, even as its rider sailed past him.

Stunned for a moment, he felt the weight of the horse pressing against him and realized he was trapped beneath it. The fallen rider tried to pull the horse from August, but it was an impossible task for one man.

Then the cavalryman also was felled by a bullet, and August lay helplessly on the ground. His pistol had been knocked from his hand, but at least he still clung to the sword, though how he would be able to use it was doubtful.

All around him, he heard the shouts and cries of the wounded and dying as soldiers ran past him in both directions. He tried to move his legs, but he was pinned. It would take several men to release him. Already, breathing was becoming difficult, the dying horse's weight unbearable.

"Ah, an officer," a soldier said in French. "Waiting to be butchered."

Perhaps it wasn't a good thing that he spoke the language fluently.

Replying in French, he told his enemy, "Move along. You see I am helpless. Where is your honor? Would you kill a defenseless man?"

"With great pleasure. Even if you are an Englishman who speaks flawless French."

The soldier stepped on August's left wrist, tearing away the saber.

"I shall claim this beauty for myself," he said matter-of-factly, already smiling at the sword.

August knew death was only moments away, most likely at the hands of his own weapon.

The Frenchman laughed and swiped the blade across the throat of the horse, which shuddered and then stilled. Then he swung the sword high, bringing it down. August threw up his left hand, trying to protect himself, feeling the blade slice through fingers and part of his palm. Pain shot through him, and he gasped, his right hand clutching the damaged left one, bringing it to his chest. Blood poured from the hand, and he saw three of his fingers barely attached.

His enemy cackled, swinging the sword high again, bringing it down once more. It struck the top of August's head, moving down to his brow, his eye, and slicing open his cheek. The white-hot pain sizzled, making him feel as if he were on fire. Blood poured from his left eye, clouding his vision.

It was over. His life would end on this Spanish field. All the risks he had taken, all the bravery he had shown, and he would die at the hands of a foot soldier who showed him no mercy. But he would meet death and look it straight in the eye.

August raised his face to his attacker, the blood freely flowing down his face, the gloating Frenchman standing over him laughing.

Then the laughter died. A perplexed look came over his killer's features.

And August saw the sword protruding from the man's chest.

He blinked several times, realizing someone had run a sword through the Frenchman from behind, the blade entering his body and coming out the other side. He watched as one of his own men placed his foot on the Frenchman's back and yanked hard, withdrawing the sword, as another man in his command pushed the dead body hard.

"We'll get you out from there, Captain," he was promised.

August continued to hold his injured hand to his chest, taking shallow breaths. Enough men must have been summoned because suddenly the weight of the dead beast was lifted.

Someone grabbed his legs, dragging him away. He could breathe again, gasping as he filled his lungs with air.

Then he was lifted and being carried, a voice saying, "Get him to the surgeon. Now."

As he was jostled along the uneven ground, he heard the others who carried him tell him that the 48th had collapsed France's second line's attack and that Lapisse himself was supposedly dead.

He could smell the grass fires, though, as they swept across the battlefield, the wounded calling out in desperation to be moved before they burned alive. August closed his eyes again, but he could not close his ears.

He would hear those screams for the rest of his life.

If he lived.

After what seemed like an eternity, the men jogging with him came to a halt, and he determined they had reached camp.

"Get me to Morrow," he commanded. "He is the best."

"Yes, Captain!" his three saviors cried in unison.

He must have passed out from the pain because when he awoke, he was on a makeshift table, probably a barn door, the most common thing used to act as a surgical base during operations.

"He is coming around. Pour plenty of brandy down his throat. I'm going to have to take the eye—and possibly the hand."

August looked up, seeing Dr. Morrow with his right eye, the left still a bloody mess.

"You can't save the eye?" he asked weakly.

"No, Captain." The surgeon placed a hand on August's shoulder. "But I will try to save what I can of the hand."

Someone helped him to sit up, and a bottle was brought to his lips. He caught the strong scent of brandy and was urged to drink. He continued to do so, knowing it would help dull the pain. He prayed he would pass out from a combination of drunkenness and pain, and he did.

When he awoke, August ached everywhere. He was prone,

on a cot, and sensed many others around him. Slowly, he raised his left hand, seeing the thick bandage around it. He tried flexing his wrist and found he could. That something was still on the other side of it. He then tried to wriggle his fingers, but the bandage was wrapped too firmly about his hand.

He brought his right hand up to his face. The left side was swathed in bandages. Without being told, he knew the eye was gone. His brow and cheek were also covered in gauze. Letting his hand fall, he closed his one good eye and surrendered to sleep again.

The next time he awoke, it was because someone shook him.

"Let's try to sit up, Captain," someone suggested. "I've got broth for you. You need something inside you."

As he allowed the soldier to help him move to a sitting position, he heard Dr. Morrow say, "The broth can wait. Let me speak to him first."

"Yes, Doctor."

August moved his legs from the cot, placing his feet on the ground. He felt woozy, from either blood loss or from having drunk too much brandy. Or both.

The surgeon knelt before him. "You still have your hand, minus the last three fingers. They had been cut through the bone and were only hanging on by a thread of skin. Having your thumb and index finger will help, though."

"Help me do what?" he said, not bothering to disguise his bitterness.

Morrow looked at him with sympathy. "Live."

"What about infection?" he growled, knowing oftentimes it was infection which killed an injured man and not the wounds themselves.

"We are keeping an eye on that, Captain Holt," the doctor assured him. "Both on your hand and your head and face."

He lifted a hand to touch it, but Morrow guided it down.

"The less you can touch it, the better. At least, that is what I have found. You are lucky to be alive, Captain."

"I don't seem to feel so lucky," he said. "You know what this will mean?"

The surgeon nodded wearily, having seen it all too often. "You will be ordered to sell your commission. The crown is grateful for your service to His Majesty, but an officer with one eye cannot lead troops into battle."

"Exactly. I might as well be dead."

Morrow laid a hand on August's shoulder. "Don't say that, man. Never say that. Life is too often taken for granted. By God, I've saved yours."

"If infection doesn't kill me," he added morosely.

"True. But you will get to go home to England. To peace. No more fighting. No more killing. No more scent of death in your nostrils, so deeply ingrained that you will never be rid of it."

"There is that," August said, seeing the green of Edgefield in his mind.

"Eat the broth. The more liquids we can get in you, the better. The sooner you have regained at least some of your strength and can move about, the quicker I can send the papers to your commander that will let you go home."

Home. What truly was there for him?

August was a second son. He would return to England a damaged man. There would be no title. He would be hideous to look at. He supposed he could retreat to his father's country estate. Edgefield was in Surrey, just five miles from Surrey's border with Kent. Perhaps he would be granted a cottage and live out his days in the woods, far from others.

"Bring the broth then," he commanded. Softening his tone, he said, "Don't think I am not grateful, Morrow. I am. I simply will have to adjust to a life I have no wish to live."

"You are a resourceful man, Holt. I think you might surprise yourself and find something worthwhile to do."

He accepted the broth from the private who offered it, even asking for a second bowl. Once his belly was full, he lay back on his cot once more, falling into a dreamless sleep.

The next days passed in the same fashion. He slept. Awoke. Saw Dr. Morris and had his wounds redressed. Ate. Then slept some more.

After a week, he noticed very few were still around him, and figured they had either died or been sent back to the front. He asked about the battle and learned the majority of Joseph Bonaparte's force had fallen back to defend Madrid. Casualties for the French at Talavera numbered over seventy-three hundred, while Wellesley's losses made up more than a quarter of his forces. Because the commander had lost so many men and Soult had a fresh army threatening to cut all lines of communication, Wellington had withdrawn his army once more to Portugal, leaving behind the wounded.

Even Dr. Morris was about to leave to rejoin Wellington's troops and came to say goodbye to August.

"I spoke to your commanding officer on your behalf, Captain Holt," the army doctor said. "He came to see you early on."

"I do not recall that at all."

"He put in for the papers which would allow for your commission to be sold. Records stated that your father, the Marquess of Edgethorne, had purchased it on your behalf. Once sold, the monies will be sent to his solicitor."

His father wrote to August upon occasion, while his brother wrote with regularity. August wondered if Father would allow him to keep the proceeds from the sale of the commission in order to live on. He thought it a reasonable request, especially after all he had given to his country.

Withdrawing parchment from his coat, Dr. Morris said, "This letter came for you the day of the battle. I held it until now, waiting for you to be well enough to open it."

Morris offered his hand. "I am leaving, Captain Holt. I must catch up with our troops in Portugal. You are to stay here another three days. At that time, your bandages can come off both your hand and face. Let me give them a look and change your dressings for the final time."

He forced himself to sit patiently as the doctor examined him. Normally, August was a restless man, never staying still for long, but Morris had taken good care of him and showed more concern for him than August would have expected.

The doctor applied some type of salve and then fresh bandages were again placed upon his wounds.

Holding up the jar of salve, Morris said, "Keep this. It is almost full. Even after the bandages come off, place it upon your face, in particular, until it runs out. You might also wish to consult a doctor once you return to England."

"How bad do I look?"

He had never asked to see a hand mirror, and none had been offered to him.

"You will be given an eyepatch to wear. Keep it on at all times unless you are sleeping. I will be frank, Captain. You are not a welcomed sight. I stitched up where your eye was, and that doesn't look half-bad. You will have a scar, though, on part of your forehead and the length of your cheek. It is angry and red now, much as you are angry inside for losing control of your life. But it will fade in time."

Morris looked at him in sympathy, gentling his voice. "Try to also let your anger inside fade, August. I know you did not ask for this. That it is something you will live with the rest of your life. But do not let it control your life."

He snorted. "Easy for you to say, with your pretty looks, Doctor."

Morris laughed. "At least your sense of humor is returning. But I am serious. Don't let this injury affect how you view yourself."

Shaking his head, he said, "It will be the very first thing others see when they look at me, Morris. You and I both know people judge others by what they see. I will be ridiculed. Pitied. I cannot help but be angry. Some worthless, nameless French bastard has ruined my life. I no longer have my good looks, much less my position in His Majesty's army. My life might as well be over."

"You may feel that way now, Captain, but I hope your attitude will change in time. That your family and friends will accept you because they know the man you are. Will others judge you by your appearance? Most certainly. But their opinions are not important. Be true to yourself, Captain Holt."

Dr. Morris paused. "Write to me. Tell me how you fare. And I don't mean once and think your obligation is ended. Write to me in six months' time. Again, in a year. Even five years from now. Once those five years have passed, I will excuse you from that obligation."

"Obligation?"

Morris smiled. "Then shall we call it a request? I do want to hear from you. And I believe as the years pass, your attitude will soften toward your appearance. That you will find the important things in life and enjoy those simple things."

He shrugged. "We shall see."

"Read your letter then, Captain Holt. I hope we will meet up again someday."

The doctor left, and August turned his attention to the letter. The handwriting was unfamiliar to him, and that did not bode well.

He opened it, his eye falling immediately to the closing, seeing it had been written by a P. Thomas, a name he could not recall ever hearing before. He returned to the top of the page.

1 May 1809

Dear Captain Holt —

I know we have not been introduced, but I have been Lord Edgethorne's solicitor for the last several years. I regret to inform you that your father passed away last week, and he was buried in Surrey, in the Edgewood churchyard, two days ago.

His affairs were in excellent order, and your brother has assumed the title. Unfortunately, his poor health prevented him from leaving London and traveling to Surrey for the burial service.

I do not by any means wish to be presumptuous, Captain Holt, but I must express my concern regarding your family's holdings. Lord Edgethorne—that is, your father—spent the bulk of his time in London and rarely went to Edgefield. Now that your brother has become Lord Edgethorne, his health is even more precarious. I fear he will not be long for this world.

My professional advice would be for you to sell your commission and come home to see to the business affairs of your family. Your brother shows no interest in them nor any inclination to remedy things left undone during your father's time of holding the title. Because you are now the heir apparent, I suggest you return to England at once, not only to care for your brother in his last days but to see to your family's affairs.

I hope you will be able to make due haste and return to England, Captain Holt. It would be for the best.

Your humble servant,
P. Thomas

His father dead. Peter apparently dying. And him now half a man, one whom the army no longer had any interest in.

"Well, I shall be home sooner than I expected, Mr. P. Thomas," August said aloud.

CHAPTER ONE

London—September 1809

AUGUST LEFT THE ship which had brought him from Spain to England.

To home . . .

But would home ever be the same to him again?

He was coming back to an England he probably remembered in a different way than before he went to war. He had only been in His Majesty's army four years, but those years at war had hardened him. Changed him. Once, he had been a handsome, charming, lighthearted bachelor. Attending university during the year and then events of the Season before he graduated and took up his commission. He had danced with pretty girls. Flirted with them. Bedded willing widows. Life had been joyful. Worries, nonexistent.

All that was over now. England might not have changed—but August Holt most certainly had.

He had only looked at himself once in the mirror when the bandages came off his face, trying to hide his horror at the reflection staring back at him.

While Dr. Morris had told him the scars would fade with time, they were still a bright, angry red, fresh in appearance.

Now, he sported a black eyepatch to cover where his left eye had once been. He left it on all the time, except when he slept. He could not imagine going without it. Since leaving the army hospital, he had received looks ranging from outright curiosity to disgust to horror—and that had been from the hardened sailors aboard this vessel. August tried to prepare himself for the reactions he would see from members of the public.

As they floated down the Thames toward the London docks, he went to find the captain.

"I wanted to thank you for making room for me on your vessel, Captain. As you know, it is imperative that I reach home as soon as possible."

The grizzled seaman nodded. "I want to thank you for your service to England, Captain Holt. Somehow, some way, I hope that Britain and her allies can stop this monster called Bonaparte."

"I have every faith we will, sir."

August said his farewell and returned to the miniscule cabin he had been given, collecting the rucksack which held all his worldly goods. A change of clothing. His shaving razor. And the letter he had received from Thomas, the solicitor.

As he made his way back to the deck, he wondered if he should go and see this solicitor first or head directly to his father's townhouse. No, Peter's townhouse, he corrected himself.

He would want to meet with Peter's doctor to understand his brother's diagnosis, as well as see if what Thomas had written was true and that Peter only had a short while to live.

The old August would have barreled into the situation without a backward glance. The new, more introspective man he was quickly becoming decided a visit to the solicitor would be his first step upon arrival.

As they sailed along the river, he watched the people scurrying along the docks. It would be good to be back on English soil and get a decent cup of coffee. Even small things such as a scone now took on greater significance. August had put up with army rations for years, and he was ready to indulge in a good meal and take his time digesting it.

The ship came to rest in its slip, dropping anchor, sailors hurrying to and fro on the deck. The gangplank was quickly lowered, and before it was barely in place, a group of dock workers hurried up it. He assumed they would be unloading the cargo below brought back by the ship. Very few passengers were aboard, only two that he knew of beside himself, both of them injured soldiers such as himself. One had lost a leg and had kept to his cabin, eating all his meals there. The other soldier had been blinded in a cannon attack, and he, too, had remained in his cabin, having all meals brought to him.

August tamped down the bitterness that filled him, thinking of those two men's predicaments. At least he had all four limbs and could get about, as well as the sight from one eye.

He glanced down at his gloved left hand, wistful for the missing fingers. His fingers would never again grace the keys of a pianoforte. Still, he had his right to use when he ate and wrote. He only wondered what his life would consist of now.

The rush of workers ended, and the gangplank was empty for a moment. August took the opportunity to descend, finally stepping onto English soil. He walked a few minutes, heading away from the waterfront, caught up in the hustle and bustle of the crowd, trying not to shy away from the noise. He had been the bravest of officers, leading men into battle, but since his injuries, he wanted nothing to do with being around noise or large groups of people. He supposed a quiet life in the country would be the most satisfying one and determined to go to Edgefield as soon as possible, where he could avoid the stares of strangers.

Peter had never enjoyed life in the country. His precarious health had prevented him from the pursuits August enjoyed so well—riding, hunting, and fishing. His brother had been drawn to his books and studies, first attending school, and then finishing with a tutor at home. Even as children, August had protected his older brother from bullies at school. Though two years ahead,

Peter had always been small and slight, weak, and perpetually out of breath. Walking across a room brought his brother to the point of exhaustion. Boys at school had picked at Peter constantly, and August had fought every one of them. He had gained many a black eye—as well as given several—in defense of the brother he loved.

He passed a food vendor's cart, and the smell of the pies caused his belly to growl angrily. Retracing his steps, he paused in front of the cart and simply inhaled.

"Smell good to you, Captain?" the old woman manning the cart asked.

Grateful she had not flinched, nor mentioned his condition, he said, "It smells heavenly. I would like two meat pies. Please," he added, thinking he needed to get used to such niceties again in everyday speech.

The woman handed the pies over to August, and he held them under his nose, inhaling deeply.

"I have just returned from Spain, and this will be the best meal I have eaten in years," he told the woman.

Reaching into his pocket for a coin, she waved it away when he tried to hand it over.

"For your service, Captain," she said, smiling, revealing a gap where teeth should have been. "My boy is in the army now. Couldn't be prouder of him. It's the least I can do for one who has fought so well."

August doffed his hat to her. "My thanks, madam. You have warmed this soldier's heart with your graciousness. I hope your boy comes home soon and with his health intact."

"I pray for that very thing each night, Captain," she said. "Godspeed."

He walked the street slowly, chewing thoughtfully on his pies as he did, not rushing, wanting to savor each bite. It truly was the best thing he had eaten since the farewell dinner his father had held in August's honor before he had left to take up his commission and enter officer training.

He hadn't yet dealt with his father's death, deliberately pushing it from his mind. The old man had been hard on him, twice as hard as he should have been, but even back then, August had realized he was being pushed for two since his father could not discipline Peter. August had gained a grudging respect for the marquess, and it hurt to think he would never see or speak with his father again. Thomas' letter did not give any details regarding the marquess' death, and that would be something he would ask the solicitor about.

The pies eaten, he withdrew the solicitor's letter from his coat pocket, once more checking the address of the man's offices. Flagging down a hansom cab, August gave the address to the driver, who couldn't bring himself to look his passenger in the face. It took a good three-quarters of an hour to get through the busy streets of London, but he didn't mind. He looked at the sights, seeing new buildings which had sprung up during his absence.

The driver pulled up, and August paid him, exiting the vehicle. He entered the building and stopped at the first desk he came to, where a clerk looked up.

"May I help you?" the clerk asked. Then his eyes widened, and he visibly swallowed as he took in August's appearance. To his credit, though, the man steadied himself and said, "Thank you for your service, Captain."

It surprised him how many people recognized his rank based upon his uniform. Then again, Britain had a long, illustrious history at war, and the newspapers were always full of accounts of the army and navy and the various battles fought upon land and sea.

"My name is August Holt. I received a letter from Mr. Thomas regarding the death of my father, the Marquess of Edgethorne."

Recognition appeared in the clerk's eyes at hearing the name. "Mr. Thomas will certainly want to visit with you, Captain Holt. If you would have a seat, I will let him know you are here.

Presently, he is with a client, but he shouldn't be engaged but for another quarter-hour or so."

"Thank you," he said, taking a seat on the bench the clerk had indicated.

As he waited, his eye roamed about the office. It was a habit of those who had gone to war. A soldier, especially an officer, constantly assessed a situation and his surroundings. Within seconds, he knew how many workers were in the office. Their locations. Whether they would pose a threat or not.

He shook his head, trying to clear it. These men were civilians. They held no threat to him. He would have to change his mindset now that he was back in a civilized place.

A gentleman in his late thirties appeared, looking satisfied, and August judged him to be the client Mr. Thomas had been with. As the man sailed through the office, he did not bother to stop and thank anyone.

When he reached the area where August sat, the man froze in his tracks, his jaw dropping. His eyes widened as he studied August a moment, and then he shuddered violently, giving him a wide berth as he left the office.

As if August's scars were catching.

The clerk he had spoken with rose from his desk and disappeared down a long hallway. He was gone several minutes and when he returned, another man accompanied him.

The man had to be Mr. Thomas. He was in his early forties, with graying temples and light blue eyes. Apparently, the clerk had warned his employer regarding Austin's appearance because the solicitor approached him without trepidation.

The solicitor offered his hand. "I am Mr. Thomas, Captain Holt. It is good to see you back in England."

He shook the man's hand and joked, "I consumed two meat pies the moment I left the ship which brought me here. It was the best meal I have eaten in years."

Thomas chuckled. "I have heard rumors of how pitiful army food can be. Is it the same fare for officers as other soldiers?"

"Upon occasion, officers dine a bit better than the men in the field. For the most part, however, we eat from the same stewpots and chew on the same moldy bread as did others."

The solicitor had a little trouble meeting his client's eye, but he said, "Shall we go to my office? I am sure you have questions, and I am happy to answer them."

As they walked past the other desks, he was aware of the surreptitious glances he received. He would have to learn to ignore them because they would be a part of his life from now on. Even if he did not bear the horrible scar from the sword, others would always be curious as to why he wore an eyepatch.

They entered a cozy office, and August took one of the chairs in front of the desk as Thomas sat behind it.

"Could you tell me about my father's death?" he began. "Your letter mentioned he was buried in the churchyard at Edgewood, but I would like to know the particulars."

"Of course," Thomas said. "From what I gather, it was a massive heart attack. Lord Edgethorne was in the card room during a ball, in the midst of a winning streak. A witness shared with me that your father placed his cards upon the table—four kings—and begin raking in his winnings. His last words were supposedly, 'I will take every man at this table for whatever he ventures to gamble tonight.'

"Then Lord Edgethorne clutched his chest, and his head dropped to the table, his face buried in the chips he had just won. It was instantaneous, Captain Holt. The marquess did not suffer."

August nodded. "Then he went out as he would have liked. My father was known for his luck at cards."

"I accompanied his body back to Edgefield, along with Redding, his butler in town, and Pole, his valet. Unfortunately, your brother's health did not allow him to make the trip."

"You wrote of Peter's unstable health," August pressed. "Frankly, he has been fragile his entire life."

A grim expression crossed the solicitor's face. "I would not have advised you to sell out and come home immediately if I did not think Lord Edgethorne's death imminent."

He sighed. "I had no choice but to come home, Thomas. The army no longer wanted me in the condition I am now in. Thank you for being polite and not asking me about my injuries."

The solicitor looked uncomfortable. "I assumed the injuries were recent, Captain. It is not my place to comment on a client's appearance, however."

"I fear many people will comment about it, either to my face or behind my back." He rose. "I will go to see my brother now. Do you know his doctor's name? I will wish to speak with him, as well."

"Dr. Brown lives in Lord Edgethorne's household and has for several years now, in order to care for your brother." Thomas paused. "We have many things to discuss, Captain Holt."

He frowned. "I assume you mean estate matters."

"Yes."

"Everything can wait until I see Peter," he insisted. "When the time comes and I am responsible for everything, you and I will have a long chat. Until then, Thomas, my brother is the marquess. I have no say—or power—in his affairs."

He rose, and Thomas also came to his feet, sympathy filling his eyes. "Be warned, Captain. Your brother is gravely ill. You must be ready to assume your responsibilities sooner rather than later."

"I will not let down the tenants or anyone else," he declared. "But now is not the time to speak of the title or finances."

"I understand," the solicitor said.

"I will be in touch," he told the man, leaving the office.

He was tired of sitting and decided to walk to Mayfair. It would only be two miles or so. August regretted the decision, however, seeing the stares. Hearing the titters. Observing people move away from him. The sooner he could escape the throngs of London, the better.

His knock was answered by a footman, who gasped loudly when he caught sight of August. He recognized the servant and smiled wryly.

"I have come home, Wilson."

Recovering, the longtime footman said, "Come in, Captain. You are in time. Barely."

"For?" he asked, dreading the answer.

Reddening, the butler appeared. Stoic as ever, he said, "It is good to see you, Captain Holt. Please come with me. His lordship is almost gone. You are in time to say your goodbyes to him."

Hurt, mixed with anger, ran through him. Even knowing that Peter was in poor health, he had figured they would be able to spend some time together. Now, he was being cheated out of that.

As they went up the grand staircase, Redding said, "Lord Edgethorne did not relocate to the ducal rooms upon your father's death. Dr. Brown thought it unwise to move him."

"I see."

The butler led him to the rooms Peter had always had and opened the door without knocking. The two men slipped inside the darkened room, the heavy curtains having been drawn against the incoming sunlight.

A man stood at the bedside, and August determined him to be Dr. Brown. He turned and motioned August over.

He moved slowly, his eye focused on his brother. Peter lay in the bed, looking so frail and pale, August wondered if he still might be breathing.

He came to stand at the foot of the bed. "How is he?" he asked the physician.

"It is the end," the doctor said bluntly. "He will not live to see another day. I assume you are his brother?"

"I am." Anguish filled him as he studied Peter. "Can nothing be done?"

"Lord Edgethorne suffers greatly, Captain Holt. The rheumatic fever from his childhood caused permanent damage to his heart. He has also developed rheumatism, unrelated to the fever, but it has inflamed his joints and muscles, causing him constant pain. I was about to give him more morphine to ease his suffering."

"Don't, yet," Peter said weakly from the bed. "It dulls my mind. Makes me sleep." He gave a half-hearted smile to August. "Good of you to make it home, Brother."

He moved to the side of the bed and sat, taking Peter's hand in his. "I came as soon as I could."

His brother winced, moaning softly. "I see you have suffered as I have. At least you did so in honor of king and country." Peter sighed. "I'm certain there's a story to tell behind that eyepatch."

"Not to mention the scars," August said lightly. "You must grow stronger so that I might tell you about it."

"No," Peter said softly. "My strength is gone, August. My life is at an end."

"Don't say that," he insisted, his insides crying out, his love for Peter great.

"I am ready to go," Peter admitted. "I have suffered greatly these last two years. I am just sorry to be leaving you in such a mess."

"What mess?" he asked.

"Father never cared much for Edgefield. You must do a better job and see that it runs the way it should. That its people are cared for."

"I will do so," he promised solemnly.

"You must also wed."

"What? You talk of marriage at a time such as this?" he protested.

"I do. You are all that is left, August. You will soon be Edgethorne. You need to wed and have a house full of children."

He shook his head. "Has your sight also been affected, Peter? What woman would have me, looking as I am?"

"Several. You will have a title and money. Looks won't matter. You will have women chase you, wanting to be your marchioness. Promise me you will wed, August. That you will attend the Season next spring and choose a bride."

He said nothing, thinking Peter wrong. What woman would want to be with a scarred beast of a man such as himself?

"Promise," his brother insisted, his voice growing weaker. "That you will attend. Marry. Have children. Have many of them, August. Love them. Shower them with love. I know Father was so hard on you. I think you can teach children respect and love them without spoiling them."

Peter suddenly shuddered, groaning loudly, arching in the bed.

"No more talk," Dr. Brown said. "Lord Edgethorne, I am giving you the morphine."

August stood and stepped away from the bed as the physician injected Peter. It only took a few moments for a dreamy look to appear on his face.

"August?" he said, his voice faint.

"I am here, Peter," he said, returning to sit on the bed, holding his brother's hand once more.

"This is it. Promise . . . me. You'll wed . . ."

"Dammit it, Peter." Frustration filled him, but he wanted his brother to have peace. "All right. I promise. I'll find some chit this coming Season."

"Thank . . . you. Love . . .you . . ."

"I love you, too," August said, his voice breaking.

He was aware of Dr. Brown's presence in the room as he concentrated on his brother's face. It grew peaceful. Peter's breathing evened out—and then slowed.

Minutes later, a stillness set in, and he knew his brother was now gone. Still, he held onto Peter's hand, already regretting the promise he had made.

One which he was honor-bound to keep.

Despite his brother's warning, August thought it would be difficult to find a woman in Polite Society who would agree to wed him. If he did find a lady desperate enough to do so, at least they could couple in the dark so she wouldn't have to look upon him.

Releasing Peter's hand, August stood.

"He is gone," he told Dr. Brown.

Now, he was the Marquess of Edgethorne.

CHAPTER TWO

London—February 1810

Lady Georgina Strong awoke and rolled over, eager to tell her twin about the silly dream she had had.

But Pippa wasn't there.

Georgie flipped to her back, still getting used to the idea of not having her twin with her anymore. Pippa had wed Viscount Hopewell six weeks ago, and the couple had set off on a honeymoon which would take them around the world. It had been an adjustment, not having her twin by her side each day, sharing all the little things that happened. It would be even more difficult going into her come-out Season without Pippa by her side, but Georgie had encouraged her twin and Seth to go ahead and take their honeymoon.

More than anything, Georgie yearned for love. She knew it existed because she had seen how happy Pippa and Seth were together, along with their brother James and his recent bride Sophie. While Georgie had counted on her twin's advice as they hit the Marriage Mart, she knew now she must trust her own heart in making the most important decision of her life.

Finding a husband whom she could love.

They had come to town yesterday, her entire family, so that

gowns could be made up for this upcoming Season. Georgie and Mama had already been fitted by the modiste when they came to London before Christmas to see to Pippa's wedding gown and wardrobe, so Madame Dumas had begun work on their wardrobes.

Today, though, it would be the other Strong siblings and cousins who went to Madame's shop to be measured and start the process. Alongside Georgie in this come-out would be her sister Mirella and her cousins Allegra and Lyric, who had grown up in the Strong household. If anyone could manage the come-out of four girls at the same time, it would be Mama, the most capable woman Georgie knew. Mama would have help from Aunt Matty, who was also looking forward to the upcoming Season since neither Aunt Matty nor Mama had attended one during the last three years. The Duke of Seaton had been gravely ill during that time, bedridden thanks to an attack of apoplexy, and her father had passed away from its lingering effects.

That was all in the past now. It would be a new Season, one which Mama would participate in, alongside all but the youngest of her girls. Pippa and Georgie had encouraged their mother to look for a new husband. Mama had been ordered to wed the Duke of Seaton during her own come-out Season, when she was only seven and ten. She was still the most beautiful woman Georgie had ever seen, and she hoped that her mother could find lasting love, perhaps even have another child.

After ringing for a maid and Kitty dressing Georgie for the day, she went downstairs for breakfast, learning she had already missed James and Sophie. Her sister-in-law owned Neptune Shipping Lines, which had been in direct competition with the family's own shipping line. It was unusual for a woman of the *ton* to own anything, much less run a business empire, but Sophie was a most unusual and capable woman. She went to her shipping offices most days when she was in town, and James was also taking an active role in Strong Shipping since his return from being a captain on the Seven Seas.

Mirella and Effie were already at breakfast, Effie teasing her older sister about having stolen the bedclothes from her last night.

"If you do not stop hogging them," Effie said, "I shall move next door and sleep with Georgie."

"Hah!" Mirella said. "Georgie snores. Pippa always told us that. Do you want to be kept up all night, listening to her snoring?" Mirella teased good-naturedly.

Lyric and Allegra entered the breakfast room. The twins had been born on the same day as Georgie and Pippa had been. Their mother died in childbirth, however, and their father had given the infants over to the Duchess of Seaton to raise. Uncle Adolphus preferred sons to daughters, and he left her cousin Theo, who was the oldest of the siblings, along with his brother Caleb, in his household. Georgie hadn't seen her uncle or Theo in several months, not since Papa had passed and James had become the new Duke of Seaton.

As for Caleb, he was their steward at Shadowcrest, the country seat of the Duke of Seaton. She liked her cousin Caleb quite a bit and had enjoyed getting to know him once they had returned to Shadowcrest after Papa's death.

Mama and Aunt Matty came in together and took their seats, as well, making breakfast a lively meal.

"We will leave for Madame Dumas' shop once we have all finished our breakfast," Mama told their group. "Since there are so many of us, we will take two carriages."

An hour later, both of those carriages pulled up outside the modiste's dress shop. The women disembarked and entered, and Madame Dumas and her assistants greeted them.

"I have many gowns ready for Her Grace and Lady Georgina to try on," the modiste proclaimed. "My assistants will get the measurements of you other ladies, and we will sit and talk patterns and fabrics afterward."

They went to the rear of the store, and she and Mama tried on all the gowns which had been made up for them since their last visit to town. After the others had been measured, Madame instructed her assistants to take them to the front of the store so that they might begin looking at various fabrics under Aunt Matty's guidance. Even Effie was measured and would have several new gowns, though she was too young to make her come-out at this time.

Georgie liked every gown which had been prepared for her, feeling she looked like a princess in a fairy tale. She had high hopes of finding a husband during her come-out Season, but she also knew she would settle for nothing except love. James and Pippa had made love matches, and she was being encouraged to do the same even by Mama. Papa had married Mama simply because she was young, and he wanted to get sons off her, his first wife having died, leaving him only with James. Georgie still thought it amusing that Mama had given the duke four daughters instead.

She was being assisted out of the last gown when Lyric returned.

"Oh, Georgie, that is simply beautiful. Pippa was right. You are going to be the most beautiful and envied debutante of this Season."

"Have you found some fabrics you like?" she asked her cousin.

"Several, in fact," Lyric replied. "Allegra and I do not mind trading gowns, however. You know we are of a similar size though her breasts are a bit larger than mine. I doubt anyone will notice if we do so. She can wear some first, and then the bodice can be cut down to fit me."

Georgie thought otherwise, having heard the women of the *ton* gossiped furiously, especially about gowns. She would let Mama deal with that, however. Mama would see no reason for the twins having to share dresses.

She told Lyric she would be out in a moment, and her cousin started to leave the dressing room but stopped in her tracks as Madame Dumas asked Mama, "I hate to bring up such matters,

Your Grace, but how am I to bill everything?"

Georgie glanced to her cousin and saw Lyric had stepped through the curtains but still lingered there.

"Why, send everything to His Grace," Mama said.

"Even the Misses Strongs' gowns?" the modiste pressed.

"Especially their gowns," her mother confirmed. "His Grace will pay for everything regarding Allegra and Lyric and their come-outs."

She looked at her cousin and saw her lips thinning. Lyric whirled and was gone.

She didn't think James paying for her cousins' gowns was anything to be concerned about. As the Duke of Seaton, he was quite wealthy. From what Caleb had shared, Shadowcrest turned a healthy profit each year, as did all the other ducal estates scattered through England. Then there was Strong Shipping, one of the largest and most profitable businesses in the country. Yes, a come-out was quite expensive because of the large number of gowns to be made, but Lyric shouldn't concern herself with the costs.

The assistant helped Georgie into the gown she had worn to the shop, and she lingered, watching Mama try on the last gown which had been sewn for her. Her mother still possessed a stunning figure after having produced four girls early in her marriage. She thought perhaps Mama might even receive an offer of marriage before Georgie herself did.

Mama was dressed again in her own gown, and she and Madame Dumas discussed the remaining gowns which would be made up for herself and Georgie.

"Now, we must go and see about the others," the modiste said. "We can take as long as necessary, Your Grace. I have closed the shop for the day. With all the gowns I will be making for the Strong women, I doubt I will take on any more clients this Season."

"Remember, I am perfectly happy to hire another seamstress or two if that will help you, Madame. They can even live at our townhouse. That might be more convenient for fittings."

They adjourned to the front of the shop, where Aunt Matty and the others were in an animated discussion. Her aunt had already selected the material she wanted, saying she only needed a handful of gowns.

"At my age, few look at what I am wearing, but it will be nice to show off to my friends, whom I have not seen in a long time."

Left unsaid was how Aunt Matty had been banished to the country by Uncle Adolphus when she had challenged how her brother had taken over the ducal household, assuming all the power and wealth which came with the title, even though his brother still held it. Her uncle had kept the Strong women virtual prisoners in London, not allowing them to go anywhere and keeping them from seeing Papa. Aunt Matty's outspokenness had earned her a trip to Shadowcrest, where she had remained until her brother passed and James claimed the title, appearing unexpectedly after years of being thought dead.

She thought it had served her uncle right, and Georgie had not been unhappy to see him and Cousin Theo depart from their household.

Mirella eagerly began talking, showing Madame and Mama several fabrics she had chosen, and the modiste began sketching designs for those gowns.

Effie, who sat next to Georgie, leaned over and sniffed. "I know Mama wanted me to come to see what this was all about, but I am bored to tears," her sister proclaimed.

Effie was a tomboy, much as Pippa had been, and preferred living in the country. Her youngest sister was forever bringing home strays, which was harder to do in town.

"Do you think Mama would allow me to return to Shad-owcrest?" Effie asked. "I am going to have to do all this social swirl on my own soon enough. I would rather have my freedom at home this spring and summer."

"Soften your request when you ask her," she advised. "Tell her you wish to be here for the first part of the Season but that you long for the country, especially when the weather grows warm. Mama will have her hands full with our four come-outs. I think if you coat your request with sugar, she will let you go home sooner rather than later."

"That is a wonderful compromise," her sister said. "Besides, I want to make certain Starlight is being exercised properly."

Her sister referred to Pippa's beloved horse, which her twin had asked Effie to exercise regularly until she returned from her honeymoon.

"You might want to mention Starlight when you talk with Mama. That might aid your case."

When Mirella was finished and Mama turned to Lyric and Allegra, she said brightly, "We need to start on designs for the two of you."

Neither of her cousins seemed excited by that prospect, however.

"We do need a few gowns," Allegra said.

"Day gowns," Lyric emphasized. "But Allegra and I are re-considering making our come-outs, Aunt Dinah."

Mama looked perplexed. "Whyever would you delay this? We have planned all along for you to be brought out with Georgie and Mirella."

Allegra's mouth set stubbornly. "A few new gowns, Aunt Dinah. That is all we need."

Lyric nodded in agreement. "We must discuss things with you, Aunt. When we get home," she said, her tone emphatic.

Mama would never have been one to cause a scene in public, and so she nodded diplomatically. "Then let us talk about your day gowns." Turning to the modiste, she said, "Madame, would you please draw up a few designs for the twins now?"

Madame Dumas looked confused but did as the duchess requested. Allegra and Lyric liked what the modiste drew, and Lyric firmly said, "We will commit to these and no others."

Mama smiled graciously at the dressmaker. "You have plenty to start on now, Madame Dumas. Georgina and I will return in three days' time for our final fittings for the gowns you have already created for us. I know you still have many more to sew for us, as well as the ones we have discussed today. I will have a more definitive answer for you at that time regarding the rest of the wardrobes being completed."

"Of course, Your Grace," Madame Dumas replied.

As they were leaving the shop, Sophie entered. "Oh, have I missed everything?"

Mama smiled. "It was a madhouse for a while, but you should have peace and quiet for your own fittings."

"I have been coming regularly over the last few weeks, and this should be the last of what I try on for the upcoming Season. I cannot thank you enough, Dinah, for recommending Madame Dumas to me. She has such a wonderful reputation. It will be divine being seen at a *ton* ball in one of her creations." Sophie smiled wickedly. "And showing off my deliciously handsome duke to Polite Society."

"Will you be home for tea?" asked Georgie.

"I only have two gowns to try on, so yes, please expect me. James will also be there."

She was famished after having spent so many hours at the modiste's shop. She was also curious as to what Lyric and Allegra had up their sleeves and thought to speak to them about it during the carriage ride home.

Unfortunately, her cousins followed Mama into one carriage, and Aunt Matty joined them. That left Mirella, Effie, and herself to ride in the second one.

The minute their coach door closed, Effie asked, "What was that about?"

"You mean Allegra and Lyric not wanting to be fitted for ballgowns?" Mirella chimed in. "Or even *make* their come-outs? It is as if everything changed within the span of a few minutes."

Effie looked to Georgie. "Do you know anything about this? Everything was fine at breakfast."

She shared with her sisters what she had overheard, saying,

"Madame Dumas asked Mama who would be paying for the gowns she made up for Allegra and Lyric. Mama said James would. Lyric was with me and overheard that. Her entire demeanor changed. I am certain she went and informed Allegra of the conversation. Why they would not want James to pay for their gowns, however, baffles me."

"Well, Uncle Adolphus should be paying for their come-outs," Mirella said matter-of-factly. "It is a most expensive undertaking. After all, he is their father and should be responsible for doing so."

"But James is quite wealthy?" said Effie. "What are a few ballgowns to a duke?"

"Apparently, you were woolgathering," Georgie told her younger sister. "Mama has mentioned we are to have up to sixty ballgowns created, along with countless day gowns for social activities."

Effie's eyes bulged. "Are you *serious*, Georgie? That is outrageous! Why would someone need that many ballgowns?"

"Because if you do not wear a different gown to each ball, you are practically ostracized," Mirella informed their youngest sister. "If the *ton* is known for one thing, it is gossip. They will seize on the slightest thing and talk it to death. They will criticize what people wore. The food which was served. The musicians who played. And they will skewer the reputation of someone in the blink of an eye."

"I was reluctant to make my come-out in Polite Society before," Effie said, looking uncertain. "Now, I am doubly so, hearing what a vindictive group the *ton* is."

"Not all of them are so bitter," Georgie said, trying to placate Effie. "Mama has said it is only a small fraction who actively participates in such gossip."

"They may be minority, but they are a strong voice," Mirella pointed out. "Their gossip—and the rumors they spread—has a life of its own. That is why Mama wants everything we do to reflect well upon us because whatever we say or do, it will reflect upon all of us. Even Mama herself. It could affect her chances of finding a husband."

Effie's eyes widened. "*Mama* wants to find a husband? No one tells me anything," her sister huffed.

She nodded. "Pippa and I have encouraged her to do so, Effie. Mama spent many years in a loveless, unhappy marriage, one not of her own choosing. While Mama has devoted her life to raising the six of us, she has put her own happiness aside."

"She still is very beautiful," Effie agreed. "Why, I think it is a good idea if Mama decides to wed again."

Mirella asked, "I wonder if we will learn at tea what our cousins are thinking in regard to their come-outs. Do you think they will discuss it in front of all of us, or will they wish to speak to Mama and James privately?"

Georgie shrugged. "We will simply need to watch things unfold. We should not express our opinions. What we need to do is support Lyric and Allegra, no matter what."

She had a feeling her cousins were going to turn down a come-out Season. What had started as the come-out for five girls—Pippa, Mirella, Allegra, Lyric, and herself—was now dwindling fast.

CHAPTER THREE

G EORGIE WENT TO the drawing room early, not certain what was going to happen during teatime. She believed that she owed it to James to warn him as to what was on her cousins' minds.

When she entered the room, the only person present was Sophie, already back from the modiste. Georgie crossed the drawing room as her sister-in-law greeted her.

"How did the fittings for your gowns go?" Sophie asked pleasantly.

"They went extremely well. I am so happy with all that Madame Dumas has done for me. And you?"

Sophie smiled gently. "It has been a long time since I have walked amongst Polite Society, but I will do so now wearing the designs of one of the most coveted modistes in town. Don't get me wrong, Georgie. I lead a very fulfilling life, with James now my husband, and running Neptune Shipping Lines. It will be nice, though, to dress up every now and then and move among the *ton*." Her eyes sparkled with mischief. "After all, we are a duke and duchess, and that should be helpful as we introduce you and the others during your come-outs."

"I want to talk to you about that, Sophie," Georgie said. "The twins are going to bring up not participating in the upcoming

Season during our tea today."

Sophie's shock was evident by the look on her face. "Did they give a reason why? I know they were present at Madame Dumas' shop today. I saw them there."

"It has something to do with their father."

Her sister-in-law's demeanor instantly changed, becoming guarded. "What did they say?"

"They are loath for James to have to pay for their come-outs. They believe it is their father's duty to do so. They are going to bring it up in a few minutes. I simply wanted to alert you so that you might tell James what is in the works."

Sophie took Georgie's hand. "Thank you. I will let James know."

"Let me know what?" James said, appearing before them.

Sophie's features were serious. "We must talk."

She led her husband to a far corner of the room as the others began entering the drawing room for tea. Mirella and Effie came in talking animatedly, while Mama and Aunt Matty looked concerned, following Lyric and Allegra. The twins both looked grave.

Maids rolled in two teacarts, and Mama asked everyone to sit. For the first time since she could remember, no one said a word as her mother and Sophie poured out for the group.

She looked to Allegra and Lyric, who had not spoken to anyone since they had arrived, merely accepting the cups and saucers Sophie passed to them.

Georgie had only had a single sip of tea when things began.

Lyric was the first to say, "We wish to speak to you about our come-outs, James."

He said, "Please do so freely."

Mama chimed in, saying, "Perhaps we should talk about this after we have had our tea."

But Allegra was having none of that. "No, Aunt Dinah. Lyric and I wish to discuss this now. Whatever would be said in private, you know we will simply turn around and share with our cousins.

They might as well hear everything at the same time as we do."

Mama nodded, a pained expression on her face. "All right. What do you wish to discuss about your come-outs, girls?"

Lyric cleared her throat. "I overheard Madame Dumas ask you at her shop today who might be paying for the many gowns Allegra and I will be wearing. Without hesitation, you said James would be responsible for our bills."

Allegra took up the banner. "It is not James' responsibility to do so, Aunt Dinah. It is Papa's. Yes, he has neglected us our entire lives. We have gone months—even years—without seeing him. Since James became the Duke of Seaton, we have not seen Papa or Theo at all. We believe it is time that Papa accepts responsibility for having fathered us. He *must* pay for our come-outs—or we will not make our debuts into Polite Society. We won't have it any other way."

Georgie watched James and Sophie exchange a glance, and then her brother looked to Mama. Mama nodded.

"We have something to share with you that will be unpleasant to hear," James told them. "You will not be seeing your father or Theodore ever again."

Lyric gasped, while Allegra demanded, "Are they dead?"

James' fingers found his wife's and as they held hands, he said, "They tried to hurt Sophie. I could not let that happen. Then—or in the future."

Sophie looked at the twins, concern filling her face, and said, "While you girls are so very lovely, your father and Theo are terrible people."

"You don't think we know that?" Lyric asked angrily. "Papa abandoned us at birth. He let Aunt Dinah raise us. He has forgotten our birthdays. Or rather, he ignored them. We only see him—and Theo—on rare occasions."

Allegra said, "We have always known Papa is a most unkind man, Sophie. Lyric and I still believe, though, that Papa should be made to live up to his responsibilities to us regarding our come-outs."

Lyric nodded in agreement. "We know what he was like when he lived here for those three years, acting as if he were the Duke of Seaton in all but name while his brother lay dying a slow death. Papa probably ran up bills all over town, thinking he might pay them once he became the duke." She sniffed. "If then."

"But things changed when you came back to us, James," Allegra said. "We know you asked Papa and Theo to leave this house. Naturally, Papa did not bother to tell either of us where he was going, and we have had no contact with him in months." She paused. "But how did he try to hurt you, Sophie?"

Sophie was silent a long moment, and Georgie thought her sister-in-law wasn't going to answer the question. Then she said, "Your father and brother tried to kidnap me and hold me for ransom."

Georgie, along with everyone in the room, gasped loudly.

"And he and Theo would have done far worse," Sophie finished quietly, tears welling in her eyes.

Georgie could not imagine what Sophie meant, but the fact that her uncle and cousin had planned to abduct Sophie and exchange her for money horrified her.

"I could not have them around," James finally said. "They would have been a continuing threat to Sophie's safety. *All* my family's safety," he emphasized.

She knew how fiercely her brother loved Sophie and the rest of them. He himself had been taken away when he was a young boy, kidnapped and put to work as a cabin boy on a ship. The family had thought James dead for many years until his recent return.

"You said they are gone," Allegra said quietly. "Where, James?"

"We decided they must leave England," James revealed. "They had no money. They were placed aboard one of the Strong sailing vessels and taken all the way to Australia. They were left there, being told they would need to work now for their living. It was the only way I believed I could keep Sophie and the rest of you safe."

Lyric shuddered. "That was harsh, James. But they deserved their punishment, nevertheless."

"We did not want to trouble you about this," Mama said, and Georgie knew her mother had also had knowledge of the scheme. "You so rarely saw your father anyway. We were going to tell you. We merely waited for the right time to do so."

"But you didn't tell us," Allegra said stubbornly. "I am dreadfully sorry Papa and Theo tried to hurt Sophie, but we should have been told what happened to them. We have already been beholden to Aunt Dinah our entire lives, and now we find ourselves further in her debt—and James', as well."

James said, "You are in no one's debt, Allegra. You are family. You are Strongs. And Strongs stick together. You will always have a home in any of my ducal residences scattered throughout England. You will make your come-outs as planned, and then you will have a new home with your husbands."

Georgie watched her cousins carefully, seeing the twins exchange glances, knowing they were silently communicating, just as she and Pippa had done so their entire lives.

"We will not make any rash decisions," Lyric declared. "We know you think of us as family, James, but we are, in effect, orphans now. Dependent upon your kindness for absolutely everything. The clothes on our backs. The food we put in our mouths. The horses we ride."

"This will take time for us to get used to," Allegra said, linking hands with her twin. "We know the expense of a come-out is astronomical. You are already paying for Georgie and Mirella to do so." She swallowed. "Lyric and I, therefore, would like to postpone our own come-outs."

"You mustn't do that," Mama said earnestly. "Please, do not worry about the costs associated with it. James can easily afford to pay for your gowns."

"What about our dowries?" demanded Allegra. "Do we even have them?"

Mama flushed guiltily, and Georgie knew that there were no dowries for her cousins. That Uncle Adolphus had squandered them.

"I do not know all the details, but your dowries are no more," Mama revealed, her voice breaking. "The solicitor has told me nothing is left."

Lyric spoke up, love shining in her eyes. "You protected us, Aunt Dinah. You took us in and have raised Allegra and me as if we were your own daughters. Do not feel responsible for something you had no control over."

"I will provide dowries for the both of you," James said firmly.

"That is most kind of you, James," Lyric said. "This is a lot for us to take in, however. Especially knowing now that Papa stole our dowries from us. Allegra and I have much to ponder."

"We still stand firm, Aunt Dinah," Allegra said, defiance in her voice. "We are not ready to make our come-outs at this time." Her tone softened, and she continued, saying, "The news will come out—it always does. Someone will ask about Papa. Lyric and I do not want to lie. Neither do we want to blacken the Strong family's reputation with our father's misdeeds. Please, let the two of us step away from this upcoming Season. Launch Georgie and Mirella into Polite Society. Let them find husbands without any scandal attached to their names. We can see whether or not Lyric and I should make our own come-outs."

"You are family," James stressed. "I won't have you leaving us out of some misguided notion. You are not to go out on your own and try to earn a living for yourselves. You are family. *My* family. And family always looks out for one another."

"I believe Allegra and Lyric have many things to think about," Sophie interjected. "The Season is quite demanding, and they are being reasonable in considering the reputations of Georgie and Mirella. Would you prefer staying in town?" she asked. "Or would you prefer to return to Shadowcrest?"

Again, the twins looked at one another for a moment.

Georgie knew they silently made their decision.

Lyric said, "We want to go to the country. We will stay until the day gowns Madame Dumas is making up for us are completed."

Effie spoke up for the first time since tea began. "Perhaps when my gowns are finished, I could also go back with you. I have nothing to do with Georgie's and Mirella's come-outs. You know I am happiest in the country. Besides, I promised Pippa I would regularly exercise Starlight." Her gaze turned to her mother. "Would that be acceptable, Mama? Keeping Lyric and Allegra company?"

"I see no problem with that," Mama said. "It will mean that you will probably be in town another two weeks or so. I will have Madame Dumas concentrate on the new wardrobes for the three of you, and then you can return to Kent. I will go with you. James and Sophie can handle the come-outs for Georgie and Mirella."

"No, Mama," Georgie protested. "You have been looking forward to this Season so much. We all think you should wed again."

She reached and took her mother's hand, squeezing her fingers. "You have had to live for others your entire life, Mama, including your daughters and nieces. It is time you sought happiness for yourself. They will be fine at Shadowcrest."

Aunt Matty spoke up. "I will be the one to return to Kent with you. You need an adult with you, beyond the servants. I am old and have lived most of my life. I can wait until next Season to see my friends."

"You don't have to sacrifice for us in this way, Aunt Matty," Lyric said gently.

Aunt Matty smiled gently. "It is no sacrifice at all, my dear. I never wed, but you six girls have been the children of my heart. I agree that Dinah should remain here and supervise Georgie and Mirella's come-outs. We will find things to do in the country, and I know the two of you will wish to do a bit of soul searching. I will be there if you have need of me."

Suddenly, everyone was on their feet, giving hugs to others.

Georgie embraced Allegra and then Lyric. "You are more than cousins to me. You are sisters. I will always support you in whatever you do."

"We know that," Allegra told her.

"And we appreciate it, Georgie," Lyric added.

"Our tea has grown cold," Mama said. "I will send for fresh pots."

Everyone took their seats again, and Georgie realized she had been right.

The number of Strong ladies making their debuts into Polite Society was now down to two.

CHAPTER FOUR

GEORGIE STEPPED OUTSIDE, ready to see off part of her family as they returned to Shadowcrest. They had been in town now for just over three weeks, and Madame Dumas' seamstresses had worked day and night, completing gowns for Aunt Matty, Allegra, Lyric, and Effie.

Now, the four women were returning to the country. Georgie was still disappointed that the twins would not make their come-outs alongside her and Mirella, but she could understand the dilemma they faced. She hated the fact that women were at such a disadvantage in their society, dependent upon the men in their families, who had absolute control over finances.

She walked out, linking her arm through Allegra's, as they went to the carriage. Footmen were loading the women's trunks into a second vehicle, and Kitty was going to return to Shadowcrest to serve as maid to them. The servant had admitted to Georgie as she helped dress her this morning that she was happy to be returning to the country, saying she preferred the quiet of it to the noise of the city.

They reached the carriage, and Georgie embraced Allegra. "Please write," she said earnestly.

"You must do the same, Georgie," her cousin replied. "We

want to know everything that is happening during the Season and if you are leaning toward favoring one suitor over another."

It still took her by surprise at times, thinking that in a few months, she might actually be engaged to be married, planning her wedding to someone she had yet to even meet.

Moving toward Lyric, she hugged her cousin, again asking that Lyric write about news from the country.

"I know you will be searching for answers within yourself," Georgie told Lyric. "I hope you find them."

Her cousin smiled at her fondly. "And I hope that you find a gentleman worthy of your love. It was wonderful seeing Pippa and Seth come together. James and Sophie, too. I am certain you will find the man meant for you, Georgie, and that we will adore him as much as we do Sophie and Seth."

She then hugged Effie and Aunt Matty and said goodbye to Miss Feathers, who had served as their governess for several years and would still be giving Effie lessons until her own come-out in a couple of years.

As the two carriages pulled from their square, Mama took her and Mirella's hands and squeezed them.

"I know it is dreadfully hard to see them go, girls. They have been a part of your lives ever since all of you were born. The twins are doing what they believe is best. It will give us time to see the two of you find good matches, though. By then, I hope they will have worked through their struggles, so that we can see they also find decent gentlemen as their husbands next Season."

As they turned to reenter the townhouse, Mirella said, "Effie will be the happiest of them, Mama. She is definitely not one for town. She will be glad to traipse about the estate with Caleb."

"Yes, Effie and Pippa have that in common," Mama agreed. "Oh, I wonder where my darling girl is now on her honeymoon. I suppose I will go in now and write a letter to her and send it ahead so that she will know her cousins have postponed their come-out Season."

"I wish to practice my pianoforte," Georgie said, knowing she would draw comfort from the music, always eager to sit at the instrument each day.

"So do I," her sister said.

Of all the Strongs, she and Mirella were the most serious about their music. Sometimes, they would listen to one another practice and critique each other's performance of a particular piece. They had not needed a music teacher in many years, simply using their skills and experience to help one another become more accomplished pianists.

"Where do you prefer to practice today, Georgie?" Mirella asked.

"I know you enjoy the drawing room for practice. I will be in the music room."

She parted from her mother and sister, retreating to the music room, where she had spent numerous hours, especially during the three years Uncle Adolphus had kept them exiled in town. Thinking of her uncle, and what he and Cousin Theo had tried to do to Sophie, still angered her. She was glad James had put the two men on a ship and sent them far away, yet Georgie knew it still had to hurt Lyric and Allegra, learning what their father and brother had been capable of and how they had tried to hurt James by abducting his wife.

Georgie seated herself at the pianoforte, realizing how fortunate she was to be a Strong. A daughter of one duke and sister to another one. The fact they even possessed two pianofortes within this household told of the Seaton wealth and the ease of their lives.

She practiced for a good two hours, which was not out of the ordinary, and then went to find Mirella, who was finishing up her own practice session.

"Are you going to paint today?" she asked her sister, who was the most talented artist in the family and painted even better than she played her instrument.

"I am in desperate need of new paints," Mirella said. "I could also use a few new canvases. I don't think I will have much time to paint during the Season, but it does not start for another six weeks. Would you like to accompany me to buy new paints?"

"I will go with you, but I think I will visit the bookshop next door while you are collecting your painting supplies. We should see if Mama also might wish to go on the outing with us."

They found Mama in her sitting room and asked if she wished to accompany them.

"No, I have a few other things I need to get done. If Millie is not free to go with you, then Libby can do so," Mama said, referring to her own lady's maid.

Georgie rang for Millie, and the maid said she would be happy to chaperone them on their errands. No coach was available since the largest ducal coach had left to take the others to Kent, and the smaller one had conveyed James and Sophie to the wharf afterward.

"It really is not that far," Mirella said. "It isn't terribly cold today. Would you care to walk?"

Georgie had always enjoyed walking and readily agreed. They went upstairs to put on their spencers for warmth and fetch their reticules.

They set out for the apothecary's shop which mixed oil paints and sold Mirella her other painting supplies. When they arrived, Georgie said to Millie, "Go with my sister. She usually takes a long time in selecting new paintbrushes and shades of paint. If it will be too much to carry home, request for the supplies to be delivered. I will be browsing next door at the bookshop. If I finish early, I will rejoin you here."

She went next door, liking this bookshop because it was so large and offered such a wide variety of books on numerous topics. Moving among the shelves, she decided to head to the section Pippa had always enjoyed most. It carried books that described the histories and cultures of lands across the world. Pippa had a fascination with the Sandwich Islands, sometimes called the Cook Islands, and Georgie thought she might purchase a book about them and read it so she would know something of the sights her twin would see when the newlyweds called there.

Turning the corner to the isolated portion of the bookshop, she reached the U-shaped section, finding a single patron present, flipping through an open book. He stopped, his attention apparently drawn to something on the page.

She halted, studying the tall, imposing stranger. He gazed intently at his book, seemingly unaware of her presence. In profile, he was the most handsome man Georgie had ever seen. His hair was black as a raven's. His coat stretched tightly over broad shoulders, and he looked both athletic and graceful at the same time. She suspected from his ramrod posture that he either was presently in the military or was a former member of it.

Despite knowing it was rude, she continued to gaze upon him, entranced by him, her heart beating wildly. A physical rush ran through her, unlike anything she had ever known. For a moment, Georgie wished Pippa were here, so that she could ask her twin about these odd, unexpected feelings.

Then a sneeze came on suddenly, out of nowhere. Georgie rarely sneezed but when the sensation hit, she always sneezed in groups of four, tiny, delicate sneezes, but four all the same.

One. Two. Three. Four. They all came in rapid succession.

When she glanced up, the handsome stranger had turned to face her. She had been right in assuming he was a military man. Looking at him now, she understood why he wore civilian clothes. Why he had been sent home.

He wore a black eyepatch over his left eye. He also had a fierce scar which started above his left eyebrow and then ran the length of his left cheek. She could not imagine how painful the injury must have been when it occurred because it still looked so dreadful. But it did not mar his beauty. In fact, she only thought the scar enhanced his good looks.

He stared at her now, one green eye piercing her.

"Bless you," he said, his head turning back to his book.

She felt compelled to engage in conversation with him and took a few steps toward him. He turned to face her again, one brow arching.

"Yes?" he asked with disdain.

"This is very forward of me, my lord—actually, quite unlike me—but I wish to introduce myself to you," she said boldly. "I am Lady Georgina Strong."

His gaze burned into her, as if he saw to the very depths of her soul.

Then he turned away, replacing the book he held onto the shelf again.

She knew he was about to leave—and needed to stop him from doing so.

"What were you looking at?" she blurted out, the first thing that came to mind. "I am here to find a book about the Sandwich Islands," hoping her words might start a conversation between them and not chase him away.

The man glanced at her again, confusion clouding his one good eye.

Georgie held her breath, hoping he would say something. Anything.

"Why the Sandwich Islands?" he asked, his voice a deep rumble, which caused her insides to wobble like marmalade.

Smiling, she said, "Because my sister has gone there on her honeymoon with Lord Hopewell. Pippa has always wished to travel the world, and she wed a sea captain. Well, he *was* a sea captain, but he recently became Viscount Hopewell. He loves my twin more than anything and wanted to take her to all the places she has read about over the years. Why, they are going to North America first. Then they will sail down and around Cape Horn. They will visit the Sandwich Islands and Australia. I know Pippa also mentioned India. She has showed me all these places in the atlas in our library, but I thought I would read up some about the places she and Seth will visit. That way, when she returns, I will have a better understanding of where she has been and what she has seen."

She finally paused, coming up for breath, praying he would

speak again. She wanted to hear his voice.

He was quiet a long moment, and Georgie was about to turn away, discouraged she had not been able to get him to engage more with her.

"Your twin?" he asked.

Relief flooded her. They were going to have a conversation, after all.

"Yes. Twins run in the Strong family. My father and uncle were twins. And on the very day Pippa and I were born to our parents, my aunt gave birth to twin girls. Unfortunately, she did not survive their births. Allegra and Lyric came to live with us."

He seemed interested. "Two sets of twins growing up in a household?"

"Oh, it was wonderful. And then Mama had Mirella, and later Effie, so there were six of us growing up together."

For the first time, the stranger smiled. "Six girls in one household? It must have been quite lively."

"It was ever so much fun."

She proceeded to tell him a few stories about their antics, thrilled that it brought another smile to his sensual lips. She had never noticed any man's lips before, but she could not stop staring at his as she continued babbling about her family. Usually, Georgie was a bit reserved, but it was as if the floodgates had been opened and she simply could not stop talking.

She wondered now what it would be like to kiss those lips.

Her thoughts caused heat to rise in her cheeks, and she glanced away, self-conscious of the blush. She focused on the shelf of books in front of her, not really seeing any of them, thinking how foolish she had been to approach a stranger and talk his ear off.

"The books about the Sandwich Islands are somewhere," she said, trailing her finger along the spines of the books near her.

"They are over here," the man said, taking a few steps away. He indicated a shelf and then removed a book from it, returning to her side and handing it to her.

"You might enjoy this one."

She accepted the book from him and flipped through it. "I will purchase this on your recommendation," she said brightly, trying to cover her embarrassment. "I will learn all I can about this group of islands, and Pippa will be impressed when she finally returns home."

"She will be gone a long time if she is to visit all the places you mentioned."

Georgie nodded. "Seth—that is, Lord Hopewell—said they would be gone anywhere from a year and a half to two years. The weather will play a large factor in the amount of time they are gone. Seth sailed for Strong Shipping Lines. He was a captain. The same as my brother."

"Six girls and a brother?"

"James was lost to us for many years," she said quietly, surprised that she was sharing such intimate details with a man whose name she had yet to learn. "He had gone to the Strong Shipping offices with his father. Our family owns the line. James was abducted on the docks and made a cabin boy on a sailing vessel. He was so young and treated so miserably, beaten every time he tried to tell them who he really was."

She shrugged, swallowing painfully. "He finally stopped trying. His memories faded, and he did not really recall who he was after a few years."

"But he came back?" the stranger pressed.

Georgie nodded. "After seventeen years. We all thought him dead. Pippa and I were only a year old when he vanished without a trace, so we have gotten to know him since he has returned to England. He has also wed recently, and we simply adore his wife."

Worried that she had overstepped her bounds by babbling to a complete stranger, she hoped to make amends for her forwardness and still show this man a kindness.

"Perhaps you might like to come to tea, my lord, and meet them." She paused, staring at him. "Then again, I would be hard pressed to tell them who you were or where to send your invitation since you have neglected to share your name with me. I know Polite Society demands that a third party introduce strangers to one another, but there was no one around to do so for us. I have told you that I am Lady Georgina Strong, but you have yet to reveal your name to me. Unless you are some criminal and on the run from the authorities for the crimes you have committed, it would only be polite if you did share your name with me, sir."

He gaped at her and then burst out laughing. His laugh sounded rusty, as if he had not used it in a very long while. Then again, if he had been at war, as she suspected, war was no laughing matter.

"My name is August Holt," he told her. "Until last summer, I was a captain in His Majesty's army, fighting in the Peninsular Wars."

A shadow crossed his face. "My reasons for coming home were twofold." He raised a hand, pointing to his face. "You can see the injuries I suffered. I was deemed unfit to maintain my command, and so I sold out."

She clucked her tongue. "Simply because you lost an eye in battle does not mean you would be unfit to continue as an officer."

He cocked his head, studying her. "You believe that to be true, my lady?"

"Of course, I do, or I would not have said so. If you were capable before with two eyes, why would missing one matter? I assume a captain is a good rank, one which you had to earn. You are no less the leader—nor less a person—simply because you no longer possess that eye."

His gaze pinned hers. "And what of my scars, Lady Georgi-na?"

"What of them? I do not see how having something mar your cheek changes your intellect. It would not affect your skills, nor the experience you brought to the battlefield. If your commanding officers forced you out simply for those reasons, then they are fools," she declared.

He smiled, and Georgie felt herself drawn in by it.

"I also came home because my father had just passed," the former army captain revealed.

"Did you inherit his title? Usually, it is a second son who goes to war."

"No, my brother Peter did. But he was in poor health for many years. He passed the day I returned home. Fortunately, I was able to speak to him before he was gone."

Moved by what he had revealed, Georgie placed her hand on his forearm, a gesture she thought would bring him comfort. Instead, an electricity passed between them, and he yanked his arm from her.

"Good day, my lady," he said curtly, striding away before she could say anything more to him.

She leaned against the bookshelves. The encounter had intrigued her. The way it ended had stunned her. And though she had learned his name, she had yet to learn the title he held.

Georgie was determined to discover his title—and invite August Holt to tea.

CHAPTER FIVE

AUGUST FLED THE bookshop—and Lady Georgina Strong—as if the place had caught on fire.

He instructed his coachman to head to the tailor's and quickly hopped inside the vehicle, afraid Lady Georgina would have the audacity to follow him out and demand that he finish their conversation.

She was the only person beyond a servant he had spoken to in months. After Peter's death, August had retreated to the country to lick his physical and emotional wounds. He had buried his older brother beside their father, standing at their graves a long time after the other mourners had left the cemetery. Those mourners who had attended the funeral gawked at him openly, making August withdraw even further into himself.

He had returned to Edgefield, the only visitor being the local doctor. Dr. Winters had served as an army doctor fresh from his medical training, gaining experience on the battlefields of North America. Winters had heard the villagers gossiping, appalled by August's scars, and the physician had come to offer his services to the new Marquess of Edgethorne.

Winters had told August it was important to keep the wounds moist and covered, different advice from what Dr. Morrow had offered. Morrow had kept August's bandages on for two solid weeks after his injuries before removing them, saying they needed air to heal.

Dr. Winters was of a different mind, saying the bandages would protect August. He also recommended honey to keep the itching and painful swelling down, especially since the salve Dr. Morrow had provided to August was now used up.

He agreed to leave the dressings on his face for another solid month, changing them out himself daily after washing the wounds with warm water and a mild soap and then coating them in honey before redressing the wounds.

After the month, he had begun leaving the dressings off, noting the color of the scars had faded from bright red to a softer shade of red. All these months later now, his scars were pink, obviously still visible, but a sight better than what they had been six months ago. He couldn't help but be mildly pleased that his appearance wasn't as harsh.

Dr. Winters had assured him the scars would continue to fade until approximately the one-year mark. At that point, any further change was unlikely. The physician had been very pleased that the honey had reduced the redness and that no infection had set in. Winters had agreed with Morrow in that minimizing movement was important. Neither physician wished for him to overexert the area, so he had spoken rarely since his battlefield injuries.

The only course of action open to August now, according to Dr. Winters, was to gently massage the scars which had formed. He recommended doing so for a few minutes each day, saying the massage would help break up any scar tissue which might form. August had kept to the routine, doing so upon awakening each morning.

Of course, there was nothing to do for his missing eye. Winters had August remove his eyepatch, and the physician had complimented Dr. Morrow's neat stitches. He had thanked the village doctor but had not seen him again after that.

He had remained on his country estate, learning everything

he could about its management. He had an efficient steward who explained the overall needs of the estate and its tenants and then narrowed the scope, teaching August about crop cycles and rotations, planting and harvesting times, and leaving some fields fallow for a year. Edgefield also had livestock on its grounds, and he had gotten to know more about it, as well.

If it were up to him, he would have remained in the country his entire life.

But the promise he had made to Peter on his brother's death-bed haunted him. August knew he would need to attend the next London Season in order to find a bride. He would look to the wallflowers, the plain, homely girls he had never paid any attention to in the past. They always hovered in a corner, grouped together, their demeanor forlorn, knowing they had little in looks to offer a man.

A few of them, he recalled, were decent looking, simply shy in nature, gravitating toward those who would not judge them or force them to speak. At one time, he would have had his pick of the litter, attracting the most beautiful women to him. He had danced with diamonds of the first water when he was a carefree bachelor, before his army days. Now, he doubted any of them would even speak to him because of his appearance.

He vowed to take a wife this Season. His title and wealth alone would attract a good number of ladies of varying ages. At least, he hoped they would.

The one thing he did not want was a woman who pitied him. His marriage would be for procreation only. His wife would need to produce the expected heir. Hopefully, a spare, as well. They would then lead separate lives. He would allow the marchioness to raise their children as she saw fit. Perhaps she might even wish to remain in town and allow him free run at Edgefield.

August yearned to be in those children's lives, but he was afraid his looks would frighten them. He felt only part of a man these days. He would simply look with care for a woman of character and integrity, one worthy to be his marchioness and raise his children.

His thoughts drifted to his recent encounter with Lady Georgina Strong. She was definitely a beauty, and she would be sought after at any event she attended. The odd thing was that she had not blanched when she had seen his face, unlike servants in his own household. She had conversed with him as if he looked like he used to. It must have been her good breeding and inherent polite manners which caused her to be able to do so.

Yet August wondered why she had struck up a conversation with him to begin with. She herself had pointed out that it was inappropriate for them to even speak with one another, having not been introduced by a mutual acquaintance. She could have simply browsed the shelves without ever glancing in his direction. Yet not only had she started a conversation, but Lady Georgina had also continued it for some time. As if she wanted to talk with him.

In the old days, a woman such as Lady Georgina would be the exact woman he would be attracted to. She had dark brown hair and an unusual shade of eyes, what he would term cornflower blue. She was about five inches over five feet, tall for a woman, with ample breasts and wide hips. She was very feminine in her manner and dress, and he would have maneuvered her into the gardens at a ball and made sure he thoroughly kissed her soft, full lips.

Those days were over now. Even if she had prodded him for his name so she might ask him to tea, August believed she was merely being kind. Perhaps their paths would cross at some point during this next Season. He had not thought to dance any, but now he longed to do so.

Just one dance with her.

His carriage rolled to a stop, and the footman opened the door for August. He climbed from the vehicle and entered the tailor's shop, on time for his appointment.

The clerk who met him swallowed his shock and asked, "May I help you, my lord?"

"I have an appointment with Mr. Ragland. I am Lord Edgethorne."

"Of course, my lord. Please wait a moment, and I will fetch him."

He watched as the clerk went to a far corner of the shop and began an earnest conversation with an older gentleman who had a thick thatch of white hair. He assumed the man to be Ragland, and August watched as he slowly approached him, seeing he steeled himself.

Bowing, the tailor said, "Good afternoon, my lord. May I extend my condolences regarding your father's passing? His lordship was a loyal client for many years, and I enjoyed dressing him and your brother."

Ragland frowned a moment. "I thought you were . . . the . . ." His voice faded, and August knew the man only now realized that Peter, too, was gone.

He had not placed a death notice in the London newspapers, and he now regretted that choice. At the time, he had been so grief-stricken, he had not thought of things such as that, merely fleeing to the country and burying his beloved sibling.

"My brother has also passed," he confirmed. "It is why I now hold the title."

"I see. So, you wish to commission a new wardrobe, my lord?"

"I do."

"Then we must measure you first."

The tailor led him to a back room, where August stepped onto a raised platform and was measured from head to toe.

"What are your needs, my lord?" Ragland asked.

"I have left the military and truly have nothing beyond my uniforms, which I have now discarded. My father and I were close in height and build, so I simply commandeered some of his wardrobe since my return to England."

Ragland nodded. "I thought your coat and waistcoat looked familiar, but you are slightly larger than Lord Edgethorne was.

We will make certain your new pieces fit you better than these castoffs have."

The tailor hesitated and then asked, "Might you be considering attending the Season?"

"Yes. I will be attending some events." He knew Ragland thought him too hideous to darken a ballroom, but August would not break his promise to Peter.

Surprise showed in the tailor's eyes, but he shook it off. "Then let me go over what I recommend we make up for you, Lord Edgethorne."

As Ragland spoke, he was taken aback at how many items he would commission. Then again, a man of his station and wealth had a certain image to project in Polite Society, especially if he was looking to land a bride.

"I will go along with whatever you suggest, Mr. Ragland," he informed the tailor. "The number of pieces and fabrics will be at your discretion."

"I assume you will be needing shirts, hats, and boots, my lord."

"Yes, I am starting from scratch."

The tailor recommended others to him, and August spent the next day going to their various shops. He had three pairs of boots made up, along with a couple of pairs of shoes. The shirtmaker suggested three dozen shirts to start, and he acquiesced to the request. He would be wearing these clothes for a long time, and it would be good to have enough choice to rotate through them over the years. He never intended to return to London again, much less attend another Season. He wasn't a political man and had no interest in sitting in the House of Lords. He merely wanted to retreat from the world and live out his life in solitude.

When he finished with the hatmaker, his last stop, August decided to return to the bookshop he had gone into yesterday. He had merely been browsing after seeing his solicitor, waiting for his upcoming appointment with Ragland. He returned now, though, and went back to the same section which held books about various places around the world.

He would not admit—even to himself—that he hoped to find Lady Georgina Strong there.

The area, however, was void of customers, and August spent a good half-hour skimming through various books in complete solitude.

Then he came across one which featured the Sandwich Islands. Removing it from the shelf, he couldn't help but think about Lady Georgina's interest in these islands and how she wanted to learn more about them in order to have a knowledgeable discussion with her twin sister once Lady Pippa returned from her honeymoon. He knew how close he and Peter had been and could not imagine the even closer bond twins must surely have. To have shared time in the womb and then growing up must have made Lady Georgina and Lady Pippa extremely close. He hoped both women were doing well being separated for such a lengthy amount of time.

August decided to purchase the book. He had no personal interest in the Sandwich Islands, nor did he believe he would ever get on a ship and visit them or anywhere else. Yet something compelled him to buy this book. He placed it under his arm, looking on the shelf and seeing the one he had taken out to show Lady Georgina was now missing. He assumed she had purchased it after he left yesterday.

Suddenly, the back of his neck prickled in awareness. He wasn't alone.

And he knew exactly who was present.

Turning, he found Lady Georgina standing there.

"Ah, you have returned to the scene of the crime," she said, a smile playing about her soft, pink lips.

"I thought we had established yesterday that I was no criminal on the run, my lady," he teased.

No. Flirted. It had been so long since August had done so that he did not recognize it as flirtation at first. The old August—the handsome, carefree devil—flirted with ease and without thought, the playful, teasing words coming naturally to him. The new August—a scarred Lord Edgethorne—should refrain from doing so. After all, when a man flirted, it was to show his interest in a lady.

He could not be interested in the woman before him. He simply couldn't.

"It was a crime of omission," Lady Georgina continued, reaching for the book under his arm and pulling it out.

Her mouth formed an *O* as she saw its title, and then she smiled brilliantly at him. "I see you, too, have a newfound interest in the Sandwich Islands, my lord. Perhaps we should each read our own books and then exchange them and read the other's. Then we could talk about what we had read and compare."

Why was she thinking they were going to have future contact?

"Why, I thought we might become friends, my lord."

"Good God. Did I say that aloud?" he asked, horrified.

She laughed, and he knew he could become addicted to her laughter. To the sparkle in her eyes. To the curve of her breasts.

He took the book from her hands and placed it back on the shelf. "I have changed my mind about purchasing it," he said curtly. "If you will excuse me."

"No, I will not."

August halted in his tracks. "What?"

"You asked if I would excuse you. I told you that I will not. Once we have finished our conversation, you will then be free to go, my lord."

"We have nothing to say to one another, my lady. You yourself have pointed out that we should not even be conversing with one another."

She smiled at him, causing his pulse to race. "But we *are* talking now, my lord, and I would like to continue our conversation over tea. I told you yesterday that I wished to introduce you to my brother and his wife. They stay in town a majority of their time because Sophie is running her shipping line, and James is learning more about the business."

"Wait. Your sister-in-law is . . . *running* this business?"

"Yes, she first wed a man at an early age, a man who started Neptune Shipping Lines, and he taught her all he knew about the business. He was quite a bit older than Sophie, and when he passed, he left her the company."

August frowned. "Didn't ownership pass to your brother upon their marriage?"

"No, James would not have taken the company from Sophie. He loves her too much to do so. He had the marriage settlements drawn up so that she would maintain control of it. While their future firstborn son will inherit James' title and Strong Shipping Lines, their other children will own and manage Neptune."

He couldn't help but shake his head in disbelief. "You come from a most unusual family, Lady Georgina."

"That is why I thought you might enjoy getting to meet them. At least some of them. Mama and my sister Mirella are also in town. We are having gowns made up since Mirella and I are making our come-outs. Pippa no longer has to do so since she married Seth."

He was at a loss for words, having never met a female such as Lady Georgina Strong.

"Will you share your title with me now, my lord? While I can informally invite you to tea here and now, Mama has always believed a written invitation should also be extended, as well. I need to know whom to address it to—and where you live."

"I . . . I am . . . the Marquess of Edgethorne. I live on—"

Lady Georgina squealed. "What a coincidence! Why, you are our neighbor. We share the same square, Lord Edgethorne. There is the private garden between us, of course. Do you ever go and sit in it?"

August was still reeling from the fact that she and her family lived so close to him. He had known that an older duke lived in the townhouse but had never truly paid attention since the small park lay between them and the duke had no sons who had gone to school with August. You could not see one townhouse from the other.

Smiling brightly at him, Lady Georgina said, "I will go home immediately and have Mama write out the invitation to you, my lord. Are you free today? Or should we schedule our tea for tomorrow?"

He did not want to go to tea. He already liked this woman far too much and knew nothing could happen between them.

"I am afraid I am unavailable both today and tomorrow, my lady. My regrets."

She waved his words away. "Then you may come the day after, my lord. Good day."

Lady Georgina whirled and was gone before he could protest. August knew it would be churlish to turn down the invitation of a duchess.

He resolved to attend this one teatime and then be done with Lady Georgina and the Strong family.

CHAPTER SIX

GEORGIE HURRIED FROM the bookshop, not about to let Lord Edgethorne catch up with her and turn her down again. Grabbing Millie's elbow, she pulled the maid down the Mayfair street, quickly turning a corner.

"But this isn't the way home, my lady," the maid protested. "And you're practically running."

She slowed a bit, still walking briskly. "I simply thought we would go down this street, Millie."

The servant's eyes narrowed. "What have you gotten yourself into, my lady?" Millie stopped in her tracks. "It wasn't a gentleman you went inside to see, was it? Oh, Her Grace will have my head if you've been sneaking off seeing some gentleman."

Georgie now altered her pace to a normal walk. "I did happen to see our neighbor, Lord Edgethorne, while in the bookstore."

"Who?"

She remembered the maid was fairly new to their household, having come with Sophie when she wed James at the end of last October.

"You know the garden in the middle of our square? On the other side of the street, out of view, is another townhouse. It belongs to Lord Edgethorne."

"Oh," Millie said, slightly placated.

"And I did ask him to come to tea," she continued. "I told him Mama will send over a formal invitation. He is new to his title, you see, and recently home from the military. I thought it would be nice for him to meet His Grace since he also is new to his title and of a similar age."

They walked the several blocks back to the Seaton townhouse and just before they reached it, Millie asked, "Where is the book you went to purchase, my lady?"

"Oh, one of the pages was torn," she lied. "The clerk pointed it out when I went to purchase it. He did not wish to sell me a damaged copy, and so they will order a new one for me. They will send a note around when it comes in."

They entered the townhouse, and Georgie removed her spencer. She handed it and her reticule to Millie, asking that the maid take the items up to her bedchamber for her. Then she found the footman whom she had asked to stand watch outside the bookshop and passed him a coin.

"Thank you for helping me out today, Freddie," she said.

"Happy to oblige, my lady," he said, pocketing the coin. "It wasn't far to the tearoom where you were." He paused. "Don't worry, my lady. I won't say a word to anyone."

She hoped not.

Georgie hadn't known if August Holt would return to the bookshop. It was the only clue she had to go on, though, so she had sent one of their footmen to stand across the street and watch those who entered. She had described the gentleman as best as she could and told Freddie if he entered the bookshop, to come and find her. She would either be at the modiste or the tearoom next door.

Madame Dumas had been surprised to see her since she had no appointment. She had been able to try on a few more gowns, however, and then extended her visit by looking at numerous fabrics. When she had outstayed her welcome, she had told Millie they would stop for tea. They had dawdled there, and Georgie was about to leave when she saw Freddie peering through the window, motioning to her.

Quickly, she had paid their bill and hurried Millie down the street to the bookshop, telling the maid she had forgotten she was to return to pick up a book which they had not carried yesterday but had gotten from another bookseller.

Georgie went to find Mama now and located her arranging flowers, one of her favorite pastimes.

"Hello, darling. What have you been up to?"

"A little of this and that," she said vaguely. "But I did run into our neighbor, Lord Edgethorne, at the bookshop a few minutes ago."

"Oh, he was out in public? That surprises me."

"Why so?"

"I saw the death notice in the newspapers of Lord Edgethorne's passing last summer. His older son, Lord Peter, has been in failing health for many years and rarely sets foot from their townhouse."

"That is not the Lord Edgethorne I met, Mama. It is the other son. Lord August. He is home from the military. He mentioned his brother's passing."

Mama looked perplexed. "I had no idea he was gone. I saw no notice in the newspapers."

"Perhaps the new Lord Edgethorne did not place a notice there. He said he had returned home last summer from the Peninsular Wars."

"I suppose that could be the case," Mama agreed. "Lord Peter's solicitor should have handled that. He must not have done so, or I possibly could have missed the announcement."

"Anyway, I thought it would be nice to ask him for tea. I told him that you would send an invitation around to him. He was otherwise engaged today and tomorrow afternoon, but he could come the day after. I think it would be good for him to meet James. They seem to be close in age, and they both are new to their titles."

"That is an excellent idea, Georgina. I will write the marquess a note now and ask him to come. That will give James and Sophie plenty of time to plan their own schedules so that they will be here to greet Lord Edgethorne."

Georgie escaped before Mama could ask any more questions, such as how Georgie might even have known who Lord Edgethorne was since they had never met. Hopefully, that would not come up in their conversation at tea.

She went to the music room and escaped into Bach.

AUGUST HAD NOT wanted to show up for tea at the Duke of Seaton's wearing his father's old clothes. Ragland had been right. August was close to his father in size but just enough different so that the coats were slightly tight in the shoulders and the sleeves a quarter-inch too short. While he hadn't minded during his time in the country, sitting down with a duke and two duchesses was quite another matter. He had moved in Polite Society before he left for war and knew many of the unwritten rules. A gentleman showing up for tea with his wrists showing would be in the poorest of taste.

He had returned to his tailor's shop, explaining that he had an important social engagement with a duke. Ragland immediately understood August's dilemma and said he would have a complete ensemble waiting for the marquess in time for his appointment.

He now stood, being fussed over by Ragland and an assistant. A second assistant had been sent to the shirtmaker's to retrieve a shirt or two, along with a new cravat, for August. His boots would not be ready, but Pole, the shared valet he had inherited from his father and Peter, had polished August's military boots so that they gleamed.

Ragland held out the coat, and August slipped his arms into it. The tailor fiddled with the sleeves a moment and then stepped back, inspecting his client.

"You cut a fine figure, my lord," Ragland told him.

Left unsaid was how his face would never live up to his build.

"Ease out of that coat and try on this second one, my lord," the tailor instructed.

He did so, thinking the fit of this coat as good as the first.

Ragland nodded sagely. "We will keep one and allow you to leave wearing the other," he declared. "The one which remains behind will be a model for us as we work on the rest of your wardrobe."

"Then I will take the one I am wearing," he said, liking the dark brown color of the coat, which picked up shades of brown and sage from the waistcoat.

Ragland nodded in approval. "You are set for your appointment with His Grace."

"Thank you for finishing this for me," he told the tailor and assistants. "I will feel more comfortable being appropriately dressed. Two duchesses will also be present, as well as a couple of the previous duke's daughters."

"Then it is a good thing you came to me and shared your plans," the tailor said. "More of your wardrobe will be finished by next week. How long do you plan to be in town, my lord?"

"Not long. There is no rush on the other items. I can claim them when I return for the Season in early April."

"Where is your country estate?" the tailor asked. "If it is not too far a journey, I am happy to bring things to you."

"In Kent. But do not worry about it. I can wear things from my father in the country. I have no engagements while I am there."

He caught the sympathetic look from Ragland and glanced away, his throat tightening.

"I will be off now, Mr. Ragland. Thank you again for dropping everything else and spending time to get me into proper attire."

"I am happy to be of service to you, my lord."

August gave him the name of his solicitor and asked that the bill be sent there. He had no secretary and saw no need for one. He could keep his own diary, doubting it would fill with many invitations.

Returning to his carriage, he asked to be taken home, where he spent an hour pacing in his study. Nerves flitted through him, worse than any he had ever experienced going into battle. He wanted these people to like him for himself, not for his appearance.

He wondered if Lady Georgina had told them of his facial scars and missing eye, preparing them.

Something told him she hadn't, and he tried to ready himself for the reactions he would receive, from the footman who answered the door to the butler who would take him up to tea.

And that didn't include those present at tea.

It was as he thought. The Seaton footman's shock when he answered August's knock. The butler quickly recovered, asking August to follow him upstairs to where the family waited in the drawing room. For a moment, he thought the butler might ask him to wait in the corridor so the servant might prepare the family for their guest's appearance.

Instead, the butler knocked and opened the door, announcing, "Lord Edgethorne has arrived, Your Graces."

The butler indicated for August to step into the room, and he did so with trepidation. Inside, his heart pounded wildly, in part because he felt he was going into battle. Another part of him, though, was eager to see Lady Georgina again.

As he crossed the room, the others stood. He avoided looking any of them in the eye, concentrating on Lady Georgina instead and not the intake of breaths he heard as the others took in his appearance.

She wore a gown of light blue, the shade complimenting her cornflower blue eyes. She also smiled at him, a genuine smile, as if she were truly happy to be in his company again.

August forced his eyes from her, turning toward the duke.

His Grace was August's exact height, three inches over six feet, with a muscular frame. He had blond hair, however, and the same shade of blue eyes as his sister.

Two women stood on each side of him, one obviously his wife, since the duke had his arm about her waist. The duchess was Lady Georgina's height, with golden-brown hair and brown eyes. The other woman was young to his mind, possibly only ten years older than August and the duke. Could this be Lady Georgina's mother?

Seaton offered his hand to August, who took and shook it.

"We are happy to have you for tea today, Lord Edgethorne," His Grace said. "May I introduce to you my duchess?"

He took the duchess' hand and squeezed her fingers gently. In the past, August would have kissed her fingers. With her tall, strong husband standing in front of him, however, August kept his lips to himself.

"It is good to finally meet our neighbor," the duchess said. "Welcome, my lord."

"And this is the Dowager Duchess of Seaton," His Grace continued. "My stepmother."

That made sense. This duke's father must have lost his first wife and wed again, choosing a much younger woman to provide more sons. He recalled she instead provided the duke with four daughters.

The widow was very beautiful, her thick hair the color of molasses. Her eyes were blue, but more an azure shade than the cornflower of His Grace and Lady Georgina.

"I knew your father, my lord," the dowager duchess said. "I read of his death. My condolences."

"Thank you, Your Grace," he said. "We lost him—and my brother—last summer. It is why I now hold the title, something I had not expected."

"Then we have that in common," the duke said. "I became Seaton only last autumn. But let me introduce my sister to you."

The duke steered August toward an auburn-haired beauty.

She was shorter than Lady Georgina but possessed the same eyes as her brother and sister.

"This is Lady Mirella," His Grace said. "She is the painter in our family and will be making her come-out this spring with her sister."

Taking the young lady's hand, August felt it safe to brush his lips against her fingers.

"I am delighted to meet you, my lord," Lady Mirella said, peering at him with great interest. "I have a tendency to be a bit talkative, but I promise to be on my best behavior today."

"And of course, you know Lady Georgina."

Looking once again to her, he took her offered hand, kissing her fingers. While he had felt nothing touching her sister's hand, August felt ripples of desire race through him as he held Lady Georgina's fingers.

"I am so glad you could fit tea with us into your schedule, my lord," she said demurely, but he saw in her eyes that she was aware of what was passing between them.

August released her hand, wishing he could snatch it back the moment he did so.

"Please, come and have a seat, Lord Edgethorne," Her Grace said, her husband leading her to a grouping of chairs and sitting next to her on a settee.

He found himself on a settee opposite them.

Next to Lady Georgina.

He caught the scent of roses and knew it came from her. He would like nothing better than to bury his nose against her neck. But that was something Old August would do. New August would sit straight and behave properly.

And never sneak kisses from this woman.

Much to his regret.

The teacart arrived, and the dowager duchess said, "You are not facing the usual crowd we have at tea, my lord."

"I know one of your daughters recently wed," he said pleasantly, as Her Grace began to pour out for them.

"Yes, usually Pippa and Seth would be here," Lady Mirella said. "We are also missing Aunt Matty, our sister Effie, and our two Strong cousins."

"While I am sure you miss your relatives, it helps me having fewer present so that I might learn names and who everyone is," he replied.

"My lord?" the duchess said, handing August a teacup and saucer. "I will let you prepare it as you wish."

The hour flew by. Everyone was gracious to him. No one brought up his injuries though Lady Mirella did ask August about his army days. Her mother had quickly changed the topic, saying that his lordship was safely at home and most likely did not wish to relive such times.

He was extremely comfortable in Their Graces' company. They talked of their two shipping empires, and he was astounded at just how much Her Grace did know about business, far more than the two men sitting in the room. Lady Mirella talked a bit about her paintings, and the dowager duchess told a story she recalled about August's mother and father. He recalled very little of his mother, and it was nice hearing her spoken of in such a positive way.

The only one who never spoke was Lady Georgina. He was aware of their legs and hips touching, thanks to the settee being smaller than usual or him being larger than most men. Probably a little of both. It was as if a humming occurred inside him, a buzzing that built. He wanted to take her hand, which would be outrageous. A woman such as her was not for him. August reminded himself he would be lucky to claim a homely wallflower from the Marriage Mart.

"You have been so quiet, Georgie," her sister chided gently. "You are the one who invited his lordship to tea."

Georgie . . .

August liked the nickname. It was playful. It suited her.

"I have already spoken to Lord Edgethorne. I wanted him to get to know the rest of you," she said. Turning to him, she added,

"It is good that you have come when there aren't four more Strongs at tea. Things can get quite unruly."

He smiled at her. "I hope I will get to meet the others someday." He doubted it, though. While he lived across from these Strongs, he had no intention of returning to London again. He would find a wife and be done with town.

"We have mentioned the rest of us are in Kent, my lord," Lady Georgina continued. "Where is your country seat located?"

"Probably not far from your family's estate," he revealed. "Edgefield is in Surrey, but it is extremely close to the Kent border." He paused. "I have also learned from my solicitor recently that I have a manor house in Scotland. Dalmara. My solicitor only told me about it when I called upon him a few days ago."

"Is that in the lowlands or highlands?" Lady Mirella asked.

"The lowlands. Apparently, my mother brought it into the family when the marriage settlements were written. The property belonged to her maternal grandmother, and it passed to my grandmother and then mother. I will need to go and see it someday."

"You could do so if you eloped to Gretna Green," Lady Mirella said.

"Mirella Strong!" her mother declared.

"Sorry, Mama," her daughter said. "But I have always heard stories of couples eloping to Gretna Green. If Lord Edgethorne wishes to wed this Season, it would be convenient for him to marry there and then honeymoon at his property."

The dowager duchess shook her head. Looking to August, she said, "It has not always been easy, raising six girls."

"I have only met Lady Georgina and Lady Mirella, Your Grace, but judging by the two of them? I would say you have done an excellent job."

"You have a silver tongue, my lord," she retorted. "But I thank you, nonetheless."

"Will you be attending the Season?" the Duchess of Seaton

asked.

"I plan to attend a few events," he said carefully.

"His Grace and I will do the same. We are rather busy, so we will only go to some of the events. His Grace has never been to any *ton* affairs. I want him to take his place in Polite Society, as well as help bring out Georgie and Mirella."

He looked to the duke. "I went to many balls and various parties during breaks from university. Hostesses are always looking for eligible men to dance with ladies making their come-outs. Too many men hide away in the card room."

His Grace shrugged. "I like cards well enough, but I will do my duty and make certain my sisters are properly introduced into Polite Society."

August wondered about Seaton calling his half-sisters his sisters, but it would be impolite to ask him why, especially in front of those sisters.

"Does anyone need any more tea?" Her Grace asked. "No? Then perhaps you could stay a bit longer, my lord. Georgie is an accomplished pianist. Perhaps you would care to hear her play."

He would stay as long as they allowed him to do so. Listening to Lady Georgina play the pianoforte would be a treat.

Because he could stare at her all he wanted to with good reason.

"I would consider it a privilege to hear Lady Georgina at the keys, Your Grace."

CHAPTER SEVEN

GEORGIE COULD NOT recall the last time she had been nervous sitting at the pianoforte.

Perhaps never.

She wanted to impress Lord Edgethorne, though. If Georgie did one thing well, it was play her pianoforte. And she would put heart and soul into her selection now.

She chose to play a selection by Mozart, tamping down her nerves as she placed her fingers on the keys. The first few notes sounded shaky to her ear, but then she did what she always did— gave herself over to the music. Soon, she was caught up in all the drama of the piece, experiencing the highs and lows intended by the composer.

When she finished, her fingers stilled, hovering above the keys before she placed her hands in her lap. She turned, her gaze moving directly to Lord Edgethorne's. He wore an astonished look, which pleased her.

And then he smiled.

She had thought both his smile and laugh rusty, thinking he hadn't found much humorous during his time away at war. One smile he had given her had already tickled her insides, but this one was absolutely brilliant. Georgie rose and rejoined the group, taking her seat again next to the marquess.

"That was quite moving, Lady Georgina," Lord Edgethorne said, awe in his voice. "You play superbly. I have sat in many drawing rooms, hearing ladies play, but you are far and above any performance I have witnessed."

"Thank you, my lord," she said demurely, secretly pleased by his effusive praise. "Mirella is also an excellent pianist. Perhaps you would also care to hear her play for us?"

Her gaze met his, and Georgie went warm all over.

"Yes, I would be delighted to hear Lady Mirella play, as well," the marquess said.

Her sister rose. "I am quite accomplished, my lord, but I should have been the first to play. It is always difficult to follow my sister."

Mirella went and sat at the instrument and began to play one of her favorites. Usually, Georgie was very attentive when her sister performed for others, but her head was lost in a swirl of jumbled thoughts, a swirl of confusing emotions.

Lord Edgethorne's presence was doing strange things to her. She was feeling an odd exhilaration within herself, simply being seated next to him. She caught a whiff of his cologne, something she never noticed about other men. He wasn't other men, though.

He was different.

And Georgie was going to pursue more than a friendship with him.

She had asked him to tea with her family because she liked him. She knew he most likely did not have many friends in town, having been away at war for several years. She had thought he and James were of a similar age and might get to enjoy knowing one another. But Georgie wanted to know the marquess for herself. She wanted to pursue what she was feeling.

If only ladies could be suitors for gentlemen instead of the other way around.

Somehow, she realized that the music had stopped. Mirella returned to her seat.

"You play delightfully, Lady Mirella," Lord Edgethorne complimented. "I would be hard pressed to say which of the two Strong sisters who performed this afternoon did better. I would call it a draw. Only know that you both are incredibly talented. I feel privileged to have listened to your performances."

Mirella chuckled. "Thank you for the kind words, my lord, but I know my sister is the better pianist."

"I should take my leave," the marquess said abruptly. "I do not wish to overstay my welcome."

He rose, and the entire group followed suit.

James said, "If you are interested at all in business matters, Edgethorne, perhaps you might like to come to our shipping offices tomorrow and see what goes on there."

"Oh, yes," Sophie chimed in enthusiastically. "We would be happy to show you around."

Georgie watched Lord Edgethorne and felt he seemed to be withdrawing within himself.

"Thank you for the kind invitation, both for tea today and to tour your business. I will not be able to take advantage of it, however. I am set to leave for Edgefield tomorrow."

"So soon?" she asked, knowing her question was out of place.

The marquess turned to her. "Duty calls, my lady. You must remember that I am new to all these responsibilities. As a second son, I was destined to spend my entire adult life in the military. I still have much to learn about being a marquess and all that comes with it."

"I understand better than most men," James said. "We must get together sometime and talk, my lord. I, too, am fairly new to my title and am learning about the vast responsibilities I hold. Fortunately, my cousin Caleb is my steward at Shadowcrest, and I know the estate is in good hands under his direction. At some point, though, Her Grace and I will need to take a tour so that we might visit the other properties which I have inherited. I need to meet the people on them and see what they are like."

James turned to Sophie, taking her hand and lacing his fingers through hers. "That will not take place anytime soon, however."

Mama said, "Well, you do have the upcoming Season to get through before you could think about traveling throughout England."

Sophie nodded subtly at her husband, and suddenly Georgie knew what they were about to reveal.

"It will have to wait for some time because I would not want to be away from my wife—and child—for any length of time."

Mama and Mirella squealed joyfully.

Georgie beamed at the couple. "I am going to become an aunt! How wonderful for the two of you—and us."

Hugs were exchanged, and Lord Edgethorne offered his own congratulations. "I hope that you remain in good health, Your Grace, and you give birth to a healthy child."

Sophie smiled gently, one hand going to her belly. "It is early yet. The babe should not come until mid-September. I will be about three and half months along when the Season begins. Because of that, His Grace and I will go to as many of the early events in April and May as we can. We want Georgie and Mirella to meet as many eligible bachelors as possible while we are present. Once June comes, however, we may cut back on our attendance at *ton* affairs."

"I couldn't be more pleased," James declared. "I had no idea how wonderful I would feel sharing our news with you."

"Again, Your Graces, congratulations on the upcoming birth," Lord Edgethorne said. "I suppose I will see you once the Season begins."

James offered his hand, and the two men shook again.

"It was delightful to make your acquaintance, Edgethorne. We are lucky to have you as our neighbor. Do let us know when you are in town again. We would like to have you for dinner. Perhaps we might even attend some *ton* events together."

"Thank you, Your Graces, for your kindness to me today."

Their group watched their guest as he left the room. The moment the door closed behind him, Mirella turned to Georgie.

"How on earth did you get to know him?" her sister demanded. "He is most interesting, but I hope he was not terribly offended when he first arrived."

"Yes, Georgie, dear," Mama said. "You should have let us know."

She looked at them blankly. "Know what?"

"About his severe injuries, dearest," Mama said gently. "We would have been better prepared when he came through the door if we had known. It is a pity such a handsome man will carry the scars of war his entire life. I fear he will be gossiped about openly once the Season begins."

"It won't matter to most, Mama," Mirella pointed out. "After all, he *is* a marquess. Most likely a very wealthy one, based upon the house he inherited. There will be plenty of girls making their come-outs who will try and look past his injuries in order to become his marchioness."

Sophie looked to Georgie and said, "Just as your sister has done. You do not see the wounded army officer, do you? You see the man."

Her cheeks filled with heat. "I suppose I do, Sophie." She turned to Mama. "I did not think to mention his injuries, Mama. I should have prepared all of you for his appearance, but Lord Edgethorne has a good heart. He is a kind man."

Her mother stepped to Georgie and embraced her. She kissed her daughter's cheek and pulled back, saying, "Then I have most certainly done my job as a mother if you look for the good inside of others, and you do not judge them on their physical appearance."

"Do you really think others will talk about Lord Edgethorne, Mama?" she asked, concerned.

Mama nodded. "Unfortunately, Polite Society seizes on the smallest tidbit and gossips ferociously about it. The fact that Lord Edgethorne is a second son and assumed the title would already give them fodder enough. Seeing he has been severely injured at war and bears the scars of battle will cause incessant chatter."

Her mother looked to the others. "Because we know him now, we must take Edgethorne under our wing. Introduce him to others. If Polite Society sees how accepting we are of the marquess, I hope they will follow suit."

Mirella spoke up. "Will it help since James is a duke, Mama?"

Mama nodded. "Dukes—and duchesses—set the tone at many *ton* events. While I do believe there will be much gossip about Lord Edgethorne, if James, Sophie, and I accept him and treat him with ease, others are bound to follow suit. Not all," she cautioned. "There will always be that element of Polite Society which chooses to look for the worst in others."

"But he cannot help the fact that he was hurt in battle," Georgie protested. "He gave everything he had for king and country."

"You are innocent in so many ways, Georgina," Mama said, something Georgie's hair. "Not everyone looks for the good in others. There are more than their fair share of those who prefer to seek out the bad. And yes, Lord Edgethorne will be judged harshly by them, simply on his compromised appearance. I hate to address this, but James and Sophie—even though they are a duke and duchess—will also suffer from some of this gossip."

"Why so, Mama?" Mirella asked. "You just said dukes and duchesses are the leaders of Polite Society."

"They are, and James and Sophie will take their places amongst the *ton*. Once others get to know them, they will see the kind of people they are, and the Seaton influence will spread from there." She paused. "At first, however, I do believe it will be an uphill battle. Rumors will be swirling about where James was all these years and if he truly is the rightful heir to the dukedom. Sophie, on the other hand, will face judgment because she has not stepped away from Neptune Shipping.

"One thing Polite Society does not ever speak about is their money and where it comes from. Yes, they all know about one another's wealth—or lack of it—but to speak about how this wealth came about is something which is deemed inappropriate conversation. There will be a handful who will think Sophie is dirtying her hands by keeping an active role as the owner of Neptune Shipping, much less going into the office and running the business herself."

Mama sighed. "We know how wonderful they are, and Polite Society will find that out for themselves. I just want everyone to be prepared for a bit of gossip regarding their status."

"Who knew that our family would be embroiled in scandal before the Season ever began?" Georgie mused. "And here we are trying to help Lord Edgethorne. Perhaps he shouldn't associate himself with us, after all."

"We will leave that up to Edgethorne," James declared. "He seems to have a good head on his shoulders and wasn't judgmental about us being involved in our shipping lines. What I am most concerned about is not the marquess. My concern is for Georgie and Mirella. We want you to make the match you wish to make."

Mirella sniffed. "I do not care what Polite Society says about James or Sophie. You are family, and I will defend you always."

Georgie slipped an arm about Mirella's waist. "I feel the same. If we have no suitors because they believe the Strong family to be scandalous, so be it. I want to find a man who can love me for *me*. One who can ignore the maelstrom surrounding us and make a commitment to me as a person. If he loves me, he will also love my family. I could not look fondly upon any gentleman who did not do so. I will not let anyone separate me from this family, nor will I tolerate anyone who cares to blacken the Strong name. If I catch anyone gossiping about us—or even Lord Edgethorne—I will call them out and then have nothing to do with them."

"It is hard to go up against gossips, Georgie," Mama cautioned. "While it is noble of you to want to defend the Strongs and Edgethorne, it would be wise to simply walk away if you overhear such gossip. You cannot change the mind of people like that, and if you confront them? They will only sharpen their claws and blacken your reputation. My advice is to ignore anything unseemly. Continue to hold your head high. Your conduct and demeanor will speak volumes and win over the majority of the *ton*."

"But Mama—"

"Your mother is right," James said. "While loyalty to our family is important, I do not want you to involve yourselves with any of the gossip. People will come to know us during this upcoming Season, and either they will like us, or they won't. I agree with Dinah. Most of Polite Society will be welcoming to Sophie and me, most likely *because* we are a duke and duchess since rank can be so important to so many."

He looked from Georgie to Mirella. "I also want to emphasize to both of you that we are not expecting you to find a husband this Season. Sophie has told me sometimes girls take more than one Season before they settle into a marriage. I want you to go into this come-out with an open mind. Have fun! You are young, and this is a wonderful time in your lives. If the right man comes into it, so be it. You will know him. But I don't want you to feel as if you must force yourself to align with a suitor. Pippa and I have made love matches, and I cannot imagine any kind of marriage other than that for the two of you."

"I agree," Mama said. "I am speaking as one who made the marriage my parents wished me to. You have no pressure to act. You may take as long as you need to find a husband who pleases you. James is right. Enjoy all the social affairs. Both of you, especially Mirella, enjoy dancing. Have fun at the balls. The routs and garden parties. Get to know as many people as you can. The wider the circle you come to know, the more likely your chances are for finding that special someone."

"I hope you will take your own advice, Mama," Georgie said. "You married the man your parents insisted you wed. Actually, you married a title and not a man. You deserve happiness, Mama. We all do."

Georgie swallowed. "And so does Lord Edgethorne."

CHAPTER EIGHT

GEORGIE WENT DOWNSTAIRS to the breakfast room, happy to see James and Sophie present. Her brother and sister-in-law had begun altering their hours, going into their shipping offices later in the day. At first, it had been because of Sophie's nausea. Georgie had learned that when a woman carried a child, oftentimes she experienced illness in the morning for the first few months.

Sophie had turned the corner and was now starting to feel much better, but she and James had started breakfasting with the family, waiting until about ten o'clock each morning before going to the wharf.

"Good morning," Georgie called as she took her seat at the table.

Mama said, "I am so glad we have finished all the fittings for our gowns. Now, if only the Season would start."

Mirella sailed into the room. "Good morning, everyone. Thank goodness the rain has finally ceased."

The rains had been constant and heavy for the last four days. She was tired of being housebound and looked to her sister.

"Would you like to go and walk in Hyde Park this morning, Mirella, while the weather is good?"

Mirella nodded. "I would be eager to do so. You know how

much I enjoy practicing the pianoforte, but even I am tired of it after being locked inside the house these past few days."

She turned to her mother. "Mama, would you like to join us and stretch your legs a bit?"

"That is a lovely idea, Georgina. I would be happy to accompany you. If we go right after breakfasting, that would be more convenient for me."

James said, "I don't believe Edgethorne has returned from the country. I sent a note around to him to see if he had come back in town. So far, it has gone unanswered. I hope he will make the start of the Season since it is upon us."

Georgie took a sip of her tea, trying not to think about the marquess. He had been gone a few weeks now, yet he still remained in her thoughts throughout each day. She was intrigued by the former army officer and wished to get to know him better. That would be impossible, however, unless he did come back into town.

"I am sure he is trying to wrap things up at Edgefield," Sophie commented. "He may not have as trusted a steward as you do, James."

"I don't know what I would do without Caleb," her brother said. "It is nice to be able to leave Shadowcrest in such good hands and not have to worry about anything there."

"I want to have the baby there," Sophie informed everyone. "I know we will stay in town through the Season, whether we are attending events or not, but I want this first babe of ours to be born on Shadowcrest lands."

"How will that work?" Georgie asked. "Will Mr. Barnes be taking care of business for you while you are in the country?"

"Yes," her sister-in-law said. "Mr. Barnes knew upon my marriage that he is to help run the company with me. That there might be long periods of time when I will not be able to come into the shipping offices. Fortunately, Kent is not so very far from London. I have spoken to Mr. Barnes, and he is willing to come to Shadowcrest every few weeks to keep me informed about things.

If there is an important decision to be made, he knows I will be the one to make it, and he will visit and provide me with all the pertinent details so that I may make an informed decision."

James added, "We feel it is important that our children come to know and appreciate the country, as well as town. Especially when Sophie has a boy, he will be my heir. I want to instill in him a love for Shadowcrest from the very beginning."

Mirella asked, "Are you wanting a boy this time, James? I assume all men do because they want an heir."

Sophie chuckled. "I can answer that for my husband. He told me that he prefers a girl. I suppose it is because he has all those sisters."

"I will be happy with a boy or a girl," James insisted. "It would be nice to have a girl first, though, since we do have so many in the family. But if you bear me a son, love, I will be happy to welcome the new Marquess of Alinwood into the Strong family."

"Son or daughter," Mama said, "this babe will be wanted and loved." She smiled. "And perhaps a bit spoiled."

After breakfast, Georgie and Mirella went upstairs to put on their spencers and bonnets. They met Mama in the foyer, and she had done the same.

"It has been a good while since we have had a long walk," her mother proclaimed. "I am looking forward to an outing with the two of you."

The trio walked the short distance to Hyde Park, and Georgie inhaled deeply. "Just smell the fresh air after all that rain. It seems to have cleansed the entire city."

"London does smell awful at times," Mama admitted. "Especially when the heat comes. That is why it is so refreshing to retreat to the country."

They strolled alongside the Serpentine, with Georgie and Mirella peppering their mother with questions regarding the Season. Mama told them about the various types of social affairs which were held.

"I believe you will enjoy all the events, but the most fun will be the balls. You both are accomplished dancers, and there is nothing like wearing a pretty ballgown and dancing until the wee hours of the morning."

"Will we stay the entire length of a ball?" she asked. "I cannot see Sophie coming home at five o'clock in the morning and then having to go to Neptune Shipping."

"Sophie and I have discussed this," Mama shared. "She and James understand their presence is important, not only to themselves, but to the two of you. Yes, we will be staying for the entire ball each time. Sophie will go home to bed and most likely rise at noon. Mr. Barnes will be calling at the townhouse and bringing her papers to sign. She decided it would be better to conduct the majority of her business from the townhouse and refrain from taking time to travel to and from the docks each day."

"It would be a hard enough schedule to maintain without being with child," Mirella declared. "I cannot believe Sophie does so much, especially now that we know she carries James' babe."

They continued moving along the path next to the Serpentine, and Georgie's thoughts turned once again to Lord Edgethorne. While she believed she should be excited about her come-out and meeting all the various bachelors, all she could truly think about was the handsome and interesting marquess. She prayed he would return in time for the first ball because she wanted to reserve the supper dance for him.

Mama must have read her mind because she said, "Let us talk about balls for a moment. I want to discuss a few things you should be aware of going into this first one. You will first go through the receiving line, where you will be introduced to your host and hostess. The hostess is usually the wife of the host. On rare occasions, if he is a widower, his hostess might be his sister or even his mother.

"Once we enter the ballroom, there will be time before the dancing begins to socialize with others. I will make certain that you are introduced to a good number of people, especially eligible men. After you have had a proper introduction, they may ask to sign your programme. It is very important that you only allow them to sign for one dance."

Georgie frowned. "Why is that, Mama?"

"If you dance twice in one evening with the same gentleman, tongues will wag. You would have to be most interested in a suitor in order to dance a second time with him on the same night. For these first series of balls, I would only advise that you dance once with a gentleman during a particular evening."

"Anything else, Mama?" Mirella asked eagerly.

"The supper dance is the most important one of the evening because you will spend an inordinate amount of time with your partner. You two have had dance lessons, and you know how lively many of the numbers are. Very little conversation can go on between partners during those country dances. However, the waltz is becoming the common supper dance tune, and because of the nature of this dance, it gives you a chance to speak to your partner. Your partner will lead you into supper, and you will spend that entire time with him. Most of the tables are set for six, eight, or ten guests, so you will be sitting most likely with friends of your partner or his family members."

Mama paused. "I would say reserve the supper dance for the gentlemen who truly interest you."

"That is good advice, Mama," Georgie said. "Anything else we should know?"

Her mother smiled. "I do have one more bit of advice. I would leave one dance open, preferably one after supper has been served."

"Why do that?" questioned Mirella. "I thought the point of going to a ball was dancing every number."

"You never know when a gentleman might catch your eye," their mother said. "If one does so, and he asks if you have room on your dance card—you do have a blank. And if no gentleman does ask you for that dance? It can serve as a respite for you. You might go to the retiring room. You might sit and speak with other young ladies who are not presently engaged on the dance floor. It is merely a suggestion, however, Mirella. I know how much you love to dance. You are the one in charge of your programme."

Georgie thought that a good piece of advice, and she was glad Mama had shared it with them. She had a fear of Lord Edgethorne not appearing at the beginning of a ball. If he came later, she most certainly wanted to have room on her dance card for his signature.

"We have walked long enough," her mother declared. "Let us head home. I wish to write to Allegra, Lyric, and Effie."

"I will do the same," Mirella said.

"I wrote to them only yesterday, so I will go and practice in the music room," Georgie told the pair.

They began heading back and suddenly, Mirella slipped on the slick ground. She went down hard, and a cry came from her. Both Georgie and Mama dropped to their knees, trying to right Mirella, whose face contorted in pain.

"I have injured my arm, Mama," Mirella said, tears springing to her eyes.

"Let us get you to your feet, dearest," Mama said calmly. "We will go home and summon Dr. Nickels to look at you."

Mama clasped one of Mirella's elbows to steady her, while Georgie took the other, causing her sister to flinch.

"Oh, it hurts so much," Mirella wailed, tears streaming down her cheeks.

They managed to get Mirella to her feet, and Mama asked, "Did you land on your arm? Or elbow?"

Mirella nodded. "Both. My arm is throbbing something terrible now. What if it keeps me from the Season?" she wailed.

"Do not go borrowing trouble, Mirella Strong," Mama said. "We will get you home and see soon enough what is wrong."

They walked on each side of Mirella, who cradled her left arm with her right hand, holding the injured arm close to her chest. A sinking feeling filled Georgie, but she did not say anything.

The moment the footman admitted them, Mama told him to fetch the doctor—and a surgeon—as a precaution. Her mother's words caused Mirella to wail mournfully, and her sobs could be heard throughout the house.

They gently led Mirella up the stairs to her bedchamber. When Georgie tried to help her sister from her spencer, her sister only sobbed harder.

"We must cut her spencer from her before Dr. Nickels gets here," Mama said, sending Millie for scissors.

"It is my favorite," Mirella protested.

"You can have as many spencers made up as you wish, Mirella. Now hush, sweet girl," Mama urged, helping Mirella to sit on the bed and then sitting beside her, putting her arm about her daughter. Mirella rested her head on Mama's shoulder as Georgie stood by helplessly.

She slipped from the room and went downstairs to wait for the doctor. He arrived, and she greeted him.

"Hello, Dr. Nickels. It is Mirella who has been injured. She slipped on the slick ground while we were walking near the Serpentine and hurt her arm. I think her elbow might be broken."

The physician clucked his tongue. "When your footman told me a surgeon might also be needed, I sent word for Mr. Busbice to meet me here. I have worked with him numerous times in the past. Take me to your sister, Lady Georgina."

They reached Mirella's bedchamber, and Dr. Nickels entered. Mirella burst into fresh tears at the sight of him.

"I am sorry you took such a dreadful spill, my lady, but I must examine your arm to determine a course of action."

Mirella finally removed her right hand, which had been bracing her left arm, but left the arm snuggled against her chest for support. It was a good thing they had cut away the spencer so that the physician could examine the arm without encumberment.

"Yes, there is swelling and tenderness, both in the forearm and elbow area. Can you bend your arm, Lady Mirella?" Dr.

Nickels asked.

She tried to do so and then shook her head furiously. "No. The pain is too great to do so."

"The good news is that it is not a compound fracture," the doctor told them. "That is when a break has occurred and the bone protrudes from the skin."

All three women shuddered hearing his words.

"From what I can see," he continued, as he ran his fingers along Mirella's arm and to the elbow, "there is one break int the forearm and a separate one in the elbow itself. A surgeon will need to set the bones in order for them to heal properly."

A knock sounded at the door, and a footman entered. "Mr. Busbice is here, Your Grace."

"Ah, come in, Busbice," Dr. Nickels urged. "You are in wonderful hands with Mr. Busbice, Lady Mirella. We have worked together on many occasions, and he is simply the best at what he does. Under his care, you will be fit as a fiddle in no time."

Dr. Nickels stepped aside, saying, "I leave things in your hands, Mr. Busbice. If you would like, Your Grace, I can leave a sleeping draught for Lady Mirella. It would help her get through today and tonight, when the pain will be the greatest."

"I would appreciate that, Doctor," Mama said.

Mama sat on the bed again, holding Mirella's right hand as Mr. Busbice examined her left arm. Georgie could see the gentleness the surgeon used in his examination.

"There are two breaks. Here. And here," he indicated. "We have three ways to set bones, Your Grace. I can use a splint or a wooden cast. Or I can wrap it in plaster."

"Which would you recommend, Mr. Busbice?" Mama asked, her worry evident.

"If it were only the forearm, we could do any of the three. Because it is also the elbow, I think plaster is the way to go. It will form a hard, protective shell and keep the limb immobile while the bones mend. I believe it will promote faster healing."

"Then do it," Mama urged.

Mr. Busbice looked at Mirella. "Once I encase your arm in the plaster, my lady, you will wear a sling. It and the plaster will keep your arm bent and close to your body. You are going to be feeling very protective of the limb. You might have fears something else will happen to it again, which is only natural. The sling will serve its purpose."

Mirella bit her lip. "How long will I have to wear it, Mr. Busbice?"

"Again, the elbow is a more serious fracture than that in the forearm, and it will prolong the time it will take for you to heal completely. I would say anywhere from eight to ten weeks."

"That long?" Mirella burst into tears.

Mr. Busbice looked taken aback until Mama explained, "My daughter was to make her come-out in three days' time. That will be impossible now."

"Lady Mirella could certainly attend the social activities," the surgeon encouraged. "She could talk with others. But there would be absolutely no dancing. She will be off-balance as it is. I would not risk dancing if it were my daughter."

"What is the good of a come-out if you cannot dance?" Mirella asked defiantly. "No, Mama, I am not going to make my come-out this year and sit on the sidelines the entire time. All of you have told me this is a time in my life I am to enjoy. Believe me, I am not going to enjoy wearing this restrictive plaster or having to tote my arm about in a sling. I plan to go home to Shadowcrest and do my healing there. I will make my come-out next Season."

The surgeon nodded. "That is a wise plan, my lady. A quieter life and the fresh country air will promote healing. You should see the village doctor once you return, and then he will be able to discuss your course of treatment and monitor when the plaster should be removed."

"Thank you, Mr. Busbice," Mama said. "Should we give her the sleeping draught now?"

"Soon. She is in a good deal of pain. You see how the swelling is. Let me prepare the plaster. Lady Mirella may drink the concoction before I put the plaster in place. By the time I finish, she will be very sleepy. I must go to your kitchens in order to prepare the plaster. I will be back shortly, Your Grace."

Mirella cried quietly as they helped her out of her gown and into a night rail.

Georgie herself unpinned her sister's hair and brushed it out, plaiting it into two braids.

"Just think how everyone will fuss over you at Shadowcrest," she told her sister. "Why, they will want to play with your hair all day long. They can figure out all kinds of styles for you to wear during your come-out next year."

Her eyes swimming with tears, Mirella looked at Georgie. "I am so sorry I have ruined things. We were supposed to do this together, especially since you didn't have Pippa with you."

"You haven't ruined anything. In fact, it will allow me to go through the Season in its entirety, and then I will be able to share all about it with you and the others. Why, I may simply kick up my heels and have nothing but fun this Season and put off looking for a husband until next year when you do return."

"You don't have to do that for me, Georgie," Mirella said. "Please, have fun—but do not wait on me."

"You know I have said I will follow my heart. I will merely see where it leads me this year."

She kissed Mirella's brow as Mr. Busbice returned. Mirella drank the sleeping draft, complaining of how bitter it was. Mama held Mirella's hand, and Georgie sat at her sister's feet during the entire process. Once the plaster had dried, they helped Mirella into bed.

"Don't go," Mirella said to Georgie, and she sat on the bed holding her sister's hand until she fell asleep.

She could not believe what had happened. A Season when five of them were to make their come-outs had now dwindled to her.

And Georgie was anxious about going through it alone.

CHAPTER NINE

IT WAS THE opening night of the Season.

Georgie was conflicted. Part of her was excited to finally take her place amongst the *ton*. Tonight would be about meeting new people and making new friends—and possibly forming an attachment with a gentleman. She still wished she could be sharing this night with her twin. Or Mirella and her cousins.

Her injured sister had traveled by carriage two days ago to Shadowcrest. Mama had insisted on accompanying her daughter home and seeing her settled, but she promised Georgie that she would return in time for tonight's ball, hosted by Lord and Lady Pennywise. Thankfully, Mama had returned home at noon today. Georgie couldn't imagine going into the opening night without her mother by her side. It was bad enough that Pippa wasn't here.

She went to the dressing table and opened a drawer, removing the letter she had received from her twin only this morning, deciding to read it again for comfort.

My dearest Georgie –

Oh, how I have missed you!

Every time I see something interesting, I want to turn and tell you about it. Fortunately, Seth is here with me, seeing and doing everything I am, introducing me to new sights and customs. These Americans may speak English, but their accents sound rather harsh to my ears! A few of them have been downright hostile, hearing my own English accent, saying they want nothing to do with King George or Great Britain, making a point of saying they have started their own country and are better for doing so.

Yet the vast majority of them have been nothing but courteous and friendly to us. We first spent time in a place called New York City. It is a bustling city, much as London is, and quite exciting. There is an electricity in the air. It is the newness of being on their own, I suppose. The food is quite good. I will have to see if Cook can recreate some of the dishes once I am home and tell her about them.

We are off to Boston in the morning with first tide, which is why I am posting this first letter to you. Traveling across the Atlantic Ocean was an adventure in itself. Seth, being a former captain, was welcomed by the captain of our sailing ship, and we were allowed to go places other passengers were not. Seth has taught me much about ships and the various jobs of the sailors onboard. The captain had us dine with him frequently, and we spent a great deal of time in his company.

Seth has also taught me some songs which I can never sing around anyone but you! They are quite risqué, but he has a wonderful singing voice, and we blend together nicely. He has also shared many legends and stories (some of them with ghosts!), and I will try to remember them all and tell them to you once we return home.

I can tell you that I am QUITE satisfied with my marriage. Married life is even better than I could have expected. Oh, Georgie, I love my husband SO MUCH! It is hard to recall what my life was like before Seth came along. He is so loving and smart and takes such good care of me. Really good care. I know you do not yet understand that, but I hope you find a husband who will kiss you senseless and make you feel *like a princess. Seth does that for me. He is always in my thoughts, and somehow, I think I love him more each day.*

I am not certain when this will reach you. I am hoping before the Season begins. If it has already started, then I hope you have become a huge success and danced until there are holes in your slippers! Know that you are (next to Seth) my soulmate. We will always be the best of friends. Just marry a man who worships you—and who will like Seth and me—because we want to be around you a lot.

Georgie, as I write this, I miss you terribly. There is a possibility that I might be with child. Me, a mother—can you believe it? It is early, but Seth says he can already see (feel!) the difference in my body. He says my breasts are slightly larger (which I have always hoped for), and that is an indication I am increasing. I will know for certain by the next time I write.

I hope you are happy and enjoying all the social events of the Season. We will head to Canada after a short time in Boston, and then it will be many long days at sea after that. Seth says things are too volatile for us to go ashore in South America, so it won't be until we reach the Sandwich Islands before I write again and post a letter to you. No, I can actually write again and have the letter sent home to you from Canada. That is what I will do!

I miss you. I love you. I hope you are well and happy.

All my love forever and ever!
Pippa (Lady Hopewell!)

Georgie couldn't help but smile. The letter was all Pippa, down to the numerous exclamation marks throughout it. She was delighted her twin was so happy in her marriage and perhaps even a bit envious that Pippa might be with child. More than anything, Georgie longed to be a mother. Still, she would not rush into a marriage simply to become one. She would take her time and hope her heart whispered to her which man was the one for her.

Placing Pippa's letter in the drawer again, she took a sip of tea. Mama had a cup sent up to Georgie, saying it would soothe her before the whirlwind began.

An hour later, she was dressed in one of her favorite gowns Madame Dumas had created for her. The modiste and her seamstresses had almost completed all the gowns for Georgie and Mama and was done with those for Sophie. Madame had even taken on a few other clients since three of the Strongs had chosen not to make their come-outs, giving the modiste more time.

"You are a vision of loveliness," Mama said, her eyes misting over as she looked at her daughter.

"You are beautiful tonight, Mama," she replied. "Every gentleman present at Lord and Lady Pennywise's ball will be vying for a dance with you."

Mama laughed and then motioned to Libby, her maid, who had come and dressed Georgie's hair, sweeping it high on her head, allowing a few curls to frame her face.

Libby handed Mama a box, and her mother presented it to Georgie.

"Open it," her mother insisted.

She did so, removing a gold locket on a thin chain. Engraved on the locket was a G.

"It is lovely, Mama. Thank you so much."

Her mother took the necklace and placed it about Georgie's neck, fastening it. She sat at the dressing table and admired her image in the mirror, fingering the locket.

"It has a lock of your hair inside it. I saved it from when you were a baby, always intending to present you with the locket on the night of your debut."

Georgie motioned, and Millie knew to provide a handkerchief. Wiping her eyes, Georgie shook her head. "It is a wonderful gift, Mama."

"I gave Pippa hers before she and Seth left for London and their voyage."

"Oh, that is wonderful!"

Mama shook her head. "I also had lockets engraved for Mirella, Lyric, and Allegra. Even Effie because I wanted all of them to match and thought it would be wise to do so at the same time. The others will have to wait for theirs."

"Do you think Allegra and Lyric will ever make their come-outs?" she asked.

"I have not addressed the issue with them," her mother admitted. "I was so busy seeing to Mirella when I was at Shadowcrest that the matter never came up. However, your cousins seemed happy. Effie, too. Then again, Effie is like Pippa—happiest in the country, with all her animals."

"I think Mirella made the right decision to postpone her debut," she said. "You know how much she enjoys dancing. From what I gather, married ladies do not dance much at all. It would have been a shame if Mirella caught the eye of a gentleman and wed him, only for Mirella to find herself siting with all the other matrons."

"Your sister will be fine. You are the one I am concerned about now."

"I will be in good hands, Mama. Do not forget that Pippa and I want to see you happy, too."

"Whatever comes my way, I will be open to it," Mama promised. "But we should go downstairs. James and Sophie will be waiting for us."

When they went to the foyer, only Sophie was present.

"You look lovely, Sophie," Mama said to her. "You are glowing."

"Thank you, Dinah. I am feeling a bit odd."

"Why so?" questioned Georgie.

Her sister-in-law blushed. She leaned closer to the pair, so as not to be overheard by the nearby footmen, and whispered, "My breasts are actually larger these days. The gown was a little snug on me. I am a bit self-conscious about them."

"It goes with the territory of giving birth. Mine grew in size each time when I had one of my girls," Mama confided. "They usually go back to the size they were before. I only had one friend whose breasts remained that large."

She wanted to mention that Pippa had written about the same thing and then realized her twin may not have shared that news in her letter to Mama. She and Pippa had always told one another things they did not tell others. For now, Georgie would keep this to herself. It was a small piece of Pippa that she would hold dear. By the next time they received a letter from her twin, she was certain Pippa would mention whether or not there might be a babe.

James emerged from his study, and Georgie couldn't help herself. "My, the Duke of Seaton certainly looks handsome tonight. And to think just a few months ago, you were a mere ship's captain. Now, here you are, decked out in all your ducal finery, making your tailor proud."

Her brother laughed, slipping an arm about Sophie, and bending to kiss her cheek. "This is the one who looks the best of us," he said, praising his wife's appearance. "However, the two of you look quite nice yourselves. This duke will be happy to claim you all this evening."

Mama laughed. "I should hope so, Your Grace."

"Shall we go?" James asked, leading the three women to where the carriage awaited them.

Once aboard it, Sophie said, "I am a bundle of nerves. I do not know about the two of you, but I fear every eye will be on me tonight."

"You will have the attention of the *ton*, Sophie," Mama agreed. "James, too. After all, you are a new duke and duchess being introduced into Polite Society. Simply be yourselves, and all will go well. I believe you will make friends, left and right, tonight."

"I wish I would have heard from Lord Edgethorne," James said. "I even went personally to his townhouse earlier this afternoon to see if my note had gone astray, and whether or not the marquess had returned from the country. His butler informed me that Edgethorne would not arrive for at least another week. Possibly two."

Hearing these words, Georgie's spirits flagged. She had wanted more than anything to dance with Lord Edgethorne this evening. Perhaps it was for the best. It would allow her to focus on meeting other gentlemen for the first time, without constantly searching the ballroom for a glimpse of their neighbor.

The carriage slowed, and Mama glanced out the window. "As always, the first night of the Season sees the roads clogged with vehicles. This may be as close as we can get. Are you able to walk the rest of the way, Sophie?"

James answered gallantly, "If my wife cannot, I will sweep her into my arms and carry her there."

Sophie blushed profusely. "You will not," she insisted. "I am perfectly capable of walking a short distance. In fact, I am beginning to have more energy."

"That is common when you are increasing," Mama said. "Those early months, you can be so very sick, and then during the middle of your term, you seem to have more life about you. Then life will have to slow down for you again in those last couple of months. You will become quite large by then. You will not want to exert yourself."

"Then I may have to arrange for a daily meeting with Mr. Barnes at the townhouse," Sophie declared.

The carriage stopped, and moments later, a footman opened the door.

"Your Grace, the coachman says this is as close as he can get you."

"Not a problem," James said cheerfully, bounding down the steps and handing each of them down.

Mama linked arms with Georgie, and they followed James and Sophie, heading to the townhouse where everyone seemed to be going. Once inside, they joined a lengthy receiving line.

Sophie leaned over to Georgie. "This is where you will begin to scrutinize others," she said, acting as a fellow conspirator might. "I am certain there will still be bachelors amongst the guests who were bachelors during my time of coming out. Some gentlemen choose to wait many years before committing themselves to a marriage, sowing their oats before settling down."

"I do not believe that is the kind of man I wish for my husband," she declared.

"Do not close any doors, Georgie," Sophie cautioned. "You do not want to judge a man by his past. Look to his present and future potential."

James said, "Well, I will certainly be investigating suitors' pasts. Any gentleman who is interested in you, Georgie, will have to go through me. That will be the true test. If the suitor is confident enough—and interested enough in you—he will make it past me. Then you can decide if he is worthy of you or not."

"The two of you must stop calling her Georgie in public," Mama admonished. "It makes her sound as if she is a seven-year-old boy. She is to be Lady Georgina at these events."

They finally reached the front of their line, and Mama introduced them to their hosts.

"It is so good to see you at an event again, Your Grace," the countess said to Mama. "I am sorry to hear of the passing of His Grace."

"While it was sad for our entire family, we are handling things well," Mama said diplomatically. "May I introduce to you the new Duke of Seaton and his duchess?"

After greeting James and Sophie, Mama indicated Georgie. "And this is my eldest daughter, Lady Georgina Strong. She is making her come-out this Season."

"Ah," Lord Pennywise said. "You possess the good looks of your mother and the confidence of your father. Gentlemen this Season will have their hands full with a beauty such as yourself, Lady Georgina. They will be clamoring for dances, and your drawing room will be filled each afternoon with a bevy of suitors."

She had no idea what to say to the earl and so merely smiled graciously.

They entered the ballroom, which was already half-full, and Mama took them to the left, pausing to speak with two couples standing there. It included two friends of her mother and their husbands, no one who would be asking Georgie to dance.

Some unspoken message occurred however, and the two couples moved on.

"We will remain in this spot," Mama told their group. "After all, James and Sophie are a duke and duchess. It is for people to come to us—and not us to go to others."

The words were barely out of her mother's mouth when it seemed that a new line formed in which to meet and greet the new Duke and Duchess of Seaton. Mama was gracious as always, introducing James and Sophie, along with Georgie. Before she knew it, she had not taken another step into the ballroom, and yet her programme was filled.

All except for one dance.

She foolishly held out hope that somehow, some way, Lord Edgethorne might actually arrive in town and choose to attend the Pennywise ball.

Their hosts entered the ballroom, and soon after, the musicians took up their instruments. Georgie had been to a few dances at the assembly room at Crestview, the village closet to Shadowcrest, and she was thrilled to be dancing again after so long a time. The first part of the evening passed swiftly, the dances all lively. She found herself out of breath a few times, and one of her more thoughtful partners fetched a glass of ratafia for her after the dance concluded, staying by her side after doing so and chatting a few minutes before it was time for the next number to commence.

The supper dance finally arrived, and Lord Blankenship claimed her. It was a waltz, as Mama had predicted, and she found the viscount to be a fairly good dancer. They did not speak during the actual waltz itself, however, and she believed he was having to count the steps to himself.

That was hard for her to imagine. Playing the pianoforte as she did, she always intrinsically felt the beat of any music she heard.

When the dance ended, Lord Blankenship bowed to her and asked formally, "May I escort you to the midnight buffet, Lady Georgina?"

"Certainly, my lord. I am happy to dine with you."

"I was going to meet up with a few friends of mine. I hope you do not mind."

"Not at all," she replied. "If I have yet to meet them this evening, then I hope you will kindly make the introductions."

They entered the room where the buffet was being held, and Georgie saw the tables about to buckle under the weight of all the food.

The viscount escorted her to a table for eight, and then he introduced her to the other two gentlemen seated there. They, in turn, introduced her to the two ladies they had partnered with for the supper dance.

Lord Blankenship asked, "Would you like to remain here and chat with your new friends while I fetch us something from the buffet?"

"That would be quite thoughtful, my lord. Thank you."

The other two ladies also remained at the table, and Georgie spent the next quarter-hour engaging them in conversation. They were cousins, both from Somerset. Lady Lida had made her come-out last Season, while Miss Markle was making her debut tonight. She found the pair quite amiable and enjoyed their time together, realizing the Season would not only be about a search for a husband but giving her time to make new friends, as well.

The three gentlemen returned, each carrying two plates. Lord Blankenship set one down in front of her.

Laughing, she said, "I am not certain I can eat a third of this, my lord."

He shrugged. "I forgot to ask what your favorites were. I suppose I was blinded by your beauty, my lady," he flirted.

She felt her cheeks pinken. "I will sample a bit of everything."

The conversation flowed easily, and Georgie could see how much fun these *ton* events would be.

Then an odd feeling settled over her. She looked up to see if anyone was watching her.

And saw Lord Edgethorne standing in the doorway of the room.

CHAPTER TEN

AUGUST HAD TRIED to stay away.

He had thought to remain in the country for a few more weeks, but the pull to see Lady Georgina was simply too great to bury himself there. He returned to town early, surprising his entire London staff, who rushed about once he had arrived. His butler told him that the Duke of Seaton himself had stopped by merely minutes earlier, checking to see if the marquess was in town and if he would be attending the opening ball of the Season this evening.

Redding had asked if August wished for a note to be sent to His Grace, but he said no. Just because he was in town again, he wasn't certain if he wished to commit to attending the first event of the Season, knowing the entirety of Polite Society would turn out for this event.

He had left to visit his London tailor, finding the shop deserted of clients. Ragland had told him everyone had picked up what they would be wearing to the Pennywise ball this evening, saying his workers were still busily sewing in the back, and would be booked throughout the entire spring and summer.

August tried on the remainder of his wardrobe which the tailor had been working on and found that everything fit him extremely well, even better than his military uniforms had. He had his footman carry the garments to the carriage and returned home, closeting himself in his study.

It was there that he found the mounds of invitations, four neat stacks sitting on his desk. He opened them one at a time, seeing that he had been invited to dozens of events over the next two months. He wondered if those who issued invitations had seen his father's death notice in the newspapers and thought they now invited Peter, the new Marquess of Edgethorne. If so, they were certain to be surprised when he set foot in the doorway. In any case, they bore the name of the Marquess of Edgethorne, and he saw the favor of reply was asked for in each instance. Since he had not responded to tonight's affair, he hesitated, wondering if he should attend or not.

He dined alone and returned again to his study, where he sipped a snifter of brandy, hoping it would calm him. Finally, he decided he would go to the Pennywise ball. It had already started a few hours earlier, and he did not think at this point it would matter if one more guest slipped in.

Summoning Pole, he had the valet help him into his new evening clothes. August studied himself in the mirror, looking at everything but his face. He still cut a fine figure in clothes, but he was worried about the reaction he would receive when others saw what he now looked like.

Still, he had promised Peter that he would go to this Season and find himself a bride. He had already determined it could not be Lady Georgina Strong. She would have massive numbers of suitors, based upon her beauty alone. He hoped those gentlemen would get to know the lady herself and her sweet nature. His greatest hope was that she might honor him with a single dance.

August would live on the memory of that for the rest of his life.

Steeling himself, he ordered for his carriage to be brought around and climbed into it. He noticed the streets were empty of vehicles, and he supposed everyone who lived in this part of town had already arrived at the ball hours ago. His carriage dropped him in front of his hosts' townhouse, and August dismissed the driver, telling him he would walk home since it was but a short distance. The coachman looked at him as if he belonged in a madhouse but knew better than to challenge the word of his employer.

Approaching the door, he removed the invitation from his inner pocket and knocked.

When the door swung open, the footman who answered it gawked at him. August presented his invitation, and the servant accepted it, his eyes resting on the invitation and not the late-arriving guest.

"Come in, my lord," the footman said.

He stepped inside, and the footman closed the door.

"Where is the ball being held?"

"Up the stairs, my lord. The ballroom is just to the right."

Presenting a confidence he did not feel, August mounted the staircase and went to the ballroom. He heard no music playing and stepped inside, finding the massive space empty, save for a lone musician, tinkering with this violin.

He approached, clearing his throat. The man looked up, his jaw dropping.

"Is the ball over?" he asked.

"N-n-no, my lord. It is the supper hour," the musician stammered, his eyes dropping to the ground so he would not have to look upon August.

"And where might supper be held?"

Keeping his gaze lowered, the violinist pointed to a set of doors across the room. "Out that way, my lord. Then to the left. You will find the other guests dining there."

"Thank you."

Moving across the empty ballroom, his heels clicked against the polished floor, echoing as he walked. When he reached the far side, he could hear noise. Exiting the ballroom, he went down a corridor, the sound of conversations growing louder as he approached.

August went to stand in the doorway and took in the scene. Dozens of tables had been set up, and the lords and ladies of Polite Society were dining on a heady variety of delicacies. His one good eye swept the room, seeing an empty spot here and there, but he had no desire to join the guests sitting at any of the tables.

Then his gaze fell upon Lady Georgina.

She was a vision of loveliness, her dark hair swept high, a few loose curls artfully escaping. Her gown was of the softest shade of blue, and he knew it would bring out her cornflower blue eyes. She was laughing at something the man on her left said, and August was shocked to realize she sat next to an old friend of his. Two vacant seats were at their table, but he did not know if they were occupied by others or not.

Suddenly, he knew he had made a terrible mistake and turned to go.

But at that moment, Lady Georgina glanced over her shoulder, their gazes meeting. He saw her lips curve into a sweet smile.

Without warning, the supper room fell completely silent. All conversation had ceased, and August could feel hundreds of eyes upon him. From those sitting closest to the door came audible gasps since those occupants were near enough to bear witness to his hideous scars. He silently berated himself, thinking the scars had faded and weren't so horrible after all. He never should have come.

He heard one man's voice demand, "What is he *thinking*, coming here, looking like . . . *that?*"

The entire room heard the man's comment, and immediately, conversation broke out across the room. It had been wrong to come here, invited or not. Wrong to make a promise to his brother which he would not be able to keep.

Turning to go, he halted in his tracks.

Lady Georgina was making her way toward him.

He could not shun her in front of this entire crowd. August mustered every bit of courage within him and stood his ground as she approached him. From the corner of his eye, he also saw someone else headed his way, most likely a footman ready to ask him to leave.

But he only had eyes for the lovely creature who had now reached him.

He bowed to her, and she curtseyed, offering him her hand. He bent and brushed his lips against her gloved fingers. The room, which had been buzzing, quietened, eager to watch the scene played out before them.

"I did not think you would be coming this evening, Lord Edgethorne," Lady Georgina said.

"I returned to town sooner than expected, my lady. It is good to see you again."

They gazed at one another a long moment, and then he heard a familiar voice say, "Edgethorne! How good to see you."

He released Lady Georgina's hand and turned, finding the Duke and Duchess of Seaton, along with the dowager duchess, standing before him. Tears prickled at his good eye, knowing they had come to greet him in a show of support.

The duke enthusiastically pumped August's hand, and then he greeted both duchesses.

"I went to see if you were in town," His Grace said. "They said you would not be back for a week or more."

"My plans changed," he said vaguely. "I am sorry I missed your call."

The duchess smiled at him. "We do not have any space at our table, but I am certain a footman can bring a chair so that you might sit with us."

"That will not be necessary, Your Grace," a deep voice said. "We have more than enough room at our table."

August smiled gratefully at Lord Blankenship, who offered his own hand.

"It is good to see you, Edgethorne. It has been quite a while since we last spoke."

"You know one another?" questioned Lady Georgina.

The viscount nodded. "The marquess and I were good friends during our Eton and university days. Come, sit with us," he encouraged.

Turning, August nodded politely at the Seatons and then followed Blankenship, who had taken Lady Georgina's hand and slipped it through the crook of his arm, heading back to their table.

The room erupted in chatter following these exchanges, and he could feel the eyes upon him as he went to the table. He greeted the two gentlemen at it, having known one from their school days at Eton and the other at university. Both men offered him their hands, but neither could look him in the eye.

Lady Georgina was the one who introduced him to the two ladies at the table. Each offered him her hand a bit shakily, appearing quite unsure as he took it. He told himself that he had expected this kind of reception. That people would be horrified by his appearance. That there would be talk. Plenty of it. But he would push through and find a bride on the Marriage Mart.

Then he looked at Lady Georgina as he took his seat, and thought it would be a false move to ask any woman to be his wife when this beauty held his heart.

August could not begin to consider her for his marchioness, however. She was the daughter of one duke and sister to another. While his title and wealth would be more than sufficient for her family, he could not burden her with the gossip he himself would face the rest of his life. Besides, Lady Georgina was a bright light who should be allowed to shine and bring happiness into the life of many. He would spend all his days at Edgefield, in self-exile. Not that she would ever consider his suit, but even if she did, it would be unfair to put her in such circumstances with that type of marriage.

"Are you hungry?" Lord Blankenship asked.

"I suppose I could get a bite to eat from the buffet," he replied.

"You might want to try the dry cake, my lord," Lady Georgina recommended. "I found it most delicious."

"I will accompany you," his friend told him, and the two men went to the buffet, which had no line at this point.

Again, August tolerated the stares from others, hearing some of their comments, which were not uttered under a breath but boldly said aloud so that he could hear them.

"It is an embarrassment to have him here."

"Poor man. No one can even bear to look at him."

"He should leave and never come back."

After taking a few items from the buffet, he looked at Blankenship and shook his head. The two men returned to their table, where August busied himself trying to force himself to swallow a few bites.

Suddenly, he felt a tap on his shoulder and turned, seeing a woman in her sixties glaring at him.

"Marquess or not," she said in a loud tone, "you have no place here, my lord. Why, your appearance sickens me so that I cannot even finish my meal."

Naturally, the room had fallen quiet again and heard the old woman's remarks to him. August started to rise and apologize, but Lady Georgina placed her hand on his forearm, urging him to keep his seat.

She turned to face the woman. "I will have you know, Lady Mills, that Lord Edgethorne is one of the kindest and bravest of men. He has sacrificed much in the name for king and country in the fight against Bonaparte. It is because of the courageous men such as Lord Edgethorne that you are able to sit here in all this splendor, wearing your diamonds and fine gown and dining upon delicacies."

Lady Georgina's eyes narrowed at her subject. "You—and others—should be grateful for the service which Lord Edgethorne has given Great Britain. Your comment was most inappropriate. Lord Edgethorne will now accept your apology, my lady," she said firmly.

The entire room took in a quick intake of breath, on the edge of their seats, leaning forward to see what might happen next.

Lady Mills seemed stunned into silence, and Lady Georgina prompted, "We are waiting, my lady."

The old woman visibly swallowed and looking in August's direction—but not directly into his face—mumbled, "Thank you for your service to His Majesty, my lord." Then she turned away.

Once more, the entire supper room erupted, buzzing about the encounter between Lady Georgina and the outspoken elderly woman.

"You did not have to defend me, my lady. But I am most grateful to you and the courage you showed on my behalf."

"Polite Society spends too much of its time judging others on their looks. It is about time they went deeper. You are a person, the same as we all are, Lord Edgethorne. None of us would wish to be treated so shabbily."

"That was a courageous thing to do, my lady," the viscount said to Lady Georgina. "I am honored to have shared this supper with you, and I thank you for defending my friend when no one else did."

The viscount looked to August. "And I will try to live up to the standard which Lady Georgina has set for us all, my friend."

"Thank you," he said humbly, knowing she had risked her reputation of the first night of her come-out.

People began exiting the supper room after that, returning to the ballroom for the rest of the evening.

August returned to his food, eating a few more bites simply because he had nothing left to say to those at his table. He heard Blankenship ask if he could call upon Lady Georgina tomorrow afternoon, and she granted him permission to do so.

He looked at the couple and thought they would be good together. He would do what he could to encourage his friend to pursue the lady.

Even if his heart would break as he did so.

"Shall I return you to the ballroom, Lady Georgina?" Blankenship asked.

"No, thank you, my lord. I wish to speak a moment with Lord Edgethorne. He is supposed to come to tea tomorrow, and I wish to confirm the details."

Their table emptied, and she turned to him. "I do hope you will accept my invitation to tea, my lord."

"How can I not, after you so bravely spoke up for me, my lady? I only hope it did not ruin your chances with other gentlemen present tonight."

She snorted. "Either they will dance with me as they are supposed to, or they will be cowards and choose not to do so. If that is the case, I would not have been interested in them anyway."

August thought how he had wanted to dance a single dance with her, and so he said, "If you find any of those gentlemen behaving in an ungentlemanly manner and not approaching you for your scheduled dance, then I would be happy to take their place. If it would not be too much of a hardship on you," he added, giving her a way to let him down gently.

She smiled brilliantly at him. "As a matter of fact, I actually have one open spot on my dance card. It is the final dance of the evening, my lord. Would you care to dance it with me, Lord Edgethorne?"

CHAPTER ELEVEN

August could not believe that he was going to dance with Lady Georgina. That she had asked him—and not the other way around. He had escorted her back to the ballroom, and then felt too many eyes upon him, retreating to the card room instead. He did not join any table, though, knowing gentlemen sitting there would be reluctant to have him sitting next to them.

As he stood against the wall, observing play, the Duke of Seaton joined him.

"Well, Edgethorne, you made quite the entry into Polite Society this evening, didn't you?"

"I had no idea the eyes of the entire *ton* would be upon me," he admitted. "I thought I was going to arrive and slip inside the ballroom, standing unobtrusively on the sidelines."

"This was my entrance into Polite Society tonight," the duke informed him. "After many, many years at sea."

"What is your story, Your Grace? I have heard hints of it, and yet I am unclear as to what really occurred."

Seaton shrugged. "I was the heir apparent to my father, his firstborn son. My mother died trying to give him his spare. He then wed Dinah, the dowager duchess. She was not even ten years older than I. She gave him Georgie and Pippa, and he was mightily disappointed, thinking a young wife should have borne him a son."

The duke paused, his gaze looking out at the card room before he continued.

"When I was taken, I did not know that my stepmother was with child again. That would have been Mirella. I accompanied my father to the wharf. To Strong Shipping. Frankly, I cannot tell you much of anything about that day because it was so long ago. I do remember it was my first time at the shipping offices. How vast I found them. Somehow, I wound up outside. I think I was on an errand for someone in the warehouse. That perhaps I was supposed to go to one of our ships and deliver something. It doesn't matter. What happened was, I was abducted against my will."

August heard the emotion in the duke's voice. He did not press the man further, wanting Seaton to be comfortable with what he might share.

Finally, the duke spoke again. "I know now, from experience, that boys are often taken from the docks. Made into cabin boys. That is what happened to me. I do remember trying to tell someone—anyone—that I wasn't supposed to be there. I was merely laughed at and beaten to within an inch of my life. Slowly, but surely, my memories of life at Shadowcrest faded. The memories of my mother and father. Of my stepmother and stepsisters. I traveled the world, being called *Boy* on those voyages, until I insisted upon being called James. I truly did not recall what my last name was. All I knew was life at sea."

August couldn't imagine what this man had experienced. To think Seaton had been robbed of his very memories of his own family. At least he had experienced a stable childhood and though he and Peter had enjoyed different pursuits, he had always loved his brother.

"How did you come back and become the Duke of Seaton?" he asked, curious as to how the duke finally recalled who he was.

"I will not bore you with the details, Edgethorne. Suffice it to say that I can home from a voyage and while drinking in a tavern,

I met a man from my past. My former tutor. He recognized me. Said enough things to jog my memory. I began recalling things I hadn't thought about in years and years. And so I sought the truth. *My* truth."

Seaton fell silent again, and he and James stood together without conversing. Having experienced trauma of his own, August was respectful and did not push this man for more information.

After some minutes, the duke spoke again. "I put enough of the pieces together to recall my last name. To know the house to go to. I learned my father had been struck with apoplexy and had lain in his bed for close to three years. My uncle Adolphus, his twin and only younger by a few minutes, had taken over the entire family. My father died shortly afterward, and I was able to assume his title. Because of certain things my uncle and cousin did, I banished them from England to keep my family safe. There is nothing I wouldn't do to protect my family."

"So, you have not been in Lady Georgina's life that long," August noted.

"No, but it was almost as if no time had passed. I knew Georgie and her twin. I quickly came to understand them. Pippa. Effie. Mirella. Even my uncle's twins, who were foisted upon my stepmother.

"Tonight is my own coming out in a very new world to me. Polite Society is seeing for the first time the new Duke of Seaton and wondering about me, having vanished for all those years. We have not explained to anyone where I was, and I doubt we ever will. It is a private, family matter. That alone causes me to be a topic of conversation for the gossips tonight."

Seaton's story made August aware that he wasn't the only one with the eyes of the *ton* upon him tonight. The gossips would be eager to glean all they could about this man and would most likely invent outlandish tales about His Grace which were far from the truth.

The duke sighed. "Then there is Sophie herself. Wed to a

man not of the *ton*, a wealthy merchant who built a shipping empire. He took her under his wing and taught her all he knew about business. My duchess has the brightest mind of anyone whom I have ever met. She knows everything about business, and her instincts are always correct. She, too, is being gossiped about this evening. Studied. Raked over the coals. I have worried that the gossip involving both my duchess and I might pose a problem for Georgie during her come-out."

He smiled ruefully. "And then I came into your lives. For some unknown reason, your sister feels very protective of me."

The duke nodded. "She certainly stood up for you. More than once this evening. Her going to greet you was, in and of itself, a statement to the *ton*. But the dressing down which she gave Lady Mills?" he smiled, his eyes gleaming. "That, my friend, was priceless."

"Am I truly your friend, Your Grace?" August asked. "You already come with quite a bit of baggage yourself. I do not wish to be a further burden to you or the Strong family. I know what I look like. It is dreadful to gaze upon me. I can barely look at my own image in the mirror."

The duke studied him carefully. "And yet my sister has seen something within you, Edgethorne. I have told Georgie it is up to her to make the match she feels most comfortable with. She is a strong-willed, stubborn woman, despite all her sweetness. Georgie has told us that she will settle for nothing else but love. I wonder if you are the man who could give that to her in abundance."

Immediately, August shook his head in denial. "No, I am not the man for Lady Georgina. True, she has shown me a great deal of kindness, even standing up for me when she did not have to. But she deserves a man who will walk amongst Polite Society. A man who has a sterling reputation. I am definitely not that man."

"Then why have you bothered to come to the Season?" the duke pressed.

"I was extremely close to my brother. When I arrived home

from war, Peter was on his deathbed. He insisted that I promise I would find a bride. That I would provide an heir to the title. A new Marquess of Edgethorne. That is the only reason I am present tonight. The only thing that will convince me to attend further events of the Season."

"So, you were telling me that my sister is not someone you are interested in as your marchioness? Is that correct?"

More than anything, August yearned to be the special someone in Lady Georgina's life, but his physical appearance prevented him from seriously pursuing her.

"No. I am not interested in your sister," he said flatly. "I know because of my altered looks, I will be limited in my choice of a bride. I hope to seek a wife from those whom Polite Society has pushed aside. Hopefully, I will find someone who might look past my appearance and be willing to wed me and provide me with an heir."

"If that is the case," the duke said, "then you should be in the ballroom. Out on the dance floor. I suggest you dance with my duchess. I would also say my stepmother, but from what I have gathered, her programme is filled for this evening."

"Is the dowager duchess seeking a new husband?" August asked.

"Georgie and Pippa have encouraged their mother in this endeavor. She wed my father when she was but seven and ten. He was considerably older than she was. Her Grace gave birth to four lovely daughters and raised my uncle's two girls, as well. She was a faithful, devoted wife, caring for my father during the years he was an invalid. The twins believe she is still young enough to find a husband and make a good marriage. To find happiness."

"I hope she can do so," he said, liking the dowager duchess quite a bit.

"I owe Sophie another dance, Edgethorne. We shall return to the ballroom. Once I have danced with my wife, you can take the next number."

"I am supposed to dance with Lady Georgina. The final dance

of the evening," he revealed.

Seaton cocked an eyebrow. "Oh, is that so?"

The men returned to the ballroom, and the duke claimed his duchess from the matrons who were seated together, watching the dancing. August stood against the wall, watching the dancers in motion, finding Lady Georgina. He couldn't help but follow her. She had such an expression of joy on her face. She was truly enjoying this night of her come-out.

After the Duke of Seaton danced with his duchess, he brought her to August.

Smiling, Her Grace said, "I believe we are to dance the next number, my lord."

Still unsure of himself, he said, "Only if you are up to it, Your Grace."

She thought a moment. "I suppose I could use a bit of rest."

"Then let me escort you to your seat."

"Oh, no," she told him. "I still want a dance with you, Lord Edgethorne. I would like to catch my breath, however. Perhaps we could have a glass of ratafia and sit out this dance, then join in the next."

"I can agree to that."

"Let me accompany you," she said, and August knew she did not want him to be by himself.

They claimed a glass each and took a seat so they might watch the dancing as they spoke.

"Thank you for being seen with me," he told her.

"Why would I not want to be seen with you?"

He looked at her steadily. "You know why. You have heard the comments. Seen the stares."

"His Grace and I have also endured a few gaping at us. Nothing what you have experienced, but we can sympathize somewhat with what you are going through."

"His Grace told me a bit about his past. And yours."

She sighed. "At the time, I thought my life had ended. Wedding a man outside the *ton*. Being excluded from every social event. Though Josiah was quite wealthy, not a single invitation crossed his desk. And then I saw there was life outside Polite Society. My husband was quite brilliant, my lord. He was a self-made man, building his company slowly until it became a shipping empire. He shared all his knowledge with me. For that, I am grateful."

The duchess watched the dancers. "This life is artificial. Oh, I do see a point to some of it, and His Grace and I will attend some events simply for Georgie's sake. These social affairs will never consume us as they do others, however. What is important is the family we have. The family we will create. And the legacy we bestow. We both own shipping companies that bring goods which benefit many citizens in Great Britain, as well as transport goods to others around the world. I believe that is much more important than a ball." She smiled. "Even if I do enjoy dancing. I will simply have to curtail it as I continue to increase."

"I told His Grace that I promised my brother I would attend this Season. Peter was in poor health his entire life and never wed. He wanted me to do so, in order for the title to be passed down to my own son. After my reception this evening, however, I doubt even the homeliest of women would care to be stuck with me."

She frowned and sternly said, "You are more than the scars on your face, my lord. You have much to offer a woman. I will venture to say that you will find one who looks past them and sees the good in your soul."

"I hope you are right," he said, still doubting that would occur.

A cotillion was the next dance, and he led the duchess onto the ballroom floor. They needed to join three other couples. For a moment, he thought they would be refused. Then again, his partner was a duchess, and a group formed around them.

The dance began, the moves coming back to August after years of no dancing, and for the first time in too long to count, he felt a buoyancy within his soul. He had always enjoyed dancing and allowed himself to feel the music. As partners were switched, he saw the reluctance melting away, as the women who danced with him seemed to accept him for his dancing skills and not his beastly appearance.

The cotillion ended, with August returning to the duchess. Her cheeks were flushed as the music ended, and he escorted her off the dance floor. Seaton waited for them.

"You dance remarkably well, Edgethorne," the duke said. "My duchess has had me taking lessons with a dance master. Perhaps I should switch out and have you teach me to dance instead."

"I am done for the evening," the duchess said, fanning herself. "I am retreating to sit with friends." She looked to August. "Thank you, my lord, for partnering with me."

"It was my pleasure, Your Grace."

"Perhaps you might come to tea tomorrow," she added. "It has been a while since we saw you."

He smiled. "Lady Georgina has already asked me to do so."

"Splendid," said the duke. "We will see you then."

The couple retreated, and August found himself alone again. He kept to himself but was surprised when two different people passed him, complimenting him on his dancing. Perhaps he wouldn't merely be judged and then discounted because of his appearance. It gave him hope that he might have a chance to wed. It would still be an uphill battle, but tonight had given him a sliver of hope, despite the harsh words and ugly glances tossed his way by some of the *ton*.

The last dance arrived, and he sought out Lady Georgina. He had continued to watch her on the dance floor. She had not lacked for partners and was easily the most beautiful woman making her come-out this year. August planned to enjoy the dance he would have with her.

And then he would need to let go of any fantasies he secretly held of making her his.

Stepping to her, he said, "I believe this is our dance, my lady."

She placed her hand on his sleeve, and he led her onto the dance floor.

CHAPTER TWELVE

ANTICIPATION HAD BUILT within Georgie ever since she had brazenly asked Lord Edgethorne to dance with her. She was grateful that Mama had given her the advice to hold back a number. She wasn't certain why she had reserved the last dance of the night, but she was happy to have done so.

Because it was a waltz . . .

She had danced one other waltz this evening with Lord Blankenship. She liked the viscount quite a bit, and she had been surprised to learn he was a friend of Lord Edgethorne's. When he called upon her tomorrow, Georgie would be certain to thank him for asking Lord Edgethorne to sit at their table.

The way the *ton* had reacted to the marquess' appearance bothered her a great deal. Yes, he wore an eyepatch. Yes, he had a few scars. But it appalled her that people were so shallow as to think appearance made the man.

Her most recent partner escorted her to Mama. She had seen her mother dancing several times throughout the evening and hoped something good would come from it.

"Are you engaged for the last dance, Mama?"

Her mother consulted the programme hanging from her wrist. "I am. Are you?"

Georgie nodded. "I will be dancing with Lord Edgethorne."

Mama nodded sagely. "That was the dance you held in reserve, wasn't it?"

"It was. Did you see him dancing with Sophie?"

"I think the entire ballroom had their eyes on the marquess and our Sophie," Mama said, chuckling.

"He is quite the dancer, isn't he?"

"He is most skilled." Mama touched Georgie's cheek. "Just be careful, dearest."

"What do you mean?"

Her mother smiled brightly. "We will talk later. Your partner is here."

Georgie looked up and saw the marquess now stood before her. He cut a fine figure in his elegant, black evening clothes.

He bowed. "Your Grace. Lady Georgina."

"It is good to see you dancing, my lord," Mama told him. "I hope you accomplished all you needed to while you were at your country estate and can focus on the Season now."

"I am still learning, the same as His Grace. He shared a bit of his story with me this evening, so I feel comforted I am not the only one in the room trying to sort things out, having come into my title."

Another gentleman stepped up to claim her mother, and the marquess turned his full attention to her now.

"Are you ready for our dance, my lady?"

"I was in the group next to yours when you danced the cotillion with Sophie. You are a superb dancer, Lord Edgethorne."

"Thank you for your kind compliment. I always did enjoy dancing. Unfortunately, I have done none during the last several years."

He glanced over his shoulder. "We should go out onto the floor. The others are assembling."

She placed her hand lightly on his sleeve, sensing something pass between them. Something that only occurred with him. None of her partners this evening had generated the physical reactions and strange emotions Georgie was feeling within herself.

Only this man . . .

As they strolled onto the dance floor, she told him, "It is a waltz we will be dancing. I have heard it will become custom to close a ball with this dance during the Season."

He smiled, causing her to glow from within. "Then I suppose I will have you all to myself."

The musicians took up their instruments, and Lord Edgethorne took her hand in his, placing his other one against her back. Again, the ripple of physical sensations new to Georgie caused her heart to skip a beat.

Then the music began, and he swept her into motion.

He was the most skilled dancer she had ever partnered with. He—like her—seemed to feel the beat of the music. He moved her effortlessly about the floor, twirling her until she was almost dizzy.

They did not speak during the dance, for which she proved grateful. While she had wanted to have further conversation with him and thought this dance would be a good opportunity for that to occur, it was pure bliss to dance the way they were, as one, swaying to the music, transported to another place.

All too soon, though, the last strains of the waltz sounded. For a moment, Lord Edgethorne held her, their gazes connecting. She felt something for this man. It was nameless. For now. She would not try to attach a name to it until she was certain.

But her heart was most definitely speaking to her.

He released her, placing her hand atop his sleeve, guiding her back to where her mother, James, and Sophie now stood.

Bowing to her, he said, "Thank you for a most delightful time, Lady Georgina."

"You haven't forgotten that you are to come to tea tomorrow, my lord?" she asked anxiously.

"I will most certainly see you at tea. All of you. Good evening."

Lord Edgethorne moved away from them, melting through a

crowd which parted, giving him a wide berth. Georgie wanted to shout at them how foolish they were to behave in such a despicable manner. She had better sense than that, though, and held her tongue.

"Shall we attempt to locate our carriage?" James asked.

Her brother escorted them from the Pennywise ballroom and down the stairs. She called goodbye to several others she had met this evening, a few who had even asked to call upon her tomorrow afternoon.

Once they were inside the carriage, Sophie asked, "How was your first ball, Georgie? Was it everything you thought it might be?"

She said, "It was ever so much fun. Dancing in a ballroom, wearing a beautiful gown, somehow seems different from dancing in the assembly room at Crestview."

Turning her attention to Mama, she asked, "What about you, Mama? What was it like to dance at a ball? I know it has been many years since you have done so."

"I am like you, Georgina. I have always loved to dance. I did several times this evening. Not too much, because I do not want it to be obvious that I might be in search of a husband. Still, it was the most enjoyable evening I have had in many years."

"I do believe our drawing room will be packed tomorrow, containing suitors for the both of you," Sophie declared.

James frowned. "Does that mean we must be present to chaperone? I thought we were going to try to do a little business in the afternoons."

Sophie said, "I have decided because of my delicate condition that I will be conducting Neptune business from the house, my love. The carriage ride to and from the shipping offices would take up quite a bit of time. I intend to have Mr. Barnes come to me around noon each day with matters of importance. That does not mean you have to stick to my schedule."

"It would be helpful if you made an appearance every now and then during these calls," Mama suggested to James. "However, I am a perfect chaperone for Georgina. And if Sophie concludes her business and can venture to the drawing room some afternoons, that will be even better."

"I suppose I can be there whenever you wish me to do so, Dinah," James said with reluctance. "Then again, I may be taking dance lessons from Lord Edgethorne."

"The marquess is giving you dance lessons?" Georgie asked.

"I teased him about doing so because he is so light on his feet and moves so well," her brother said. "It was in jest, but perhaps the marquess might show me a few steps. I don't want to trample any more toes, as I did this evening."

"Perhaps when he comes to tea tomorrow, we could go to the ballroom," Sophie suggested. "Georgie could partner with the marquess, and you will be stuck with me, Your Grace," she teased.

"Oh, Edgethorne is coming for tea?" Mama asked.

At the same time, she and Sophie replied, "Yes."

"You were quite brave when you went to meet Lord Edgethorne in the supper room," Mama told her. "I know you have a kind heart, Georgina, but you must also be aware of the gossips."

"How could I not be aware of them?" she challenged. "Not only did people openly gape at Lord Edgethorne, but I am certain that you heard some of the ugly comments they made because they did not keep their voices down."

"Do not misunderstand me," Mama continued. "I like Edgethorne quite a bit, but if you are not careful, Georgina, people will begin to couple your name together."

"What if that is what I want?" she countered.

Mama slipped her hand around Georgie's. "If he is the man you choose, then we will all support your decision, dearest. It is early, however. I want you to thoroughly enjoy your Season. Meet as many gentlemen as possible. Only then—if your heart speaks to you—should you make a decision and commit to one."

She squeezed her mother's fingers. "I understand, Mama."

But Georgie's heart was already leading her in the direction of the Marquess of Edgethorne.

MILLIE HELPED GEORGIE change into a fresh gown in order to receive her afternoon guests.

"Oh, my lady, they are gathering in the drawing room even now. You must have made quite the impression last night. The entire room is filled with bouquets."

"Some of these callers will be for Mama," she told the servant.

Millie's eyes widened. "Her Grace is considering remarrying?"

"Lady Pippa and I have encouraged her to do so," Georgie said. "Mama is still quite young. She deserves to find some happiness. Whether that is in a second marriage or not, we shall have to see."

She took a final look in the mirror, patting her hair. "Thank you, Millie. That will be all."

"I will have your ball gown ready for this evening, my lady."

"Thank you."

Georgie made her way to the drawing room, quickly counting just over a dozen suitors within. She recognized most of them from last night, but she hoped they would reintroduce themselves because so many names were swimming in her head.

One gentleman she did recognize was Lord Blankenship. He was the first to make his way to her.

The viscount bowed, and she offered her hand to him. He took it and briefly kissed her fingers.

"You look lovely today, Lady Georgina. I appreciate you allowing me to call upon you."

She did like him a great deal, and so it was easy to tell him, "I enjoyed our dance and conversation at last night's ball, my lord. Will you be at tonight's ball?"

He smiled. "I will indeed. Perhaps you might consider saving a dance for me?"

Another tidbit Mama had passed along was not to promise dances in advance, so Georgie said, "If you approach me and wish to sign my programme this evening, I would be more than happy to have you dance with me, my lord."

Lord Blankenship chuckled. "I understand what you are saying, my lady. You cannot blame me for trying to get ahead of the others, though." He glanced about. "I do not wish to monopolize your time. I hope you will enjoy the bouquet I sent."

He bowed to her again and stepped away.

That move broke the dam, and half a dozen men swarmed around her after that. She was grateful when most of them reminded her of their names. All of them mentioned having sent a bouquet of flowers to her, and she promised to go around and look at them after everyone left.

James and Sophie were both present, and she saw them circulating about the drawing room, trying to speak to all the suitors. She looked toward Mama and was pleased at how happy her mother appeared. While Mama was a beautiful woman, she had looked younger ever since Papa had passed. The burden of caring for her husband lifted, Georgie could see the difference it now made.

Each of the callers spent about a quarter-hour before leaving, being replaced by new visitors. Georgie made certain to speak to everyone, whether they were here for her or Mama.

Finally, the last of them left, and she sat, exhausted.

"Is this going to take place every afternoon?" she asked.

"Most likely so," Mama confirmed. "Unless a garden party is being held. Of course, we can reserve one day a week to make morning calls upon friends ourselves, but you will need to make that day known so that no suitors turn up and find you absent."

She glanced about the room. "Did they all send flowers?"

"If they are interested in you, they most certainly did," Sophie said. "The larger the arrangement, the greater their interest. Or their need to outdo the other bachelors."

Her words caused them all to laugh.

"I would assume every man who walked through that door today sent something," Mama said. "There may even be a few arrangements which were sent by gentlemen who were not able to call today."

Georgie went about the room, reading the various cards attached to the bouquets, collecting them as she went.

"Must I write thank you notes for all these, Mama? If I do so, I will miss tonight's ball!"

"No, it is not custom to do so. You have proven to be quite popular, Georgina. I believe our house will be filled with fresh flowers for the next several months."

She bent and sniffed a set of roses. "It seems such a shame. All these flowers coming to one person. Might we distribute them throughout the house, Mama? Put them in various rooms? Why, I would even like to give some to the servants to brighten up their bedchambers."

Taking a seat next to her mother, Mama smoothed Georgie's hair. "That is a lovely idea, my dear. I will have Powell take care of it."

"At least this afternoon gave me a chance to speak a bit with new people," James said. "I spent some time in the card room last night. It was full of older gentlemen, most of them married. This gave me an opportunity to know the young bucks who are vying for the two of your hands."

The clock chimed four, and their butler opened the door, announcing, "Lord Edgethorne, Your Graces."

Hearing that caused Georgie's heart to flutter wildly. She had not had that reaction to any suitor who had called this afternoon. It seemed to be reserved for the marquess alone.

"Send him in, Powell," James said.

Lord Edgethorne entered the drawing room, stopping a moment to look about at the plethora of flowers before continuing across the room to meet them.

"Thank you for inviting me to tea this afternoon," he said. "I suppose I am remiss since I did not think to send flowers."

"It isn't necessary, my lord," Sophie assured him. "These arrangements came from suitors interested in Her Grace and Lady Georgina."

Georgie thought she would give away every bouquet simply to spend time with Lord Edgethorne.

CHAPTER THIRTEEN

"AH, HERE IS the teacart," James said. "Who knew talking with visitors would have me so famished? Have a seat, Lord Edgethorne."

It was just the five of them, so James sat beside Sophie and the marquess took a seat next to Georgie. She caught a hint of his cologne, and it brought back memories of last night, dancing in his arms.

Mama sat in a wingback chair nearby. As Sophie poured out for them, Lord Edgethorne asked, "Did you have many callers this afternoon?"

"Quite a few," Sophie replied, handing the marquess a cup and saucer. "I told His Grace he does not need to be present every afternoon."

"And I believe with all those bachelors coming around, I need to be here to evaluate their character and see if they are good enough for my sister or not," James said. He glanced to Mama. "I think Her Grace can determine whether or not a suitor is worthy of her."

"You know perfectly well that I am as capable as Mama of deciding on the worth of a suitor," Georgie said, accepting the saucer from Sophie.

"Your brother is right, my lady," the marquess said. "Some

men will appear utterly charming and not show their true nature when wooing a lady. I assume, being a duke's daughter, that you have an ample dowry. As a man who once attended balls with regularity before I left for war, I can tell you that many gentlemen are only interested in the dowry a bride can bring to them. You should appreciate your brother aiding you in your search for a husband. He might be able to unearth if any suitor has an ulterior motive better than you could."

"I am not truly searching for a husband this Season, my lord," she told their visitor.

"No?" he asked, frowning.

"I will merely enjoy the social activities of the Season," she emphasized. "Would I like to find a husband? Of course. But Pippa, my twin, wed for love. So did James and Sophie. They are shining examples to me, and I plan to do the same. That means I am not actively on the hunt for a gentleman to wed this Season— or any Season. I do not believe you can force love, my lord. If I cross paths with a man whom I have much in common with and who holds the same values I do, my heart will tell me if he is the one."

Georgie took a breath, surprised she had shared so openly with Lord Edgethorne. Then again, she wanted to give him an idea of what she was looking for.

And perhaps, he might be the one.

The marquess grew thoughtful. "I do not know of many in the *ton* who make love matches, Lady Georgina. My parents' marriage was arranged, as a majority of marriages are."

"But I have *seen* love, Lord Edgethorne," she said earnestly. "I have witnessed the joy on James' face when Sophie walks into a room. I watched how Pippa and Seth were with one another, falling more deeply in love each day. I want that for myself. I refuse to settle."

She paused, adding, "But already, too many men have fawned over me because I have a pretty face. I want a gentleman to see beyond that. He needs to get to know me, beyond my appearance. The man who does that and who touches my heart will be the one for me. He will become my best friend and the love of my life. He will not merely sire our children. He will actively help raise them. You see, I not only want love for myself. I want a man who is not afraid to show love to his children. My own father barely said anything to me in the years he was alive. I want my husband to be a true part of my life and our children's.

"And I do not believe that is asking too much."

Lord Edgethorne looked taken aback by her revelations. "You are seeking quite a bit, my lady."

"I disagree, my lord. I only want what my heart wants. To be heard. To be seen. To be loved."

He looked at her a long moment with his one eye, the green startling in color.

"I do hope you find happiness, my lady."

No one said a word. Georgie had thought her words might provoke the marquess into revealing what *he* was looking for in a wife.

"Are you seeking happiness, my lord?" she asked, hearing Sophie's quick intake of breath. "Would you wed for love?"

He rested his saucer on the table. "I no longer have that luxury, Lady Georgina," he said stiffly. "Not that I thought I would ever marry, much less for love. As a man now holding a title, however, I promised my brother that I would attend this Season and find a bride."

Edgethorne shook his head. "You saw the reception I received last night. Despite my family's good name, my title, and wealth, it will be an uphill battle to find any woman who would consider marriage to me. To answer your question? I do not seek happiness, nor do I expect to ever find love. The best I can hope for is a marriage of convenience, where my wife will receive the title of marchioness."

She frowned. "Would that not bore you, my lord?"

"On the contrary, I think it is the best solution. I plan to retire to the country upon my marriage. My wife may remain in town.

Or perhaps I will go to Scotland and Dalmara, so that she and the children could spend time at Edgefield."

"You said the children. Not *our* children."

"Yes, I did," he said evenly. "I will not see my children penalized because of my appearance. I will not have them bullied or talked about. The best thing I can do for them would be to allow their mother to raise them, be it in town or Edgefield. Or a combination of both. Having me around would do them no favors." He shrugged. "In all honesty, it would break my heart to see how frightened they would be of me. I know what I am now, my lady. I am a beast. Scarred beyond hope."

He held up his left hand, and for the first time, Georgie saw he was missing three of this fingers.

"It would be hard to lift a child, much less play with one, with my damaged hand." Lord Edgethorne shook his head sadly. "I will do my duty and see that there will be an heir to the title. I would not make my wife suffer by having to live with me every day and look at me. If I did, she would grow to curse me."

The marquess set down the saucer and stood. "I am sorry to have put such a damper on teatime today. I simply have to live with the reality of what I am. Polite Society will be done with me soon enough. As soon as I can find a woman willing to wed a monster, I will be gone and never darken London again."

Glancing to Sophie, he said, "Thank you for your invitation to tea, Your Grace." He looked to her mother. "It is always good to see you, as well, Your Grace. I will see myself out."

Georgie's throat grew thick with unshed tears. She wanted to rush after him but sat frozen in her seat.

When the door closed behind him, James said, "That poor man. He is a good soul, trapped with such a disfigurement."

"I like him a great deal," Sophie said. "I hate that he will settle for a marriage of convenience. Then again, I understand how very few ladies would wish to become his wife."

Mama nodded sadly. "If he makes known that he not only seeks a marriage of convenience, but also that he will grant his marchioness a great deal of freedom in their marriage, I believe he will find a bride rather quickly. It is too bad. You can see he was a handsome man."

She stood, fisting her hands. "He is *still* a handsome man, Mama," she spit out. "Why no one, least of all Edgethorne, can see that is beyond me."

She rushed from the room, no longer wanting tea or to be around anyone. If she went to her bedchamber or the library or to play her pianoforte, one of them was bound to follow her. Georgie decided to go sit in the park in the center of the square. It was the only place she could think of where she might truly be alone.

Not bothering with a bonnet, she went to the foyer. The footman on duty stood.

"May I assist you with something, my lady?" he asked.

"No. I am merely going to go and sit in the park and think. The day is pleasant. After so many visitors today, I need some quiet time to myself."

"Of course, my lady."

He opened the door for her, and she felt his eyes upon her as she crossed the street and entered the private garden area. It wasn't large, but it held several benches and had become her place of refuge over the years when she wanted time to think.

Plopping on a bench, she blew out a frustrated breath.

Lord Edgethorne wanted a marriage of convenience. He wanted nothing to do with his wife or children. He wanted to retreat to Scotland and become a recluse. All because of the wounds of war.

Anger filled her. He had no right to go and hide away from society. He was an interesting man. And a handsome one. She didn't understand why others didn't find it easy to look past his scars. They weren't that bad. They actually made his face more handsome. And who cared if he only had one eye? The one he did have was a vivid green, drawing her in.

He deserved more from Polite Society for the sacrifices he

had made. He was a good man and would make for a wonderful husband and father. She just knew it. In her heart. In her soul.

Georgie burst into tears.

She wanted Lord Edgethorne as her husband.

"Oh, bloody hell!" she shouted, leaping to her feet. "Bloody, bloody hell!"

She had fallen in love with the blasted man. With a man who did not seem to believe love existed—or at least that it could never exist for him, what with his altered appearance.

How had this happened?

One minute she was simply being nice to him. Liking him. Wanting her family to help befriend him and ease him into Polite Society. Then the next, her heart had gone off and done the unthinkable.

She simply couldn't love him. She couldn't *be* in love with him. She deserved a man who would return her love. Who would be by her side during the good and bad times in their marriage. A man who would hold her hand and tell her he loved and worshipped her, even when her belly was swollen with his child and she looked like a beached whale. She needed a man who would not only love her, but also love their children. One who would let them ride on his shoulders and tell them stories and sing to them.

Not a man who ran away to Scotland and abandoned his wife and family.

Georgie angrily wiped at her tears, turning to go.

And ran into a solid wall. No, not a wall. Merely a very tall, very broad, very muscular man.

"You!" she cried, pushing hard against his chest with the heels of her hands.

He didn't go anywhere.

"Are you all right?" Lord Edgethorne asked.

She eyed him. "Do I look all right to you, my lord?"

He flushed. "No, you don't, my lady."

"Why are you even here?" she complained. "This is *my* spot.

My thinking spot."

The corners of his mouth turned up slightly. "I thought this park was shared by our two families."

"Well, I am using it now," she said stubbornly. "So you can leave. Just like you left tea. That was incredibly rude, you know."

He nodded. "I do know. And I apologize." He paused. "Why are you crying?"

"Because I am frustrated," she told him. "About a lot of things. But mostly, about you."

"Me?"

"Yes, you," she said firmly. "Now, please go away so I might think. If you don't, I will not be able to ponder my problems sufficiently, and I will be in a foul mood at tonight's ball. Which— if you ask me to dance—I will not do so. I am not one of your supposed wallflowers who wish to wed you for your money and title, my lord."

"You would not dance with me if I asked nicely?" he asked, his tone teasing.

"No. I would not," she said stubbornly, no longer willing to allow him to hurt her. "I must focus on eligible candidates for my hand. You are not amongst that group. We are definitely at odds, Lord Edgethorne. I wish for a man who will treat me with respect. A man who is man enough to tell me that he loves me. Multiple times a day. My husband will be someone who surprises the *ton* by treating me as his equal. And he will love his children madly. Just as passionately as he loves me.

"You, on the other hand, want nothing to do with love. Or even the things a good marriage is supposed to be about. You want to marry a stranger whom you tempt with your title and wealth. Get her with child and have her produce an heir for you. And then abandon them." Georgie sniffed. "You are the last man I would ever wed, my lord."

The marquess placed his hands on her shoulders. The heat from his fingers seemed to singe her through her clothes.

"What about kissing me, Lady Georgina? Am I the last man

you would wish to kiss?"

Lord Edgethorne did not wait for Georgie's answer.

He simply kissed her.

CHAPTER FOURTEEN

AUGUST HAD NO control over himself. He had spent years being a disciplined person. His father had a rigid standard which August had always tried to live up to.

Georgina Strong tempted him beyond all reason.

Still, he reined in the passion flowing within him and kept the kiss fairly chaste, holding her in place, his lips pressed firmly to hers. She felt stiff in his arms for a moment, taken by surprise by the sudden kiss. He believed it to be her first one, having come to know her, and decided if it would be the only one between them, it must be memorable—for both of them.

Slowly, he began brushing his lips back and forth against hers, feeling her body relax. He started a series of soft, gentle kisses, touching his lips to hers briefly. Breaking the kiss. Doing so again and again.

Her hands came to the lapels of his coat, and her fingers bunched the material, now holding him in place. He couldn't help but smile against her mouth at her assertiveness.

August now let the kisses go for a longer period of time. Need began building within him, though, and he knew he must stop soon.

Before he lost his head.

Before he took too much from her.

Before he gave her his heart.

He kissed her a final time, wistfulness filling him, knowing he could never build a life with this woman. Reluctantly, August broke the kiss and then lifted his head. Staring down at her, he saw she kept her eyes closed for a few moments before opening them to look up at him.

"That was my first kiss," she shared, awe in her voice. "It is much better than kissing a pillow," she added, chuckling.

"You kiss your pillow?"

Lady Georgina nodded. "I thought it would be a good idea to practice on it. To be ready for when I did kiss a gentleman."

"So, I was better than your pillow."

"Yes. I liked your kisses quite a bit, my lord, but I did not lose my head as Pippa said I would." She paused, her brows knitting together slightly in thought. Then she gazed up at him. "I think . . . I think you were holding back," she mused. "Pippa said she becomes lost in Seth's kisses. That he uses his tongue when he kisses her. While I enjoyed what we did, I still was able to think about what we were doing."

She released her hold on him. "This confirms to me that you are not the one for me, Lord Edgethorne. That somewhere in Polite Society is a man who will make my head spin. I will admit that seeing you makes my heart speed up a beat, and my belly fluttered in a very odd but interesting way when we were kissing. But I kept my head. I knew we were kissing. I suppose I can thank you for that."

"You are thanking me for letting you know I am not the man for you," he said flatly, perturbed by her words.

August did not want another man kissing Georgina Strong. He did not want her senseless in another man's arms.

He wanted her for himself.

Now.

Catching her waist, he jerked her to him, a gasp flying from those soft, rosebud lips.

"If you truly want to know what kissing is about, my lady,

then let me be the one to show you."

His mouth came down on hers, seizing control. He kissed her hungrily, need coursing through him. He softly bit into her plump lower lip, causing her to moan softly. His tongue licked the place, soothing it. Then he used his tongue to sweep back and forth across her bottom lip, over and over. Her body began softening, her breasts pressed against his chest. August eased one hand from her waist, anchoring it along her back. His other moved to her nape, keeping her in place.

Then he persuaded her to open to him, his tongue moving inside her mouth, her gasp swallowed by him.

He found her tongue and allowed his to glide along hers. Time stood still as he thoroughly explored her sweetness at his leisure. Taking. Taking. Taking, again and again.

She began kissing him back. Their tongues began to play together. War together. But in this game, they both were winners.

August kissed her until the world outside this park became irrelevant. There was only her warm body. The scent of roses rising from her heated skin. The feel of her lush curves against him.

Finally, he broke the kiss, exhausted both physically and emotionally. He rested his brow against hers as they both fought to catch their breath.

Lifting his head from hers, he was pleased at the dazed expression on her face. Their gazes connected, and he saw the wonder in her eyes.

"That . . . was incredible," Lady Georgina said breathlessly. "*That* is what Pippa tried to tell me about and had no words to explain. How you kiss and become lost in that kiss. How you experience such pleasure and yearning at the same time."

She paused, thinking a moment. "Was it . . . I mean . . . did you enjoy our kisses, Lord Edgethorne?"

Gruffly, he replied, "I would not have kissed you for as long as I did if I had not enjoyed doing so, my lady."

He still held her against him. He did not think she even realized, and he was reluctant to release her.

"This changes everything," she said. "Now, I am beginning to understand what my twin told me." She boldly asked, "Do you have feelings for me, my lord?"

Her question took him aback. Immediately, he released her, and brusquely said, "I was merely showing you what a kiss could be, Lady Georgina. You had questioned the veracity of the kisses that came before it. I wanted you to understand what could pass between a man and a woman with a kiss."

She seemed to grow small, retreating inside herself.

"I see," she said quietly. "Your words indicate to me that nothing has truly changed between us."

Confused, he asked, "What do you mean?"

Impatience flickered in her eyes, and she crossed her arms and tapped her foot. "I was asking if the kisses we enjoyed together changed your feelings about *me*. And about your attitude toward marriage."

"I will not hide the fact that I physically desire you, Lady Georgina," August admitted. "I have not changed my opinion regarding marriage, however. You are correct to assume that we sit on opposite sides of the fence. What you want from a marriage is diametrically opposed to what I need from one."

She gazed at him in astonishment. "So, you find me physically attractive. You know we would suit one another well in the bedroom. Yet you stubbornly refuse to acknowledge anything other than a marriage of convenience. I might add, *your* convenience."

Much as he desired this beauty, he could not drag her down.

"We would never suit in a marriage, my lady," he said coldly, putting distance between them with his harsh tone. "You want a partner who is both lover and friend in your husband. You want a man who is involved in the lives of his children. I do not wish for any of that."

"Were you always like this?" she demanded. "Did you always

believe you would wed out of convenience?"

"I did not believe I would wed at all," he said honestly. "I was committed to the military. As an officer, my life was dedicated to king and country, along with watching out for my men. I knew there was a distinct possibility that I might die on the battlefield in service to my country, while protecting those men. I never considered the possibility of marriage."

He swallowed painfully. "Now, however, as the Marquess of Edgethorne, it is my obligation to provide an heir. To keep the family name going. Because of that, I will do my duty and take a wife."

He paused, their gazes meeting. "And because of my monstrous appearance, my chances of making a match have dwindled considerably. Yes, there will be someone in Polite Society who will become my marchioness. Most likely, some father will tell his daughter it is worthwhile to wed a scarred beast because of the prestige which will come to her by being a marchioness. Just because I wed, though, does not mean I wish for my wife to be tied to me. I want her to be able to live her life to the fullest. What I can give her in exchange is the trappings of a comfortable lifestyle. My name—and the title which accompanies it. Hopefully, children will also be a part of our union. I want to give my wife as much freedom as possible in exchange for locking her into a marriage with a man such as myself."

"You are a fool, my lord," Lady Georgina pronounced. "You are so much more than your looks, and yet you continually harp upon them."

He seized her shoulders, shaking her a moment, trying to have her make sense of things.

"Do you know what it is like to catch sight of myself in the mirror? To continually be horrified by my own appearance? I try to avoid doing so as much as possible. It is difficult enough for me to live with what I now am. I do not want that to hurt my wife or children. The less they have to do with me, the better."

August released her, retreating a few steps. They glared at

one another, no words passing between them.

"I will leave you to your thoughts, my lady," he said. "Now that I know this space is your retreat, I will avoid coming here."

She wet her lips, causing a rush of desire to run through him, and said, "I will hand it to you, Lord Edgethorne. Your kisses have awakened something within me. I understand this is but the tip of the iceberg in regard to physical intimacy between two people. At least I know what a good kiss is—and I plan to kiss several men in the future. I will find one whose kisses make my head spin. A man who is not so shallow as to only think of his physical appearance. I intend to find a man who believes in love. With me."

Her words were like a knife to his heart. August couldn't bear the thought of her sharing intimacies with another man, yet he could not ruin her life by tying her to him through marriage. It might ostracize her from the *ton*. He was not willing to hurt her so deeply.

Giving up Lady Georgina Strong would be the greatest sacrifice he had ever made. He had held her in his arms for a few stolen moments. He would have to live on the memory of those kisses.

Bowing to her, he said, "I will not approach you again at any social event, my lady. I will never ask you to dance, so you will not have to publicly reject me. I wish you the best in finding happiness. And love."

He turned away, his heart shattered, and strode from the small garden. He would keep to his word and avoid the place in the future, knowing that she came here. It was a place they could be alone, and that meant it was a place of temptation to him. August could not be around her. He would avoid her at *ton* affairs. He could never seek her out again. Never speak to her. If anyone in her family asked him to tea, he would politely send his regrets. He must cut off all contact with Lady Georgina and the Strong family. It was a pity, because they had been some of the few people who had supported him at last night's ball.

He would also need to avoid Blankenship. While he would give anything to renew his friendship with the viscount, he believed his old friend might make a match with Lady Georgina. Because of that, he would avoid Blankenship and his friend's entire circle at all costs.

August retreated to his study and poured himself a snifter of brandy. He sat in the chair by the window, staring out at the park that separated his townhouse from Seaton's.

A single tear rolled down his cheek from the one good eye he possessed. He allowed it to fall, feeling his life was over.

CHAPTER FIFTEEN

GEORGIE WAS GETTING ready for that evening's ball. She had thought the Season would be fun. It was—to an extent—but nothing had been the same since her spat with Lord Edgethorne.

And those heavenly kisses . . .

She closed her eyes, the memory of being in his arms overpowering.

Then she opened them, staring at her perfect image in the mirror. Georgie knew she was blessed with beauty. All the Strongs were immensely attractive people. Yet she was so much more than her face and figure. That was what she wanted Polite Society to see.

The townhouse had been inundated with flower arrangements and suitors for the past week. Gentlemen complimented her left and right. One had even told her she sneezed more ladylike than any woman of his acquaintance. That had been too much, and she had laughed to the point of making herself sick, causing the gentleman to flee from her vicinity.

She knew she was the sum of many things. Her appearance. Her intelligence. Her experience. Her education. Her family relations. Her thoughts and emotions.

Why couldn't Lord Edgethorne see that he, too, was more

than his scarred face? At the same time, she understood how recent his disfigurement was. It must be jarring for him to think of himself as he once had been—and then to look into a mirror and see what was, in effect, a stranger. It upset her that she would never truly comprehend the level of his struggles.

"How is that, my lady?" Libby asked.

Georgie's eyes went to her image in the mirror, but her thoughts remained on Lord Edgethorne. She wished the *ton* could see past his scars and missing eye as she did. It hurt her to have heard his name whispered during this past week, knowing the disparaging remarks being bandied about. Of course, no one directly mentioned his name to her. Then again, she had been the one who had pleasantly greeted him when he arrived at the Pennywise ball.

She saw the man—the real man—who lay beneath the scars. And she loved him, much to her dismay.

His kisses had confirmed what Pippa had talked about. Georgie had been captivated by them. By him. The marquess was the first thing she thought about upon waking each morning. She tried to surreptitiously look for him at each social affair she attended. No one—so far—had caused her pulse to race as it did when he was near. She had met several very nice, attractive men, chief among them Viscount Blankenship. He had been most attentive to her. She could even see herself wed to him. They would have a good life together. An easy life with no complications.

But it wasn't the life she wanted. It wasn't the man she wanted.

How could she make Lord Edgethorne want her?

"My lady?"

Georgie blinked. "Oh. Yes, Libby. I quite like this style. You have done an excellent job," she praised.

"Her Grace thought it would suit you. Will there be anything else, my lady?"

"No, thank you."

The maid left, leaving Georgie to her thoughts again. Something told her that Edgethorne was a stubborn man. He had made up his mind and would not consider offering for her. The only alternative would be to offer for him.

That was *not* the done thing. Even Georgie knew it would be going too far for her to be so brazen as to ask him to marry her. Worse, even if she attempted to do so, her heart told her he would scoff—and then reject her proposal.

"Blast!" she said, frustration filling her.

He was not for her. He had made that obvious. She was going to have to put aside her infatuation with him. That is what others would label it, a foolish, obsessive love for a man who brushed her off. Georgie told herself Lord Edgethorne was not the only man she could be interested in. Others offered just as much, if not more, than Lord Edgethorne. She was being called a diamond of the first water and had her pick of any gentlemen she might wish for. Surely, another could capture her attention as Lord Edgethorne had.

Glancing at her image in the mirror, she proclaimed, "I will be open-minded. I will cease to think about the Marquess of Edgethorne. I will enjoy myself, my surroundings, and the company I keep. I will continue to meet new people and see what they have to offer. I promise myself to be happy. To stop wanting someone I cannot have. To stop fixating on Lord Edgethorne."

It was times like these when she missed Pippa dreadfully. Her twin knew her inside and out and would have given Georgie the exact advice she needed to hear. She wistfully thought of Pippa, married and in love, sailing the Seven Seas with her husband, having the adventure of a lifetime with the man she adored.

Tears welled in Georgie's eyes, and she dabbed them with a handkerchief. She was not truly jealous of Pippa. She was thrilled that her twin had found love with Seth. Georgie only hoped she, too, would be fortunate enough to find love. She loved Lord Edgethorne, but could it be love if the other person did not love her in return?

No, a one-sided love was no love at all. Love needed love to flourish, or it would die. Even if Georgie thought she loved the marquess, he was mulish by nature. He would not compromise and yield. She swore she would not throw herself at him ever again. She would have nothing to do with him.

But she would continue to keep an eye out for him. Watch to see if he attended an event. Observe who he was drawn to. She believed that he would look to the plainest of girls. That meant the wallflowers. Georgie decided to get to know some of them in order to see which ones might be good enough for him. Not that he would want her opinion on the matter, but she decided she would give it to him anyway. He might not want her.

But she wanted him to find happiness.

She joined her mother in the foyer, and James and Sophie soon appeared.

"Ready for another ball?" Sophie asked. "I hear Lord and Lady Hoffman are quite the hosts."

An idea came to her. "You should host a ball," she told them. "After all, you are a duke and duchess. Everyone would come simply because of that."

"Why, that is a splendid idea," Mama said. "I would be happy to help you organize it."

Sophie shook her head. "It would take so much planning, Dinah. I am already splitting my time between Neptune Shipping and *ton* events. I don't see how I could pull it off."

"Leave it to me," Mama said happily. "I have planned several over the years. It would be good to open up your home to others, not to mention it might help Georgina's prospects."

"Do you think so?" James asked. "And what of other events? I know we have received a plethora of invitations. Is there even room for another event?"

"Most hosts issue invitations a month or more in advance. It is only late April now. How about holding it during the first week in June? We can review what events are to take place then. I know the two of you had mentioned pulling back and only rarely attending an event as June began, due to Sophie's increasing. Why, it would be a wonderful way for you to exit the social Season. You could even announce your happy news at that ball. It—and your sister's come-out—could be the reasons for the celebration."

"I like that idea," Sophie said, linking her arm through Georgie's. "What do you think?"

"I like it, too. And I know Mama loves to give a ball. We girls used to watch all the servants decorating the ballroom in years past. Cook would let us sample the buffet items before the menu was set. It was ever so much fun."

"Then we shall host a ball," her brother declared. "Begin to mention it tonight," he told them. "Do not give an exact date. We will need to decide that tomorrow after we review the invitations we have already received. But it wouldn't hurt to build a bit of excitement about it."

"I agree," Mama said. "Thank you, James. I will handle everything. You and Sophie will not have to lift a finger."

Sophie chuckled. "Well, I wouldn't mind sampling various dishes. That part sounds like fun."

They went to the carriage and soon found themselves at the Hoffmans' townhouse. Their hosts looked to be in their early forties, and Georgie thought Lord Hoffman to be a bit too flirtatious toward both her and Mama while his wife was engaged with James and Sophie.

As they moved toward the ballroom's entrance, she whispered to her mother, "Did you find Lord Hoffman a bit forward?"

"He has a terrible reputation," Mama confirmed. "He and Lady Hoffman have three children, but I have heard he has sired another four out of wedlock."

"Then why do people come to their balls?" she asked. "Shouldn't they be showing their disapproval for his atrocious behavior?"

Mama looked pained as she said, "Many gentlemen of the *ton* conduct these extramarital affairs, dearest. Wives simply turn a blind eye, as does most of Polite Society." She sighed. "If we were to stay home from events hosted by philandering noblemen, we would rarely leave the house."

"You do not think James—or Seth—would ever have an affair, do you?" Georgie asked worriedly.

"No," Mama assured her. "They are those rare men who have made love matches. They will be loyal to Sophie and Pippa."

"Was Papa true to you, Mama?" she asked, her voice small, already knowing the answer.

"I tried not to think of those things. Ah, Lord Blankenship. How good to see you this evening."

The viscount greeted Mama and then Georgie, asking for a dance with her.

"Might it be the supper dance again, my lady?" he ventured. "I so enjoyed your company during supper the opening night of the Season."

"Yes," she agreed.

It was impossible to truly have a decent conversation at any social event, and balls, in particular. Most of the dances were so lively and exhausting that conversation was simply impossible. She had thought when suitors called upon her the next day that she might delve into deeper topics to get to know them better, but they stayed for such a short period of time, that never seemed possible. Supper was the one time at a ball when you could talk to someone at length. It was time to get to know Lord Blankenship better.

And perhaps even kiss him. No, definitely kiss him. The viscount would the first gentleman she would kiss so that she might compare his kiss to that of Lord Edgethorne.

Georgie allowed the viscount to sign her programme, and it only took a few more minutes for it to fill up. Not entirely, however. She stuck to the idea of keeping one dance open. Not for Lord Edgethorne, of course. They had both made it perfectly clear they would not be speaking to one another, much less dancing together.

With her dance card filling so early, she decided to circulate about the room by herself. Mama had a bevy of men surrounding her, laughing easily, making everyone feel comfortable as she always did. James and Sophie were engaged in conversation with another couple. No one would note her absence.

She headed for a line of chairs. Not the ones for matrons. The ones where the wallflowers sat. Already, a few of them stood nearby the seats, ready to take them when the music began.

"Hello," she said brightly, joining a group of three. "I hope you do not mind me stopping by."

One, a mousy brunette, gaped at her. "Why would you wish to talk with us?"

"Because I am trying to meet as many people as possible this Season," she said honestly. "I am trying to enjoy myself. I know it is not proper etiquette for me to approach you without an introduction, but we are already marching through the Season, and I have yet to meet you."

The second young lady sniffed. "I do not know why you would bother to meet us, Lady Georgina."

"Oh, you know who I am?" she asked.

The last of the trio snorted. "Who does *not* know of you, my lady? Every young buck has gone sniffing around you. You dance every dance. You are obviously having the time of your life, and why wouldn't you? With your looks and figure, you can charm anyone."

"I would still like to get to know you," she said quietly, knowing it might be one of these three women whom Lord Edgethorne could choose as his bride.

The last two women who had spoken to her looked as if she had gone mad. One excused herself, and the second one followed her, leaving Georgie with the first woman she had spoken with.

"Might you tell me your name, my lady?" she asked gently, seeing the woman look in desperation at the friends who had deserted her.

Turning to face Georgie again, she said, "Miss Bancroft. My

father is a viscount whom I am certain you have never heard of, my lady. My mother passed away when I was only ten years of age. My aunt managed my come-out three years ago and still insists upon dragging me to *ton* affairs, despite the total lack of interest any gentleman displays toward me. My father hasn't said a dozen words to me in the decade since Mama has been gone. When the Season rolls around each year, I know it will be months of misery for me, being forced to attend all these events."

Miss Bancroft glared at her. "I am plain. My dowry is so small, I might as well not possess one. While I am clever, no gentleman spends any time with me in order for me to show I am more than my looks. So, off you go, Lady Georgina. You must go and enjoy yourself as a diamond of the first water should."

"I can hear the hurt in your voice, Miss Bancroft. Hurt from having been ignored for so long. Hurt because you are solely judged on your looks." Georgie paused. "I would like to be your friend, though."

"Why?" Miss Bancroft asked, baffled by the words.

"Because I do believe others have something to offer beyond their looks. I am constantly judged on my looks. Flattered by sycophants. No one wishes to get to know me."

She paused, deciding to set the stage. "Our neighbor, Lord Edgethorne, has been judged on his looks, as well."

Miss Bancroft frowned. "Isn't he the one with the terrible scars? And the eyepatch?"

"Yes, he is. But he is friendly with my family. He has been to tea. He is a lovely man. I believe it is wrong for others not to give him a chance. He should not be judged solely on his appearance. Neither should you, Miss Bancroft."

The other woman appeared stunned. "I actually think you believe what you are saying, my lady."

"I do believe it. Very much so. And I hope you will allow me to introduce you to Lord Edgethorne."

Miss Bancroft blushed. "But . . . he is a marquess. He would have no interest in someone such as me."

"You would be surprised," Georgie said. "It was lovely meeting you."

She returned to Mama's side, knowing it was almost time for the dancing to begin. Then she heard the ballroom quieten and knew why it did so.

For the first time since their spat, Lord Edgethorne had entered a social event.

Knowing if she thought about it, she would lose her courage, so Georgie did not think. She merely acted, moving toward the marquess.

He caught sight of her and started to turn, but she quickly hurried toward him, trying to prevent him from doing so.

Slipping her arm around his, she quietly said, "I know you and I are not going to be dancing with one another. But please come with me without making a scene."

Georgie tugged on his arm, and Lord Edgethorne actually moved along with her without protest.

As they walked, heads turning as they passed, she told him, "You have mentioned you would like to find a bride amongst the wallflowers. I have met a few, and I believe there is one you should meet, my lord. She came out a few years ago and is plain in appearance. However, I find her quite intelligent and think you might be interested in her."

He halted. "You are playing matchmaker for me, my lady?"

She grinned. "I suppose I am. And if you kiss her as you did me, she would most certainly accept a marriage offer from you. Come along, my lord."

They went to the far end of the ballroom, where Miss Bancroft's two friends had rejoined her. All three of their jaws dropped as she and the marquess approached.

Smiling, Georgie said, "Miss Bancroft, I would like to present to you the Marquess of Edgethorne, our neighbor and good friend. My lord, this is Miss Bancroft."

The two friends were speechless, gawking at the nobleman. Miss Bancroft's eyes cut to Georgie, and she nodded at the woman.

"Miss Bancroft," Lord Edgethorne said, bowing to her.

Somehow, Miss Bancroft managed to offer her hand to him, and the marquess kissed it briefly. A tinge of jealousy shot through Georgie, followed by acceptance.

"I believe Miss Bancroft has an open dance, my lord," she said, nudging him into action.

"May I request a dance with you this evening, Miss Bancroft?" he asked.

"Yes, my lord," she replied, her voice shaking, handing him her programme.

Georgie saw it was entirely blank.

"Do you have a preference, Miss Bancroft?"

"No, my lord," the wallflower replied, fidgeting.

"Why not the supper dance?" Georgie suggested. "That way, you will have more time to spend together, getting to know one another."

"A splendid idea, Lady Georgina," the marquess said. "Does that suit you, Miss Bancroft?" He signed the programme and returned it, saying, "Then I will see you later this evening."

Georgie slipped her arm through his again, leading him back the entire length of the ballroom, as whispers erupted.

"Why are you helping me?"

"Why not?" she asked.

What she couldn't say aloud was that she still pined for him, despite their quarrel. That if he could find a bride on the Marriage Mart and become betrothed, it would force Georgie to give up hope for the two of them ever being together. It would allow her to be free of her feelings for him.

It would let her be open to finding love with someone who could return her love.

The musicians began tuning their instruments. They reached Mama, and Georgie withdrew her hand.

"It was good to see you again, Lord Edgethorne," she said truthfully.

Her first dance partner arrived, looking warily at the marquess. "Are you ready for our dance, Lady Georgina?"

She smiled brilliantly at the man, having no idea of what his name might be. "Definitely, my lord. Lead the way."

CHAPTER SIXTEEN

GEORGIE KEPT HER eye out for Lord Edgethorne, and she saw that he danced twice before the supper dance began. He had chosen his partners from amongst the wallflowers, and she was happy to note neither time was with Miss Bancroft's disagreeable friends. She was determined to get to know more of these women. Already, she had a fondness for Miss Bancroft and thought to ask her to tea to get to know her a bit better.

Mama said, "I see Lord Blankenship coming this way to claim you for the supper dance. What do you think of him?'

"He is most amiable," she replied.

"Do you believe something might develop between the two of you?"

"That remains to be seen."

It wasn't as if she could tell her mother that she needed to kiss Lord Blankenship before she could consider him as marriage material, much less that she wanted to compare his kiss to that of Lord Edgethorne's.

Some things a girl just had to keep to herself.

The viscount arrived and bowed. Georgie accepted his extended arm and placed her fingertips atop it. He led them to the very center of the ballroom.

"My, do you wish to be the center of attention, having us

dance with others surrounding us?" she teased.

"I want to be the center of *your* attention, my lady," he flirted, and she rewarded his remark with a smile as he took her hand in his and slipped an arm about her.

The music began, a waltz, as she had expected. She did not try to talk with him, since they would have plenty of time to do so over their shared supper hour. Instead, Georgie gave herself over to the music and enjoyed moving to its rhythm. Lord Blankenship was a more than adequate dancer, yet she couldn't help but remember her one dance with Lord Edgethorne. He was a man who knew how to move to a beat.

She pushed all thoughts of the marquess from her mind, dedicating herself to this dance and the company of the man she shared.

When the waltz ended, they began moving along with the others to the supper room.

"I hope you do not mind, but I did not arrange to dine with my friends as I usually do."

"Oh, no! Have you had a falling out with one or both of them?" Georgie asked worriedly.

"No, my lady. I merely was being selfish, wanting you all to myself this evening."

He guided her to one of the few tables for two and seated her. It was in a far corner, away from most of the other tables. It would easily allow her to observe the room.

And Lord Edgethorne and Miss Bancroft.

She turned her attention back to the viscount. "This will give us a chance to have a decent conversation without interruption. Should we get something to eat first?"

"I will do so for the both of us," he told her. "Stay here so that others know this table is occupied."

She watched Lord Blankenship head for the buffet line, and then her eyes drifted across the room, delighted to find Lord Edgethorne and Miss Bancroft had joined James and Sophie and another two couples at a table. She caught her brother's eye and nodded approvingly. James winked at her.

Her eyes continued viewing the room, locating various gentlemen who had called upon her since the Season began. She found her mother sitting with a very handsome man, perhaps a few years older than Mama. She could not remember the gentleman's name, but she had heard he was a recent widower with two young children, in search of a wife to help him raise the two boys. Georgie wondered if Mama would be interested in raising another woman's children, and she supposed it wouldn't matter if Mama fell in love with this man. Her mother was so open and giving, Georgie only prayed that Mama could find happiness after such a long, unsatisfying marriage.

Lord Blankenship returned, placing a plate in front of her and then taking a seat opposite her.

"I hope I was able to choose some of your favorites, Lady Georgina. I took note of what you ate the last time we took supper together and what you left on your plate."

"That was most observant of you, my lord. You did bring me an abundance of food that time, however. I might have actually liked a few things which I left on my plate that night, but I needed to limit what I consumed so that I might still be light on my feet when I danced."

"You are an excellent dancer. I have also heard that you play the pianoforte extremely well. How often do you practice?"

"I try to every morning. Since the Season began, however, I do not always get in practice each day. I do feel at one with my instrument, though. Music has always spoken to something within me."

"Edgethorne was the same way," the viscount told her. "He could play the piano like no other. It is a pity now that he will have had to give it up, missing fingers and all."

She had not known the marquess played, much less that he played so well. He had complimented her own playing. Now that she knew he once was a musician, the compliment meant even more to her.

"So, tell me about your school days with the marquess. And your other friends," she added, not wanting him to think she was focused on Lord Edgethorne.

He told some amusing stories of scrapes they had been in during their days at Eton, and how they had also gone to university together, as well.

"We shared rooms while at Cambridge. Edgethorne is the most genial man I have ever met. Full of life and laughter. Of course, we all knew things would change when he took up his commission that sent him off to war."

Blankenship shook his head sadly. "I have tried to meet with him, but he has not acknowledged the two notes I have sent to him."

Sympathy for the marquess filled Georgie. "You must remember that he is still getting over the deaths of his father and brother," she reminded him. "And that he has assumed a title he was ill-prepared to take on. That is on top of the war injuries he suffered. Give him time, my lord. The marquess was a good friend to you once. Perhaps he can be again."

"You are right, Lady Georgina. You have a wisdom about you that few others possess."

He looked at her longingly, and she believed the time had come for her to see if they were meant to be together.

"The supper room has grown extremely warm," she commented, hoping her words might nudge him into action.

He took the hint. "Would you care to stroll in the gardens until the ball resumes? I would be happy to escort you there for a brief respite."

"That would be lovely, my lord."

They left the supper room through a set of French doors and were not the only couple doing so. Two others followed them and when they reached the terrace outside, she saw another couple strolling along it. She had known this was something others did, and she wondered how many of these women would receive kisses in the dark tonight.

"Why don't we go along this path?" Lord Blankenship said. "I believe we will find a bench we can sit on while we admire the view of the gardens."

"Lead the way, my lord," she said cheerfully, tucking her hand into the crook of his arm.

They moved at a leisurely pace, a comfortable silence between them. She really did like him very much. If it turned out he was not the one for her, she hoped they might continue a friendship. Then again, she did not know of any ladies amongst the *ton* who were simply friends with a gentleman.

Reaching the promised bench, they took a seat upon it. The night air was slightly cool, and Georgie shivered involuntarily.

"Would you care to wear my coat?" he asked.

"No, that is not necessary," she said. "However, you might place your arm about me to help ward off the chill."

She did not want anyone to come across them and see Blankenship without his coat on. That would give the wrong impression. She did not think an arm about her would be nearly as suspect.

He slipped his arm around her back, his hand curling about her waist. He was quite warm, and she liked the smell of his shaving soap.

Turning to say something to him, he placed his index finger against her lips.

"Let me say what I need to, my lady."

She nodded, her heart racing, and he lowered his finger.

"I find you most interesting, Lady Georgina. I like your kindness toward all and how you are interested in everything about you. Might I have permission to kiss you?"

Since this was the very reason she had come out here with him, she smiled.

"Yes, my lord. You may kiss me."

He lowered his head, his lips meeting hers, pressing gently.

She felt nothing.

Frustration filled her. Georgie liked this man. She wanted to like his kiss.

She also did not want him to know she had been kissed before, and so she kept still, not reacting.

Gradually, he began to tease her mouth open, slipping his tongue inside. She did not respond, merely allowing him to keep to his task.

When he finally withdrew, he gazed deeply into her eyes, sadness in his own.

"You did not enjoy the kiss, did you?"

She shrugged, wanting to let him down gently. "It was quite . . . nice," she said primly.

"Nice is not enough," he told her. "I was hoping there would be a spark between us, but I will admit that I felt nothing myself."

Relief filled her. "I will be honest, my lord. I enjoy your company very much. You are intelligent and handsome. Most pleasant to be around. I was very much hoping we would suit."

She paused. "But I *am* looking for that spark which you mentioned. Seaton found it with his duchess. My own twin found it with Viscount Hopewell. I promised myself I would not settle. That I want to find lasting love."

"I was not looking for a love match, Lady Georgina." He smiled wryly. "But I was hoping I might have found one with you. You do realize a love match is quite rare amongst *ton* marriages?"

She nodded. "It may escape me this Season. And in Seasons to come. Still, I have to be true to myself. It is what I want. I cannot settle."

"Then I will say it has been a pleasure—and privilege— getting to know you, my lady. I will not take up anymore of your valuable time, however. I am seeking a wife this Season, just as you wish to find a husband who will love you. I do not want to take up space on your programme. I will refrain from calling upon you, as well."

A wave of sadness filled her. "I hope that we are parting as friends, my lord."

"I believe we are, my lady," he said, smiling fondly at her. "I hold no animosity and even applaud your honesty with me. I do hope you will find what you are looking for."

Lord Blankenship leaned in and softly brushed his lips against hers a final time in parting. Then he stood.

"Shall we return to the ball?"

"I believe I will go to the retiring room."

"Then let us go," he said, offering his arm to her.

The viscount took her back to the ballroom, and Georgie descended the stairs, going to where the retiring room was located.

While she was doing her business behind the drawn curtain, she caught Lord Edgethorne's name in conversation and stilled.

"I cannot understand why Edgethorne goes where he is not wanted," a voice said.

"It is hopeless," a second replied. "Even with him now dancing with wallflowers, no lady will ever wish to wed him. Can you imagine what might be under that eyepatch he wears?"

The two tittered, and the first said, "The scars are horrid to look upon, but the hole where his eye once was?"

Laughter erupted again.

Georgie smoothed her ballgown and pulled the curtain aside, emerging. Immediately, the two women looked at her guiltily and exited the retiring room.

She washed her hands in the basin, accepting a towel from the attendant and drying her hands. Anger surged through her, and she hurried from the retiring room, catching up to the two gossips, stepping in front of them to block their progress.

"You are despicable," she told the pair. "You are raking over the coals a fine man. One who has sacrificed greatly for our country."

Knowing both of these women had brothers, she demanded, "How would you treat your own brother if he came home from war scarred in a like manner? Would you laugh at him? Criticize him? Make fun of him? No, you would still love him, scars and all, because he was the same brother you had loved your entire life. Lord Edgethorne is the man he has always been. Yes, his looks have been altered, but the marquess still has much to offer. To society. To his friends. And to his future marchioness.

"My advice to you would be to hold your wicked tongues. Gossip is vicious—and other gossips turn on one another with great regularity. You would not wish to be the topic of gossip yourself. You would not want your injured brother to be a topic of the gossips, as well. Neither should Lord Edgethorne be one."

The two women's eyes had grown large as she spoke, their mouths trembling. They ducked their heads and skirted around her.

Georgie took a deep breath, trying to release the anger still within her, anger for all those who had gossiped unmercifully about Lord Edgethorne.

She turned, ready to return to the ballroom.

The Marquess of Edgethorne stood in her path.

Embarrassment flooded her face, knowing he must have heard at least part of the dressing down she had given the two gossips.

Curtseying quickly, she said, "My lord," and rushed past him before he could say a word.

CHAPTER SEVENTEEN

I T WAS MID-MAY now, and they were into the fourth week of the Season.

And not a single gentleman had caught Georgie's attention.

She picked up the letter in her lap from Mirella. She had only written her sister once since the Season began. She had also written everyone at Shadowcrest one letter, but that included Aunt Matty, Effie, Lyric, Allegra, Miss Feathers, and Caleb—as well as Mirella. It was hard finding time to steal away from her social obligations to play the pianoforte for half an hour each day, much less write so many letters.

Still, she knew Mirella was feeling left out. Possibly even lonely. She owed it to her sister to write again. She would encourage Mirella to share the letter with the others, hopefully keeping them happy, having heard from her.

Placing the letter in a box where she stored special correspondence, she went to her mother's sitting room. Mama was just leaving the room.

"May I use your desk?" she asked. "I am going to write to Mirella."

"Of course. Give your sister my love. I am about to meet with the Powells. We still have so much to do regarding James and Sophie hosting a ball. I want to chat with them about decorations. The food to be served. And a few additions to the guest list, which has already been sent out."

"Enjoy, Mama. I know this is the kind of thing you have always loved doing."

Her mother nodded. "I do love to entertain, especially when it is a ball. It has been so long since one was held in this house. It is about time we brought Polite Society back to our doorstep."

Georgie sat at the desk, withdrawing fresh paper and opening the inkwell. She thought a moment, and then she began to write.

Dearest Mirella —

I am sorry it has taken so long to write to you. You will understand next year when you are caught up in the social whirl of the Season. I have truly missed having you here with me. I hope your bones are healing nicely and that the fresh country air is doing you good.

I had to laugh when you wrote of how you are practicing the pianoforte with one hand! It must sound odd, playing only the melody to songs without the accompanying chords. Still, I know how much pleasure music brings you, so keep up what you are doing.

You did not mention if you were painting. I hope you are since your right hand is intact. I miss the smell of your paints. Seeing a smudge of it on your cheek. Viewing your finished landscapes. I hope being at Shadowcrest has brought inspiration to your art.

While I am enjoying the events we are attending, I have yet—after a month—to find a gentleman who speaks to my heart. Well, that is not entirely correct. I know you met Lord Edgethorne when you were here. I will admit (only to you) that I am attracted to him.

We kissed, Mirella. My first kiss. It was as Pippa described to me, something that is . . . indescribable. She said I would have to experience it for myself because it is difficult to explain, not just the physical aspects of a kiss, but the emo-

tional connection you feel to the gentleman who kisses you.

Alas, Lord Edgethorne is as obstinate and uncompromising as anyone I have ever met. He has it in his head that, because of how his injuries have altered his appearance, he would not appeal to me. That is far from the truth. I have had to learn to respect his wishes, though, and watch him dance with other women at balls. I have been fortunate; I have not lacked for partners. But no gentleman has held my attention as Lord Edgethorne. None of them hold a candle to him.

I have decided I will simply continue as if nothing is wrong. I meet new individuals at every event I attend. I am enjoying myself. Music and dancing are a part of a majority of the events held, so you know I am happy in that respect.

Mama has convinced James and Sophie that we need to hold a ball. It has been decided it will take place the second week of June. Even as I write this, Mama is meeting with the Powells and Cook, creating a menu (the invitations have already gone out).

She says it will be a good way for Polite Society to meet James and Sophie, through them hosting an event in their own home. Each guest will pass through the receiving line, so they will get to speak to James and Sophie for a brief time. Sophie is letting Mama handle everything since she has experience in planning a large event.

As for Sophie herself, her face is growing rounder. If she turns and her gown clings to her, you can see her burgeoning belly. The styles of the day usually hide it. She has said that after this ball, she and James will most likely withdraw to the country. She meets with Mr. Barnes every afternoon, sorting out business. It is Mr. Barnes who will be in charge of Neptune Shipping while Sophie is away. She is hoping, since Shadowcrest is not so far from town, that he will come down every few weeks and catch her up on important things.

Mama and I will stay in town until the Season concludes, of course. I had hoped by now Mama might have formed an attachment. That is not the case. She has been incredibly popular, though. Our drawing room has been filled with as many suitors vying for her hand as have come to see me. Mama confided that she is having the time of her life, so I am happy for her in that regard. As to whether or not she will decide to wed again, that is anyone's guess.

That is all my news for now. Please give everyone my love and share the contents of this letter with them (except the part about Lord Edgethorne). It is difficult to find time to write to so many of you. I look forward to coming home to the country and suppose you and I will do a Season together next year, since it seems as if love is not on my horizon this year.

All my love,
Georgie

She read through the letter once, making certain she had not left anything out. She would let the ink dry and give it to a footman to post.

As she waited, she went and practiced her pianoforte for half an hour, playing pieces Mirella enjoyed, feeling close to her sister. She missed her sisters and her cousins dreadfully, more than she would have imagined. Georgie only hoped that Allegra and Lyric had decided to proceed with their own come-outs next spring.

After giving the letter to Dursley to post, she remembered it was Tuesday. Mama had designated this day as the one where they would not be at home to callers. She had told Georgie and Sophie that it was important to make time to rest and recover from all the events. Sophie would meet with Mr. Barnes and then nap in preparation of the evening's activities. Since Mama was still busy with the Powells, Georgie decided to go sit in the private park on the square.

She had not been to it since she had been kissed by Lord Edgethorne.

AUGUST WAS SITTING in his study, idly looking out the window, when he heard a knock at the door.

"Come," he said.

Wilson appeared, clearing his throat. "It is Lord Blankenship, my lord. Here to see you."

He cursed under his breath. Blankenship had written to August three times. He had ignored each of the notes and avoided his old friend at the few events he'd attended.

"Send him in," he grumbled, hoping he would soon be rid of the viscount.

"Lord Blankenship," announced Wilson.

Apparently, his friend had accompanied Wilson to the study's door, because he breezed in immediately and took a seat opposite August. Wilson closed the door.

"I would ask you to sit, but you have already done so before being invited."

"Don't be a curmudgeon. You used to be fun, August."

"I also used to have another eye and three more fingers," he said drily. "Perhaps they are what made me so fun and carefree."

Blankenship's look turned sympathetic. "I am sorry for that, August. No one should have to suffer what you have gone through."

"I don't need your sympathy. Or your pity," he barked.

"Can't I merely express my sorrow without you biting my head off?" his friend countered. "Come, August. We were once the closest of friends."

"That was before the war. Before everything changed."

He grew quiet, thinking over how he should be grateful Blankenship had come to see him.

"I am sorry I ignored your notes," he said gruffly.

"Why did you?"

"Because it is all so different now. You stayed here in England. I never understood what safety meant. Stability. The peace of a country day." He swallowed. "War is harsh, Silas. If you knew what it was like, you would not wish it upon your worst enemy."

They sat in silence for several minutes before August spoke again.

"I am sorry I have pushed you away. I knew you wanted to be around your old friend, but that jovial, carefree young man no longer exists. Battle beat that out of me. To live in fear—knowing you could perish at any moment—that changes a man. And not for the better."

He met his friend's gaze. "I cannot be who I once was, Silas."

"I am not asking you to, August. I merely want my friend. Yes, the man scarred by battle. The man who has seen death and lived to tell about it. We had our fun. There may still be some in our futures. But I need you, August. *You.* Whatever version of you which I can have."

August put a hand to his face, emotions getting the better of him. "I do not know how you can bear to look at me."

"You look much the same to me. Slightly older. Hardened. I know the war has done that to you."

He dropped his hand. "But these scars. They are hideous, Silas. I hate how I look."

"And yet there are those who do not see them. Such as Lady Georgina."

August stilled.

"I will admit it was a shock to see your new appearance the opening night of the Season. But when I speak with you, August, I do not see the scars. I see my friend. I believe others are the same. I have seen you with the Duke and Duchess of Seaton and a few others. Why, you have even started partnering with some ladies at balls."

His friend raked a hand through his hair. "But the one person who has never seemed to see what you think are your faults is Lady Georgina." Blankenship paused. "I have seen how she looks at you when she thinks no one is looking."

"You are interested in her."

"I *was* interested in her. Until I discovered just *how* interested she is in you."

He shook his head several times. "You would be a good husband to her."

The viscount looked at him steadily. "She doesn't want me, old friend. She wants you."

"She said that?"

"She didn't have to. I kissed her."

Immediately, jealousy flooded him. "You *what?*"

His friend grinned. "You heard me. I kissed her. Do not tell me you wouldn't have done the same. And remember—I know you."

August calmed himself. "A man kisses a woman for two reasons. One, because he wants a good time. And second, because he is looking for a wife. You are not the type to dally with a woman of such good breeding as Lady Georgina. Therefore, I am thinking you are on the hunt for a bride."

"I do wish to wed," the viscount agreed. "And I had thought Lady Georgina would be the best candidate. Of course, I had to kiss her." He snorted. "It was like kissing my sister. We tried. We both tried. But it was hopeless."

Something stirred within him. Something nameless that he refused to identify.

"We decided that we did not suit. I will no longer take space on her programme. She needs her dance card to be filled with the names of potential suitors, not rejected ones."

"Why are you telling me all this, Silas?" he asked. "You see what I look like now. Do you truly believe in my present state that I am fit for a duke's daughter?"

"If she thinks you are, then you are, August."

The viscount rose. "I will leave you to these thoughts. Are you going to the musicale this evening or the card party?"

"I accepted an invitation to the musicale. Before they truly knew what I looked like, else I doubt I would have been invited. No one—as of yet—has rescinded any invitations, but fewer are trickling in now."

"Well, I am hearing less and less gossip about you." His friend paused. "Think about what I have shared," his friend urged. "And the next time I send around a note, answer me, man!"

They both laughed.

"I will see you tonight," August promised. "I will also stop avoiding you."

"Good. Because you are stuck with me. We have been friends far too long for a missing eye to make any difference."

He walked Blankenship to the door, and they shook hands. "Thank you for coming."

After his friend left, August was restless. Though he said he would not return to the park separating his townhouse from that of Seaton's, he decided to go there now. He assumed Lady Georgina would have a bevy of callers and be nowhere close to it.

Entering the park, he decided to go to the bench where he had kissed her. He had spent far too many times thinking of those kisses as he tried to fall asleep each night.

The day was sunny as he went to the bench and was shocked to see Lady Georgina rising from it. Immediately, he knew it had been a mistake to come here.

Startled by his sudden appearance, she cried, "Lord Edgethorne! I thought you were not in the habit of coming here."

He shrugged. "I haven't been." He paused, their gazes meeting. "It is the first time I have returned since . . . since the last time I was here with you."

She blew out a long breath and sat again. "You might as well join me."

August did so, having not a clue why he did so.

CHAPTER EIGHTEEN

AUGUST TOOK A seat beside Lady Georgina, having no idea what they might discuss.

It surprised him that they sat in companionable silence for several minutes. He closed his one good eye, aware of her body heat next to him, that subtle scent of roses which always clung to her tickling his nostrils. This wasn't reality. It never could be. But for a few brief moments, he was truly content.

Finally, she broke the silence. "I just posted a letter to Mirella."

August opened his eye, ashamed he was only now realizing he had not seen Lady Mirella at any of the *ton* events which he had attended.

Lying, he said, "I know she has not been in attendance this Season. Did she change her mind about making her come-out with you?"

She sighed. "It was a twist of fate which made the decision for her."

Lady Georgina went on to explain how she, her sister, and mother had been strolling along the Serpentine in Hyde Park and how, due to the slick ground, Lady Mirella had slipped and fallen, breaking a bone in her forearm and also her elbow.

"I know the elbow, in particular, can be a painful bone to

break," August noted. "I had more than one of my men break theirs during battle."

"I have stopped myself from asking you, but what is battle truly like? As a civilian, I cannot begin to imagine it." She bit her lip. "And I am also ignorant of the politics behind it. This war has gone on for so long. It seems it has been raging on my entire life, and yet I understand so little about it."

He ignored delving into the causes of the war and merely said, "Officers receive more training than the average soldier. We are to keep our heads at all times, especially in the heat of battle. Frankly, there are many tedious hours that run over days. Even weeks. And then, swift orders come down, and the carnage begins in earnest."

"Who makes the decision on when to fight?" she asked, and he saw she wasn't merely being polite. She truly seemed interested in knowing the answer.

"It goes to the very top commander. In my case, being stationed in Portugal and Spain, that meant Wellington. The army is organized regarding its ranks. There were a few times I was allowed into Wellington's tent in order to see the battle plan and directly hear what our orders would be. An officer of my rank, that of captain, would lead men into battle. We have infantry, which consists of foot soldiers, and the cavalry, which ride their horses into battle."

The thought of horses caused him to shiver, the memory of being pinned under one flooding him with a sudden swiftness that stole his breath, and he shuddered.

Lady Georgina placed her hand atop his. "I am sorry I asked. I should not have been so forward as to do so. I have brought up terrible memories for you."

"I have never spoken to anyone about them," he admitted, not daring to look her in the eye. "I took risks. Risks that almost always paid off. The day I was injured, though, it was a series of unfortunate events which I could not have prevented, much less protected myself from."

He grew quiet, drawing strength from her hand against his—and decided he wanted to tell her what had happened to him.

"I was leading a charge. We had engaged with the enemy twice the day before and were weary from those encounters. We were outnumbered, as well, but that had never stopped Wellington from being aggressive on the battlefield. Cannons fired all around us. Soldiers shot wildly, some bullets finding a target. Others fought in close proximity, hand-to-hand combat with their bayonets."

This time, it was Lady Georgina who shuddered. "I cannot imagine being as close to my enemy as you and I are at this moment. Using my bayonet on human flesh. Being stabbed to death must be a terrible way to go."

"I feared on that last day that would be my fate," he said quietly. "A horse charging by me was struck by a bullet, its rider tossed over its head. The horse fell." He paused and then added, "On me."

He heard her quick intake of breath and finally faced her.

"You were trapped beneath that horse, weren't you?" she asked astutely.

August nodded. "I was pinned. Helpless. I lost the pistol I carried but held fast to my saber. Ensnared, I was confronted by a French foot soldier. He was not going to stab me and be done. He wanted to slowly slice me to ribbons. Cause me to suffer in the worst way."

Her hand tightened on his damaged one.

"With his first strike, I threw up my arm to protect myself. That was when I lost the fingers. The pain was greater than anything I could have imagined. While I cradled my ruined hand to my chest, he struck again. You are witness to the results of that second blow."

Instead of pity, he saw sympathy in her eyes.

"You must have escaped, or you wouldn't be sitting here with me now."

"Fortunately, one of my men saw my predicament and

rounded back to rescue me. When the Frenchman raised his saber again, my man ended his life."

"You owe your life to this soldier."

He nodded. "I do. And to the others who came to my rescue. They managed to lift the horse enough to pull me out. Took me to the makeshift hospital. That was the last time I fought for crown and country. I was told I was not fit to continue as an officer, and so my commission was sold for me while I was fighting for my very life."

August swallowed. "A majority of men do not die from the wounds they receive on the battlefield. It is the infection which sets in which kills so many. I was one of the lucky ones who managed to escape that horrible fate."

His gaze met hers. "There have been countless times, though, when I wished I had not survived."

Lady Georgina squeezed his hand again. Then she lifted it to her lips and pressed a soft kiss against the stumps where his missing fingers had once been. The gesture moved him greatly, and his throat swelled with unshed tears.

She returned his hand to his lap, saying, "I have worried about such trivial things my entire life. Whether to buy a blue ribbon over a pink one. If I should practice Bach instead of Mozart. Deciding how to arrange a group of flowers. Hearing what you have gone through makes me see how silly my life truly is."

"Do not belittle yourself and any concerns you have had, my lady. You are operating with the sphere of your position in society. But what of Lady Mirella?" he asked, wanting to move away from the war. "Is she healing well?"

"I believe she is. She will have to wear the hardened plaster two months, perhaps even longer. It makes her slightly off-balance, and she was forbidden to dance because of that reason. If there is anything Mirella enjoys more than dancing, I don't know what it is. She was not willing to compromise and appear at this Season and not be able to dance. Speaking of dancing, I see you are doing more of it, my lord. Perhaps you are seeing not everyone is repelled by your appearance and that there are good women out there."

"I believe my title and wealth are helping more than a few compromise themselves by dancing with me," he said lightly. "Perhaps, after all, someone will agree to be my marchioness. Changing topics, he said, "I just had a visit from Lord Blankenship before I came here."

"That is wonderful. You should start seeing your friends more often."

"Blankenship is one of the best men I have ever known."

August paused, searching her face for answers. "I thought at one time that the two of you might suit."

"And now?" she asked, seemingly holding her breath.

"He indicated that is not the case."

She expelled her breath. "I find Lord Blankenship to be a very fine man indeed. He is simply not the man for me, however. We can be friends—but nothing more than that."

Lady Georgina fell silent a moment, looking nervous. Finally, she asked him, "Are we friends, my lord?"

"No, my lady. I cannot be your friend."

Her face filled with distress. "Why?"

"Because friends do not wish to do this."

August lowered his lips to hers, grazing them lightly. As he did, her hand tightened around his. He brushed his lips against hers, thinking he could die happily having done so. He moved his mouth to the roundness of her cheek, kissing it. Her soft temple. Moving to her ear, his teeth tugged on her lobe, and he sensed her shiver.

She released her hold on his hand, framing his face and bringing his lips back to hers. She was the one kissing him now, having learned from their previous encounter what to do and what he liked. He allowed her to take the lead now, enjoying the feel of their mouths together.

Then she used her tongue to tease open his mouth, hers

plunging inside, seeking something from him that he was afraid to give her. Still, this opportunity to kiss her would never occur again, and so August decided to make the most of it. His hands went to her waist, and he lifted her into his lap, his arms steadying her. Her hands remained on his face, her thumbs stroking his cheeks as she continued to kiss him.

He could no longer hold back and became an active participant in the kiss. His tongue stroked hers, and he heard her contented sigh.

They continued to kiss deeply, and his hand moved up and down her slender back. He wanted so much from this woman and yet knew it would be wrong to take anything more. The discipline instilled in him, which he had been so proud of his entire life, crumbled, though.

August wanted to make a memory with her which would last a lifetime. He slipped a hand beneath her gown's hem, slowly massaging her shapely calf. She must have enjoyed his touch because the kiss intensified. He worked his way up to her knee and then danced his fingers along her thigh, finally reaching his destination.

He ran a finger along the seam of her sex, causing her to gasp into his mouth, breaking their kiss. He gazed into her eyes, seeing desire—and yearning—in them.

"I am going to touch you," he told her, low and rough. "You will let me. You will like it."

She nodded in understanding.

August thought to kiss her again and then decided he would rather gaze upon her as he brought her tremendous pleasure. He was most skilled at bringing a woman to orgasm this way. At least he had been years ago during his carefree bachelor days.

He caressed her intimately, watching her wet her lips as he did. She wriggled a bit in his lap, and he pushed a finger slowly inside her. Her eyes widened in surprise, and then her lips curved into a smile.

"Ooh. That feels . . . so good."

"Give me time and it will feel the best you have felt in your entire life," he boldly declared.

He continued touching her, caressing her, another finger joining the first, stroking her deeply. He listened as her breathing increased rapidly. She whimpered. Moaned. Writhed beneath his touch.

August sensed she was about to peak and knew it would be disastrous if they were overheard, so his mouth seized hers again, his tongue imitating the motion of his fingers.

She climaxed, shuddering violently, gasping for breath. He broke the kiss and watched her face as she moved her hips against him. Finally, she stilled in his arms, and he withdrew his hand from her.

When she opened her eyes, he saw her dazed look. "That was incredible. The most . . . moving experience of my life."

She leaned toward him and pressed a soft kiss against his lips. Withdrawing, she added, "I am beginning to see what Pippa means and why she is so satisfied in her marriage to Seth."

Talk of marriage frightened him. August wanted this woman desperately, but he would be a gentleman and not tie her to him, ruining her life. Easing her off his lap, he set her on the bench beside him, lowering and smoothing her gown.

Standing, he said firmly, "This must stay between us, Lady Georgina."

"I understand, Lord Edgethorne. Will you be at tonight's musicale?" she asked.

"It is a possibility," he said, having already replied he would attend, but not certain if he should after what had just passed between them. If anything, August needed to put further distance between himself and Lady Georgina.

She rose. "Then I hope to see you there, my lord." Looking hopeful, she added, "And perhaps we could meet here at noon tomorrow. I think it would be a lovely day for a picnic."

Picnicking with this beauty was the last thing he should be doing, yet all his willpower dissolved.

"Yes," he agreed. "Allow my cook to provide the food for us."

"Then if I do not see you tonight, I will again at noon tomorrow," she said. "Goodbye, my lord."

August watched her walk away, fighting the urge to chase her down and kiss her all over again. He realized what a fool he had been.

It had been staring him in the face this entire time—and he had ignored it—until now.

He was in love with Lady Georgina Strong.

CHAPTER NINETEEN

A UGUST WAS AT war with himself. Deep inside, he knew he should not attend tonight's musicale. Yet his growing feelings for Lady Georgina prevented his rational side from claiming victory.

He was in love with her. He wanted to be around her night and day. He also knew nothing lasting would come of his feelings. They were still at odds on the type of marriage they wanted. She was of a mind to have a loving husband who doted on their children, while he—though feeling a bit more welcomed in recent social outings—still felt the stares of a strong minority in Polite Society. A marriage of convenience would suit his purpose, allowing him to keep his deathbed promise to Peter, and still retreat from the world of the *ton*.

He had actually enjoyed the company of some of the women he had met at the social events of the past month. True, none of them had the inner and outer beauty of Lady Georgina, but they had the good breeding he was looking for in a spouse. He should pursue one of them.

And yet he allowed his valet to dress him to attend Lady Nesbitt's musicale this evening, strictly for the sole purpose of seeing Lady Georgina Strong.

Venturing downstairs, Redding approached him, presenting

him with a note.

"This came for you a few minutes ago, my lord. It is from His Grace, the Duke of Seaton."

Seaton was one of those men who had welcomed August into Polite Society, and he was growing fond of the duke. He was also finally renewing old friendships and acquaintances. Perhaps that was what gave him the sliver of hope that he might actually find his place within the *ton*.

Breaking the seal, he skimmed the contents, seeing that Seaton asked if he wished to ride in their carriage with them to Lady Nesbitt's musicale.

Folding the note, he returned it to his butler, saying, "I have no need of my carriage tonight, Redding. I will be accompanying Their Graces to the event."

The butler gave him a pleased smile. "Of course, my lord. I will notify the coachman of your plans."

He left his townhouse and cut through the gate which allowed him to allow the small garden in the center of the square. This place held treasured memories for him now because of the two times he had been here with Lady Georgina.

He found the gate leading him to the other side of the square, where the ducal carriage stood in front of Seaton's townhouse. August went to the door and knocked, being admitted by the butler.

"Glad you could make it, Edgethorne," the duke said, moving toward August to shake his hand. "We are simply waiting for the ladies to appear. They should be here any moment now."

Movement caught his eye, and he saw Seaton's wife descending the stairs. She glowed. He did not know if it was because she was increasing, or if it was the love she held for her husband shining from her eyes. Perhaps both.

The dowager duchess followed her, a very attractive woman. He believed if she truly wished to wed again, she would have her choice of husbands, based upon the flock of men he had seen gathered around her at *ton* events.

He greeted both duchesses and then that odd prickling sensation filled him again. The one which told him Lady Georgina was nearby.

Glancing toward the staircase, he saw her gracefully descending the stairs. Her dark hair was swept into a simple chignon, allowing her beauty to shine. Her gown was an iced blue shade, the faintest of colors, and he knew it would enhance her cornflower blue eyes. He had noted each of the Strong siblings he had met possessed the unusual eye color and wondered if their other siblings did, as well.

He couldn't help himself and stepped toward the staircase, holding out a hand for Lady Georgina to take as she reached the bottom. She wore a pleased expression.

"It is very good to see you, Lord Edgethorne."

"His Grace offered to share his carriage with me this evening so that we might all go together."

A hint of color splashed across her cheeks. "That is a lovely idea."

August led her to the others, and they left the foyer, going to the ducal carriage. He handed up Lady Georgina and then did the same for her mother and sister-in-law. Nodding to Seaton, he allowed the duke to enter the carriage before August himself finally did.

"Lady Nesbitt is known for her musicales," the dowager duchess informed them. "Why, at one of her events, I heard an Italian soprano who had the most angelic voice. I do not believe I have ever heard such a talent before or since."

"I do wish I could sing," Lady Georgina said. "At least I play well." She looked to August, who sat opposite her. "Lord Blankenship told me that you were quite the pianist in your youth, my lord."

"Yes, I enjoyed playing quite a bit. After having heard you play, my lady, I understood that I was technically very skilled. You, on the other hand, possess not only the talent and skill, but you also draw from deep within your soul as you interpret the music. It is what I admire most about your playing."

"Thank you," she said, smiling at his compliment.

"I received the invitation to the ball you are holding," August said conversationally, thinking he should draw the others present into their conversation.

The duchess chuckled. "His Grace and I may be hosting this ball, but it is Her Grace who has planned everything."

The dowager duchess shrugged. "I have always enjoyed social gatherings, including planning them. As the Duchess of Seaton, my husband expected us to hold regular events, both in town and at Shadowcrest. I am proud to say they were some of the most talked about within the *ton*. In a good way, of course," she added, smiling.

"I cannot imagine the effort it must take to organize a ball," he said. "Why, deciding what food to serve in itself would be a monumental task."

"It does take quite a bit of time and effort," the dowager duchess agreed. "Much thought goes into the dishes served, as well as the decorations and choice of musicians."

August smiled at her. "I would say you would compete handily with the great Wellington himself, Your Grace, regarding planning and implementing things. He might have planned and executed entire military campaigns, but I believe you might show him a thing or two about organization."

"I rather like that idea. Planning a ball being compared to planning a military campaign. I hope all will go well."

"It will, Mama," Lady Georgina told her mother. "And James and Sophie will reap the benefits of all your efforts, along with myself."

They arrived at Lady Nesbitt's residence and entered. Because of the nature of the event, no receiving line was in place. Guests were directed to the ballroom, where chairs had been arranged in a boxed shape. Within the square were seats for the musicians. A harp and pianoforte also stood within it.

Lord Blankenship joined them, greeting everyone in their

party, and then saying, "Edgethorne, I have a few gentlemen I would like you to meet."

"Will you excuse me?" he said to the others, following his friend.

August wanted to sit with Lady Georgina this evening, and he hoped stepping away would not prevent him from doing so.

"I am delighted to see you with Seaton and his party," his friend said.

"His Grace was kind enough to invite me to join them in their carriage this evening."

Silas cocked an eyebrow at him. "Hmm."

He was introduced to the two gentlemen, one whom he recalled slightly from their Eton days, the other one new to him. He was grateful he received a better reception from most others these days. True, his sudden appearance at that first ball had stunned Polite Society, and the gossips had made quick work of him. As time marched on, however, he was finding more and more that others were accepting him.

If they accepted him, could they accept him with Lady Georgina as his wife?

He enjoyed a good quarter-hour of conversation with the three men, and then the musicians moved to the center of the square, causing the guests to begin to seat themselves.

His friend leaned close and quietly said, "Go to her. I know you want to."

"Thank you," he said gratefully, bidding the other two men a good evening.

August had kept Lady Georgina in sight the entire time he had been away from her, and he quickly made his way in her direction again.

Once he joined her, he asked, "Might I sit with you this evening, my lady?"

"Yes, my lord," she said demurely, a twinkle in her eyes.

He offered her his arm, and the Seatons followed them. He noted the dowager duchess already sitting beside a distinguished-looking fellow.

They moved into their row and took their places, watching as their hostess came to stand in the middle of the square.

Lady Nesbitt was known to August, having been a hostess everyone had appreciated for decades. The countess was probably approaching sixty, but she was still a handsome woman. She had been widowed about a decade earlier, but it had not stopped her from holding musicales at her townhouse.

"I am afraid I have a bit of bad news to share with you," she began. "We are to be entertained by a famed German opera singer this evening, Fraulein Maier. Unfortunately, Fraulein Maier has been delayed."

A murmur rippled across the crowd, and August assumed the musicians who were to have accompanied the singer would merely play in her absence until she arrived.

"I thought to have this string quartet play for you an hour before we adjourned for a brief, late supper. By then, our guest of honor should have arrived." The countess smiled. "But then again, am I not known for doing the unusual?"

A few in the crowd chuckled, and Lady Nesbitt bowed her head in acknowledgement.

"I believe we have enough talent within this room. That a few of the young ladies present might entertain us."

August was certain Lady Nesbitt would call upon Lady Georgina to play. If she didn't, he would boldly suggest she do so.

"If you do not mind, there are three of you I would like to hear play this evening. I have been fortunate to hear all of you perform in the past, and I know those gathered this evening would appreciate hearing your talent."

The countess named three women. Lady Georgina was the last of those names she mentioned.

Lady Nesbitt motioned to a woman. "Come, my dear. You may play anything you wish for us."

He watched the young woman rise and move to the piano-forte. He supposed they would be asked to play in the order the countess preferred, Lady Georgina most likely playing last.

Their first surprise performer turned out to be an accomplished musician, and August enjoyed her playing quite a bit. After a quarter-hour, she rose, the guests applauding her impromptu performance.

Next, a pretty woman in her late twenties went to sit at the harp. He had always been fascinated by those who played this instrument, having never done so himself. For a good twenty minutes, the harpist plucked the harp's strings, awarded with appreciative applause when she completed the musical number.

He turned to his companion. "You are better than the both of them," he said quietly. "You play with confidence. More than that, you play from your soul."

"I will play tonight—for you."

She rose and went to the pianoforte. August felt his heart hammering in anticipation. While he knew she played beautifully, he did not know if she would be comfortable doing so in front of such a large number of people.

But her parting words had touched him. Somehow, he knew Lady Georgina would block out all those present.

Because she played for him.

She placed her fingers on the keys and struck the first notes. Within seconds, he recognized her selection. He had never told her who his favorite composer might be, but she now played Mozart better than anyone he had ever heard.

Watching her, listening to her, a warmth rushed through August. He admitted to himself that the feeling was love. His heart soared and his blood sang because he was in love with Lady Georgina Strong.

More importantly, was he willing to change his mind—and give her the type of marriage she desired?

CHAPTER TWENTY

GEORGIE AWOKE, ANTICIPATION already filling her.

She was going to picnic with Lord Edgethorne today.

The musicale had gone even better than she had hoped it would last night. After she had played for the guests, Lady Nesbitt had encouraged everyone to go into supper. Lord Edgethorne had accompanied her, and they sat with Lord Blankenship and one of his friends, as well as two other ladies. Their table had been the most jovial in the supper room, and Georgie could see Lord Edgethorne relaxing, forgetting about his scarred appearance. He told a few witty stories, and people not only laughed at them—they responded to *him*. It was as if others were beginning to see what she had seen all along.

The man beneath the scars.

And if the marquess could see he was being accepted by more and more in Polite Society, he might wish to become a part of it instead of making a marriage of convenience and retreating to Scotland to become a recluse. She hoped beyond hope that would be the case.

Because she might have a chance to make a life with him.

She knew he had feelings for her. After the intimacies they had shared yesterday, how could he not? She lay in bed, closing her eyes, reliving those moments of pure bliss. His touch. His scent. The physical and emotional feelings he stirred within her.

Should she tell him that she loved him?

She wanted to desperately, hoping if she declared her love, he might, too. Yet at the same time, Georgie did not want to chase him away with such a bold declaration.

Oh, why did Pippa had to be gone now, of all times! She most certainly could use her twin's advice in these matters of the heart. Of course, if it were up to Pippa, her bold sister would most certainly tell Lord Edgethorne of her feelings toward him. Georgie was more reserved, the same as the marquess himself. She decided to let things continue as they had been, slowly building trust with him. If the Season ended and he had not declared for her, she just might play Pippa and offer for him. But that was still a long way off.

Georgie rang for Millie, and the maid helped her to dress. Millie chose a mint green gown, but Georgie told her to save it for afternoon, when suitors would be calling.

"I have in mind the daffodil yellow for now."

"Oh, I do like you in that gown, my lady," Millie declared. "It is so flattering, and it makes your Strong eyes even bluer."

Once dressed, Georgie ventured downstairs, seeing she was the last to arrive at breakfast. She took her seat and only asked for toast points, knowing the picnic was approaching. Fortunately, James and Sophie were busy discussing business matters, while Mama finished her breakfast, saying she had more work to be done on the upcoming ball.

"I am going to the conservatory to look at the plants and flowers," Mama told them. "The ball will be here before we know it, and I want to see what we might use."

Georgie finished her own breakfast and excused herself, going to the music room to practice for a bit. She was a bundle of nerves now and thought playing might relax her.

After playing two pieces, she went to the library and pulled a book from the shelf, heading downstairs with it tucked under her arm, saying to the footman at the door, "It is such a lovely day, I believe I will go read on the square."

He smiled at her. "Have a nice time, my lady. Enjoy the sunshine. It is a beautiful day."

As she left the house, she heard the clock chiming noon behind her. Crossing the street, Georgie entered the gate to the private garden and found Lord Edgethorne already present. He had spread out a quilt for them to sit upon the grass. On the edge was an opened hamper, and he was lifting out plates for them.

Seeing her, he sprang to his feet. "Good afternoon, Lady Georgina," he said, giving her one of his rare smiles as she set her book on the bench.

"Good afternoon, Lord Edgethorne. Might I help you?"

"No, you are my guest. I will handle everything."

Georgie went the quilt and dropped to her knees before sitting, tucking her feet to the side.

"Since it is a picnic, I believe I will remove my slippers," she declared.

"Let me assist you," he said in that low rumble of his, sending chills along her spine.

She pushed one leg straight in front of her, and he untied the ribbon with his damaged hand, using his thumb and index finger. He slid the loosened slipper off with his good one. She offered her other foot, and he repeated his actions, setting the pair on the edge of the quilt.

Placing her hands flat behind her, she lifted her face to the sun. "It is a glorious day for a picnic," she told him. "I am only sorry we are not at Shadowcrest for it. There is a lake separating our property from Lord Hopewell's. I think the only thing that can make a picnic better is to hold it by the water."

"Perhaps we should have another one along the Serpentine," he suggested.

His comment gave her hope because picnicking by the Serpentine meant being seen in public together. She had refrained from going to Hyde Park ever since Mirella's accident there, not even accepting any offers to drive in the park from five to six with a suitor, the fashionable hour to be seen.

"I would like that," she said, their gazes locking for a moment. Then he turned and finished removing what was left in the basket.

Handing her a plate, the marquess said, "I asked Cook for ham sandwiches. There are also some apples and nuts. Also, fruit tarts for our dessert."

They ate and talked as they did. He asked her questions about Shadowcrest, while telling her a little about Edgefield.

"I am still eager to see my mother's property in Scotland."

"Dalmara?" she asked. "Was that its name?"

"You have an excellent memory, Lady Georgina."

They finished their food, and she knew she couldn't stay much longer without being missed.

"Much as I am enjoying myself, my lord, I am going to need to return home. I will need to change my gown in order to receive callers, who will soon arrive."

"Has Her Grace had many suitors come to call?"

Georgie smiled. "Mama has had as many as I have had. More, some days."

"And has she made her choice as to who might become her next husband?"

"She has remained silent on that issue. Sophie has teased her about it, but Mama merely smiles mysteriously."

She longed for him to kiss her but didn't think he was going to. Leaning over, she claimed her slippers.

"Allow me," the marquess said, gallantly replacing both shoes and tying the ribbons for each.

He rose and extended his hands. Georgie took them, and he pulled her to her feet. He kept hold of her hands, squeezing them lightly, saying, "Thank you for coming to the picnic today, my lady. It has been the most enjoyable hour I have spent since I returned from war."

The marquess moved his head toward hers and softly pressed his lips against hers, holding them there a brief moment. Then he broke the kiss and released her hands.

"You better collect the book you brought," he reminded, smiling. "Else people will wonder what you have been up to."

She picked it up and said, "Will you be at tonight's ball, my lord?"

"I will." He paused and then asked, "Would you reserve the supper dance for me, my lady?"

Georgie beamed at him. "I would be happy to do so, Lord Edgethorne."

She returned to the townhouse, practically floating through the air.

⬖⬗

AUGUST FINISHED PLACING everything in the hamper and then folded the quilt he had brought for them to sit upon. Returning to his townhouse, he handed things off to the footman who answered the door. He retreated to his study to think.

As he sat, he decided he would do something he had never done before. Not even in the days before he went to war.

He was going to pay a call on Lady Georgina Strong. As a suitor.

Going upstairs, he rang for his valet, shedding his clothes so he could wear something fresh for this call. Pole seemed delighted his employer was changing clothes in the middle of the day.

"Do you know where an arrangement of flowers might be purchased?" he asked.

Since he had never been serious about any lady, he had never bothered to learn where the bouquets suitors sent were purchased.

"There are florists' shops all about town, my lord. You may also find a lovely bouquet from one of the flower cart vendors."

"Where is the nearest florist?" he inquired, thinking he would head in that direction first and stop at any vendors who might catch his attention along the way.

Pole told him, and August set out. He passed two flower carts and then stopped at a third, asking the woman standing next to it, "Can you make up a bouquet for me from flowers I request?"

"Of course, my lord. What would you choose for your young lady?"

He asked for crocuses, primroses, and snowdrops.

"Would you like them wrapped in paper or placed in a vase?" she asked.

"In paper," he told her, thinking it might appeal to Lady Georgina to arrange the flowers in a fashion pleasing to her.

The vendor placed the flowers in tissue and wrapped it. August handed her a coin and told her to keep the change.

"You are most generous, my lord."

He returned to his square, heading straight for the Seaton townhouse, and knocking upon the door. The footman who opened it seemed a bit startled to find him there but greeted him by name.

"Good afternoon, Lord Edgethorne."

"I am here to call upon Lady Georgina," he announced.

"Yes, my lord."

Powell appeared and said, "Right this way, my lord."

August followed the butler up the stairs and to the drawing room, where he was announced.

The duke and duchess were present, along with the dowager duchess, who stood speaking with two gentlemen. Lady Georgina was also engaged in conversation with a pair of men. When she spotted him, though, she excused herself and came straight to him.

Glancing about the room and seeing the numerous bouquets, he handed his flowers to her, saying, "I thought you might enjoy getting to arrange these yourself."

She gave him a brilliant smile. "I will do so right now, my lord. Perhaps you would like to help me."

She asked the butler to bring a vase and shears as August told her, "I have never done so, my lady. I think I will merely enjoy watching you put a bouquet together."

Powell returned with the vase, half-filled with water, handing it to August. Lady Georgina led him to a table. He set down the vase, and Lady Georgina placed the flowers next to it.

By now, the dowager duchess had come to them and said, "What a clever idea, Lord Edgethorne. I enjoy arranging flowers myself and have taught my daughter how to do so."

"I though Lady Georgina might enjoy putting together a display of flowers in a manner she enjoys," he replied.

Lady Georgina began adding one flower at a time, occasionally removing one from the vase and placing it in another position, snipping stems and varying the heights of the flowers. Within minutes, she had completed her floral arrangement. The others present had gathered around, watching as she worked.

One gentleman declared, "This is the best bouquet I have ever seen put together, my lady. You are most talented."

"Thank you, my lord. It is all in the choice of flowers to start. Lord Edgethorne selected three of my personal favorites, so it was easy to arrange them in a delightful fashion."

She turned away, touching August's sleeve, and he followed her to the window. They both looked down on the street below.

She said, "I think we need to dance more than once this evening, my lord."

Even he knew what she was saying and asked, "Is that wise, my lady? You know if you dance with a partner more than once, the *ton*'s tongues will wag."

Gazing up at him, she said, "Let them."

"All right," he agreed. "Then besides the supper dance, I will ask for the final one of the evening if that is acceptable to you."

Her smile caused his heart to flutter like a butterfly.

"It is more than acceptable, my lord. It is my preference on how to end the evening."

August took her hand, lifting it to his lips, brushing a tender kiss upon her fingers.

"Then I will see you tonight, Lady Georgina. I look forward to our time together."

CHAPTER TWENTY-ONE

Augusta took a sip of his coffee, looking around at the gentlemen socializing at White's just before noon. He was seated with Silas and a few others as they drank their beverages and pointed out items from the newspapers to one another.

Finally, he was finding a community. A sense of belonging with a small but loyal group of men. He had thought his life over after he had lost his eye and fingers.

But not anymore.

The past month had shown him he was still the man he had been before his tragedy. No, actually a man more in tune with himself and others. He had renewed old friendships and made a few new ones in the process. He had continued to attend *ton* events, enjoying himself immensely, because of the time he spent with Lady Georgina Strong.

The ball given by the Duke and Duchess of Seaton would be held tonight, and August had decided he would offer for Lady Georgina at that time.

Because he loved her.

He believed she, too, loved him, though neither had voiced their feelings toward one another. He could feel it, though, in every glance. Every touch. Every stolen kiss. And it was right. *She* was right. Love made all the difference. He would be the husband she wanted. A loving father to their children. After having spent time around the Strongs, his gut told him that family was everything.

And he couldn't wait to start one with the woman he knew was his soulmate.

August decided he should speak with Seaton and seek the duke's permission for Lady Georgina to become his marchioness. He was having tea with the family this afternoon and decided he would pull Seaton aside and discuss the matter with him. He had no doubt the duke would allow the match for his sister.

Several times a week, he had met her in the private gardens, something they did for an hour each day at noon if they both found themselves free. They had had many wonderful conversations on all matter of topics. Lady Georgina was bright and curious, and he knew he would never become bored with her. His foolish notion of a marriage of convenience had flown out the window. August wanted a true marriage with his bride, a partner in life.

He finished his coffee and bid his companions farewell, deciding to stop at a bookshop for a few gifts to present to those at tea today. Walking a few blocks, he entered the shop and quickly found a book on India for Lady Georgina. She was continually seeking materials to inform her more about her twin's trip around the world, wanting to know what Pippa was experiencing as she called at different ports.

For the Duchess of Seaton, he decided upon a new atlas. The businesswoman had ships sailing all around the world, and August thought she would enjoy having this reference at her office.

It proved more difficult to select a book for the Dowager Duchess of Seaton. He did know she enjoyed arranging flowers, and so he spoke to a clerk, asking if they had any books on that topic. The clerk pointed him to an area, and August went down the rows of shelves, skimming titles. Finding one that looked promising, he pulled it from the shelf and opened it.

Then he heard the voices coming from a row over and recognized the sultry tones of one of the speakers. He couldn't put a name to her, but he definitely knew her from his past, when he had bedded a good number of women before he went to war.

The woman and her companion were gossiping about a couple who had been discovered kissing at a garden party two days earlier and how the gentleman had extended an offer of marriage. August supposed if the man liked the woman enough to kiss her, he should wed her, helping keep the young lady's reputation from being in tatters.

He went back to the book, flipping a few pages, disregarding the women's conversation.

Until he heard Lady Georgina's name come from the mouth of his former lover.

August stilled, holding his breath.

"It's hard to conceive Lady Georgina would attach herself to Lord Edgethorne," the sultry voice said, and both women tittered. "Though I will admit he is marvelous in bed."

"You knew him . . . in that way?" the other voice asked.

"We came together twice. Of course, that was before he went off to war. Oh, Edgethorne was a magnificent lover. Such a pity he looks as he does now."

"Do you think he has already bedded Lady Georgina?"

His ex-paramour laughed throatily. "I am certain of it. He must have, else why would she even have anything to do with him? Oh, the things that man can do. I suppose in the dark, she doesn't have to see those hideous scars."

"But Lady Georgina is the most beautiful woman making her come-out this Season," reasoned the other woman. "She could have her choice of any suitor."

A sniff sounded. "It is too bad she will be trapped in a marriage to a monster. She will never be the leader of Polite Society she could be if she marries Edgethorne. Why, who would even let their children be around the Edgethorne ones? The marquess would certainly frighten little ones, especially his own. I can hear their screams now. 'No, Papa, no! Don't come closer!'"

The women laughed merrily and then moved on as August found himself unable to move. Hurt washed over him. Then anger. Then a deep sadness.

He was keeping Lady Georgina from her full potential. She could rule Polite Society with her goodness and kindness. She could wed any gentleman she chose of any rank and would still sparkle more brightly than the largest diamond.

August had fooled himself. True, some gentlemen within the *ton* had accepted him, but there would always be that element which gossiped about him. He wanted better for Lady Georgina.

Because he loved her.

He must end things between them now. Leave London. And never come back.

Woodenly, he went to the clerk and purchased his books. He would send them with a note to the Seaton household, saying he had been called away unexpectedly on pressing business, and inform them he would not be returning for the rest of the Season. Yes, it would be best to let them all know in this way. It would keep him from having to face Lady Georgina. August knew it was cowardly, but he had no willpower when he was around her. One look at her, and he would be kissing her and asking her to be his forever. It was best to cut ties in a distancing manner. She would be hurt, but so much of the Season still remained. With him gone, he prayed she would open her heart and find someone worthy of her.

August returned home, carefully composing the note. He rang for a footman and asked that the note and packages be delivered to the Duke of Seaton's household at a quarter until four this afternoon. He almost called the footman back as desperation filled him, knowing he was ending all chances for his future happiness. But it wasn't his happiness at stake. It was Lady Georgina's, and August refused to drag her into the mud with him.

He would return to Edgefield and find some young miss in

the neighborhood who would enjoy being propelled to the level of marchioness. She would be delighted at her position in Polite Society and the wealth which would accompany it. Marrying a local would allow her to remain close to her family.

As for him, he would get an heir off her as quickly as possible and retreat to Scotland. Dalmara and solitude awaited him. It would be a lonely life, but he would live on the memories of the sweet times he had spent with Lady Georgina. As all fool's dreams must end, he had been jolted awake to reality. His would be an empty life without Lady Georgina Strong in it, but August knew his actions were for the best. He was willing to sacrifice his happiness in order to give the woman he loved the chance to make a good life and good marriage for herself.

EXCITEMENT RAN THROUGH Georgie as she readied herself for tea. They had not been at home today for visitors to call since the ball her brother and sister-in-law were hosting was being held this evening. It had still not kept the many bouquets from arriving, both for her and Mama.

Georgie wondered what Mama's plans might be regarding her future. She had proven to be quite popular throughout the entire Season, with numerous suitors appearing, trying to woo her. Mama was pleasant to all, but Georgie didn't think her mother had formed an attachment with any of them.

She had wanted that for Mama. Her mother had been forced to wed the Duke of Seaton all those many years ago, and while she would say her children were the light of her life, it was time Mama enjoyed a life—and love—of her own.

James and Pippa had both wed for love, and Georgie knew now she would do the same. Over the last month, when Lord Edgethorne had seemed to let down the walls he had hidden behind, their relationship had grown in strength. It was based upon a firm friendship, and yet she also understood the physical aspects to be explored were something they both wished to do sooner rather than later. In fact, Georgie had arrived at the conclusion that Lord Edgethorne would offer for her this evening on the night of the ball held in her honor.

She thought he might go to James first, though, seeking permission. Because of that, Georgie went to her brother's study a quarter-hour before tea was to begin. She knocked at the door and heard him call, "Come," entering and then closing the door behind her.

"Is it teatime already?" James asked. "I had told Powell to come and fetch me."

"No, you still have a quarter-hour, but I was hoping I might steal a portion of it."

James set down his quill and leaned back in his chair, pillowing his hands behind his head. "I always have time for my sisters," he told her with a smile. "What is on your mind, Georgie?"

"You know I have been seeking a love match, and I believe I have found one, James."

He lowered his arms, sitting forward in his chair. "And might it be the Marquess of Edgethorne who has claimed your heart, Sister?"

Georgie nodded. "I love him, James. I think I may have from the first time I set eyes upon him."

Her brother looked at her, his expression serious. "You have always seen the man beneath the scars, Georgie, unlike many others in the *ton*. While I enjoy Edgethorne's company a great deal, I want to make certain you know what you are getting into."

She frowned. "What do you mean?"

James hesitated a moment and then said, "There will always be that portion of Polite Society which will gossip about him, Georgie. And that means you would be included in that gossip if you become his marchioness."

"You yourself have been the victim of gossip, as has Sophie," she reminded him gently. "You are a duke, James, and you wed a woman who is not only a businesswoman, but she runs a shipping empire. Sophie does the job of ten men, and yet she still is a gracious hostess and loving wife to you. Do you—or Sophie— care about any gossip?"

A slow smile spread across her brother's face. "Not one whit," he admitted. "We love one another. Even if all of Polite Society turned their backs on us, we would always have each other. That is all that matters."

She nodded empathically. "And that is all that matters to me, as well, dear brother. I love Lord Edgethorne, and I believe he returns my affection. I have a suspicion that he may offer for me tonight, knowing what a special night it is for our family. He is, in many ways, a conventional man, and I suspect he will come to you to ask for your permission for us to wed."

James beamed at her. "I will not give him my permission, but rather, my blessing. Edgethorne is the best of men, and he if makes you happy, Georgie, then I will do all I can to support this match."

She rose and went to him, embracing him. "Thank you, James. That means the world to me. I am so glad you have come home to us after being gone for so long, and I know you and Edgethorne will become the best of friends."

"Let's not leave Seth out of things. Once he and Pippa return to England, I am sure Seth will be happy to welcome Edgethorne into our growing family."

"Pippa told me to follow my heart, and that is what I have done, James. My heart led me to Lord Edgethorne. Oh, I am so happy!"

"Then you will only be happier when we make the announcement. If he offers for you at tonight's ball before supper, let me know. I will announce the news to our guests at that time."

"I suppose we should go up to tea," she told him, a glow within warming her. "Lord Edgethorne might already be here."

A knock sounded, and Powell entered, bearing a few packages and a note.

"These arrived just now, Your Grace. They come from Lord Edgethorne," the butler said.

Powell handed the letter to James, along with two of the three parcels wrapped in brown paper. The third he handed to Georgie.

"Thank you, Powell," she said, looking down and seeing her name written across the front in Lord Edgethorne's familiar writing. Looking to James, she said, "I believe it is a book."

Her brother said, "These feel like books, as well. They are for Sophie and your mother. Shall we take them up to tea and then read this note from the marquess?"

"Of course," she said, linking her arm through his.

They made their way to the drawing room, where the others were gathered. A maid rolled in the teacart, and Mama nodded to Sophie, who began to pour out for them.

As they sat, her brother said, "These came from Lord Edgethorne."

He distributed the packages, and Georgie said, "Shall we open them one at a time and see what Edgethorne has sent us?"

"I will go first," Mama volunteered, tearing the brown paper, and lifting the book from it. "Oh, my. It is a book on flower arranging. How very thoughtful of the marquess to select a book regarding a topic I thoroughly enjoy."

"I will go next," Sophie said, opening her rather large gift, and then squealing in delight. "It is a new atlas! Oh, this will be a wonderful reference for my office. Ours is outdated, and I have had to rely on reports from my sea captains. This will come in ever so handy. I cannot wait to thank Lord Edgethorne for his thoughtfulness."

Sophie set aside the atlas. "You go, Georgie. Let us see what the marquess has gifted to you."

She tore open the package. Her eyes widened as she smiled. Holding the book up, she said, "It is a book about India. You know I have been reading about the various places Pippa and Seth are seeing, but I have yet to read anything regarding India."

Hugging the book tightly to her, she suddenly realized Lord Edgethorne should have been here by now. That he should have brought these gifts in person. He also had not appeared in the gardens at noon today. An uneasiness filled her, and she turned to James.

"Lord Edgethorne sent a note along with his gifts. Perhaps he knows we are all busy with preparation for tonight's ball, and that is why he decided to miss tea with us this afternoon."

"Open the note, James," Georgie commanded tonelessly, worry consuming her.

Her brother broke the seal and unfolded the letter. He skimmed it, a frown creasing his brow.

"What does Lord Edgethorne say?" Mama prodded James.

Her brother folded the note and said, "He sends his regrets for missing tea this afternoon." James paused and turned to Georgie. "He also writes that he has been called away on unexpected business."

"Did he say what kind of business?" asked Sophie.

James looked grim. "No, but he does reveal that he will be gone for the remainder of the Season."

The words were like a knife to Georgie's heart. All her hopes—all her dreams—seemed to crumble in an instant. Lord Edgethorne did not love her, and he hadn't the courage to tell her to her face. He had led her on, making her believe they had a future together. That future, which she had once thought so bright, immediately turned bleak.

Knowing the color had drained from her face, Georgie stood, clutching her book to her breasts. "If you will excuse me, I am in no mood for tea."

Head held high, she crossed the drawing room, knowing the eyes of the others were upon her and that they had questions which she had no answers for.

Georgie made it to her bedchamber, the one she had shared

with her beloved twin for so many years. She closed the door and locked it, flinging herself onto the bed, weeping for a life with a man which would never occur.

CHAPTER TWENTY-TWO

A FIRM KNOCK sounded upon the door.

Georgie didn't move.

"Georgie, open the door now," Mama said firmly.

Reluctantly, she pushed off the bed and went to the door, turning the lock. Immediately, the door opened. Her mother hurried inside and closed the door, concern written on her face. Though Georgie had thought she had shed every tear within her, she broke out in new sobs, falling into her mother's arms.

"There, dear, it is all right," Mama said, her tone soothing as she stroked her daughter's hair. "Weep if you wish."

She did. Hard, heaving sobs erupted as her mother guided her to the window seat. Mama sat, pulling Georgie's head into her lap. She cried for some minutes, Mama smoothing her hair, allowing her to cry.

Finally, the tears subsided. She sat up.

"Does it hurt?" Mama asked gently.

"Terribly," she admitted. "I have never been in love, Mama. And now Edgethorne has stomped upon my heart. I am so terribly sad, but I am also angry at him."

"You should be. He trifled with you, dearest. What I do not understand is why. It seems so out of character for him."

Georgie bit her lip. "I think so, too. Oh, Mama, we have spent so many hours in conversation. I thought we knew everything about one another. He has even talked to me about the war and how his injuries came to be."

Mama squeezed Georgie's hand. "Then he trusted you quite a bit in order to share that horror with you."

Her eyes brimmed with fresh tears. "My heart aches. Truly aches, Mama. Can a person die from a broken heart?"

"No. You only wish you could."

She recalled what her mother had shared with her and Pippa before her twin wed. How Mama had once loved a boy before her marriage, a lowly baron's son. Her parents had grand ambitions for their daughter, though, and had forced Mama to wed the Duke of Seaton.

"How did you survive after your parents made you wed Papa?" she asked.

Her mother shook her head. "At first, I thought I would not be able to go on. All I yearned for were those magical kisses with the young man I had grown to love. I had no desire to become a duchess. I was expected to obey my parents, however, and so I did as they demanded. I went to my wedding with a heavy heart, knowing I loved another. As a dutiful wife, I had to allow Seaton to touch me."

Mama's eyes filled with tears. "I did not think I would survive, so heavy was my heart, Georgina dearest. Then I discovered I was with child. Something primal in me awoke, knowing I was responsible for the life inside me. I could not mope about. I had something—someone—to live for. Slowly, my heart healed. I put aside all notions about my first and only love. Then I had you and Pippa to love. That changed everything."

"But I have no one else I wish to wed, Mama, much less have a baby with," Georgie said. "All I can think about is Edgethorne and his kisses."

She saw determination in her mother's eyes. "You must make a choice. Live in the past—or look to the future. It is one I made. I know you wished for a love match. That still could come to pass,

Georgina. Finish this Season. If no other gentleman catches your eye, there is always next year. But it is up to you now. How you will handle your situation. You can go to your ball tonight and laugh and dance and enjoy the company who has come to celebrate you.

"Or you can pine for a man who is not worthy of you."

She swallowed. "I do not think I can stop loving Edgethorne, Mama. At least not right away. But I know how hard you have worked to put together tonight's ball. And I want to go and dance the night away."

Mama kissed Georgie's cheeks. "A wise decision, dearest. Put aside your hurt for a few hours and enjoy tonight. You may be sad tomorrow. The day after. Even a month or six months after. But the sadness will lessen with time. That, I can promise you."

She hugged Mama fiercely. "I will wait for love, Mama. Even if I must wait a lifetime."

Her mother framed her face with her hands. "I do hope you will find it, Georgina." Mama kissed her brow.

"I hope you will find it, too."

"I had hot water sent up to my chambers for your bath."

Georgie smiled through her tears. "You mean, because I would not open the door to any of the maids?"

"Yes, there was that," Mama said, smiling. "But I thought we might get ready together."

She took her mother's hand, and they went to prepare for the ball. Georgie allowed herself to be bathed and dressed and fussed over. Her hair was simply dressed. She wore the locket Mama had given her about her neck.

Then James and Sophie arrived, and her brother presented her with a pair of sapphire earrings.

"We thought you needed something special to wear to tonight's ball," he told her.

"They're lovely," Georgie said, donning them and admiring her image in the mirror. She sprang to her feet and embraced them both. "Thank you so much. I am sorry for storming out from tea this afternoon."

Sophie touched her cheek gently. "It is quite all right, Georgie. You had every right to be hurt. I only hope you will put aside that hurt and enjoy tonight's affair."

Smiling for the first time in hours, she said, "I plan to."

"We should head downstairs," Mama said. "It is almost time for our guests to arrive. I want to look everything over one last time."

She accompanied her mother, first to the kitchens, then the supper room, and finally the ballroom itself.

"Oh, Mama! You have outdone yourself," Georgie exclaimed, turning in circles as she inspected the decorations. "It looks like a garden party, only brought indoors. And it smells heavenly."

Mama slipped an arm about Georgie's waist. "I am glad you approve. Shall we go join James and Sophie?"

They did so, and soon the receiving line was out the door of the townhouse. Georgie stood between Sophie and Mama, smiling brightly, welcoming their guests. Yes, her heart was heavy, and there were a few times she wanted to scream, but she kept her poise and nodded graciously, thanking all their guests for coming this evening.

"That's the last of them," James said, relief obvious in his voice. He looked to his wife. "Do you think we could simply steal away to our bedchamber now? The musicians could play. The people could dance and eat and drink."

"Without their hosts?" Sophie said, grinning at him. Slipping her hand through his arm, she added, "You are the Duke of Seaton, Your Grace. This is our last ball to attend before I give up social affairs for the rest of this Season." She rubbed her belly for emphasis. "And the next time we host a ball, we will go and kiss this little one goodnight before attending to our guests."

Georgie swallowed hard, seeing the tender look pass between the couple. She had wanted this for her and Edgethorne. The closeness. The love. The intimacy. She still could not fathom why he had dropped her so abruptly. Perhaps she might never know.

But Mama was right. She had a choice to make. To wallow in misery or choose to move forward. She had her family. Her music.

And somewhere out there, she might find true love.

Her gaze met Mama's, and Georgie raised her chin a notch. "Shall we go inside?"

Mama took Georgie's hands in hers. "I am so very proud of you, Georgina. I hope you realize that."

"I do, Mama. I am proud of you, too."

"Let us go open this ball," James said gruffly. "I shall dance with my duchess, then Georgie, then Mama. That will be all the dancing for me."

The four approached the ballroom doors. Georgie could hear the buzz of conversation. She paused, gathering her courage, and then stepped inside. Within moments, she was surrounded, gentlemen demanding she allow them to sign her programme.

"No, I will not worry about gentlemen signing my dance card this evening," she told those gathered about her. "But I do plan to dance often." She scanned those in front of her. "I believe I will dance with Lord Bottlesworth first."

The earl smoothly stepped forward and took her hand, bringing it to his lips and kissing it. "I will be happy to open the ball with you, Lady Georgina."

"Lead the way, my lord," she called gaily, thinking if she sounded happy and acted so, she might actually convince herself that she was.

They joined James and Sophie, and then Mama and one of her frequent suitors met them in the center of the room. Her brother nodded to the musicians, who had been tuning their instruments.

"Let the music begin," James called out.

Soon, Georgie was swept away in the music. She danced each number, from country dances to cotillions. Music had always been a large part of her life, and dancing was an extension of that. Despite the hurt she carried within, she put on a brave face and finally began enjoying herself.

Until she caught sight of Lord Edgethorne.

AUGUST HAD REMAINED locked in his study after sending the note and books to Seaton. He had told Redding he would not be dining tonight and had refused the tray Cook had sent to him. He sat in the dark now, peering out the open window, hearing the activity of carriages dropping off guests for the ball.

The ball where he was to have asked for Lady Georgina's hand in marriage.

He cursed under his breath for the tenth time. Or twentieth. By now, he had lost count. All he knew was that the ache inside him was so great that he wished it would swallow him whole. He had not felt so wretched nor been so despondent since he'd been injured on the battlefield. When he had lost his eye and fingers, along with his commission, August had thought life was over for him. Then he'd suffered the blow of losing Peter and had the title thrust upon him. His gloom and melancholy had deepened.

Yet meeting Lady Georgina Strong had changed all that. From the beginning, she had responded to August, the man—not August, the monster. She had seen past his wretched appearance, drawing him in with her goodness and smiles, slowly making him a part of her family. She had given him the courage to begin to speak to others. She had also given him her time and friendship, as well as beautiful, shared kisses.

"Bloody hell," he said to himself, a revelation striking him hard as lightning. "She truly *wants* to be with me."

Saying the words aloud convinced him of the fact. Lady Georgina Strong might be gentle and good, but she would not have spent the time with him that she had simply because she was nice. No, she had wanted to be in his company. She was a soft-spoken woman with a large heart, but she hadn't been nice to him simply to be nice. She cared about him.

And he had treated her like rubbish.

Oh, he was a fool indeed.

The small stirrings of hope began again inside him, like embers begging to be turned into a flame. If Lady Georgina hadn't cared for him, she would have politely let him know. Instead, she had met him daily. Kissed him. Talked about everything under the sun with him. And August had taken away her choice. If anything, it should be up to the lady to choose or reject him.

He bounded to his feet, racing from the room. "Pole! Pole! I must dress at once."

Servants appeared from all corners, his valet among them. "Of course, my lord. I set out your evening clothes in case you changed your mind."

"Then get me into them right away! I've a ball to attend. A very important ball."

August ran up the stairs, his heart beating wildly in his chest. He slowed his pace, walking to his ducal rooms, allowing Pole to undress and then redress him. He combed his hair and took a final look at himself in the mirror. The battle scars had faded, as Dr. Morrow said they would. They still were prominent, marring his once handsome appearance, but he found he could look past them.

Just as Lady Georgina had.

"I hope it is not too late," he said quietly to himself, bidding his valet a good evening and returning downstairs.

To save time, he crossed to the garden square and entered the gate, cutting through the small park and exiting on the other side. The receiving line would have ended long ago, and Lady Georgina's dance card would have filled by now. He only hoped he might speak to her for a few moments.

Knocking upon the door, a footman opened it, recognizing him.

"Good evening, Lord Edgethorne. The guests have all arrived and are upstairs in the ballroom."

"Thank you."

With a pounding heart and full of trepidation, August mounted the stairs, the music growing louder as he approached. He entered the ballroom, his eyes immediately sweeping across it, searching for Lady Georgina.

For the woman he loved.

He spotted her and watched for a moment. Her color was high as she danced to a lively tune. For a moment, he almost turned and left because she looked so happy. Apparently, she hadn't missed him at all.

Then she spied him, their gazes locking. She stopped dancing and stood still, looking upon him. Her partner tried to get her into step with him, but she turned, saying something to him and exiting the dance floor.

She came toward him, and August saw she trembled. He met her and caught her hands in his, holding them tightly.

"You . . . came. I thought I would never see you again."

"I am a bloody fool," he admitted, drawing her away from the others and toward a large potted fern, stepping beside it, hoping it might give them a bit of privacy, shielded by the large plant.

He still held her hands as she said, "You most certainly are, my lord. Why, I thought you were going to offer for me tonight. I was going to tell you that I loved you."

"You do?" he asked, his heart skipping a beat.

She frowned. "I should not have said that to such a coward."

He winced. "You are right. I was a coward. I should have looked you in the eyes and told you I could never wed you."

She bit her lip. "I suppose you found your courage and came to do so now."

"No, my lady. I came to tell you how much I love you." He raised her hands and kissed her fingers. "How I cannot live without you." He kissed them again. "How I was a dolt to think I could go on without you."

Color flooded her cheeks. "What?"

He shook his head. "I overheard two gossips going on about us in the bookshop today. I was going to offer for you tonight, but I let their vile words inside my head. I was afraid if we wed, you would grow miserable, being stuck with a man such as myself."

"Stuck with you? *Stuck* with you?" she repeated. "I *want* to be with you, Edgethorne. More than anything else. I love you—and have for ever so long."

August smiled at her. "And I love you, Georgina Strong. More than I could ever put into words."

She frowned at him. "You should have not listened to those gossips. They prattle on about James and Sophie, but you do not see it affecting them."

He continued to smile at her. "I know that now. But I wanted to give you the choice. To make a life with me or not."

She cocked her head and studied him. "You do recall I do not wish for a marriage of convenience, my lord."

"I seem to remember that," he said lightly. "I believe I was wrong about wanting one for myself. Instead, I want a woman who is my other half. My soulmate. My closest friend. My lover. My be-all and end-all." He paused. "No, not any woman. One woman alone. I want you as my wife, Georgina Strong. No other will ever do."

Tears misted her eyes. "Do you truly mean that, August? You want love? You want me?"

"It has always been you, Georgina. Always. You pulled me from the depths of despair. You made me want to live again. Not just exist, but live. With you in my life and by my side. You saw past all the ugliness and have brought light into my life."

August dropped to one knee, her hands still in his. "Will you have me, Georgina? Be my marchioness? The mother of my children?"

The smile that lit her beautiful face made his heart sing. "Yes, August. Yes. A thousand and one times, my answer is yes!"

He leapt to his feet and did something out of character. Or

perhaps it was out of character before he had fallen in love. Somehow, August believed he would be demonstrating his love for this woman in countless ways, both public and private, over the next several decades.

Taking her into his arms, he kissed her. Soundly. His kiss promised her all the things he had yet to say to her, but he knew she understood, all the same. They were meant to be together. Meant to love and laugh and create a family.

He finally broke the kiss, smiling down at her.

"I love you, Georgina Strong. And now that I have properly ruined you, you'll simply have to wed me."

She laughed merrily. "I hope you will purchase a special license, August. Because I do not think I can stop at mere kisses from now on."

He kissed her again, hard and swift. "I will see to it in the morning, my love. How soon would you like to wed?'

"We better give Mama at least tomorrow to plan the wedding breakfast. How about the day after, Lord Edgethorne? Are you free to wed that morning?"

"I will be happy to be groom to your bride," he said, his heart lighter than it had ever been.

She looked around. "Oh, dear. I believe we have quite an audience watching our every move."

August glanced about, seeing the crowd watching them. "Then we should give them something to talk about."

And he kissed her again.

CHAPTER TWENTY-THREE

GEORGIE SENSED ANOTHER presence close to her and August, and then she heard the familiar clearing of a throat, knowing her brother was nearby.

Turning her head, she broke the kiss, seeing not only James, but also Sophie standing next to them, along with Mama. Mama wore a bemused expression, while Sophie's was one of delight. James, on the other hand, looked sternly at her and August.

"If you are making a public spectacle of yourself and my sister, Edgethorne, then I expect you to do the right thing and offer for her immediately."

His tone might have sounded harsh, but Georgie saw James' lips twitch in amusement.

August faced her family, one arm still possessively about her as he offered his hand to the duke.

"I am deeply in love with Lady Georgina, Your Graces. I find I cannot exist without her in my life and by my side. With your permission, I plan to purchase a special license tomorrow morning, and we will wed as soon as possible."

Knowing how Mama spent hours planning any event she hosted, Georgie quickly said, "Do not worry, Mama. I told Lord Edgethorne we would not wed tomorrow. That you would need at least a day to put together our wedding breakfast. And of

212

course, we must send word to Shadowcrest so that Aunt Matty and my sisters and cousins can come to town for the ceremony."

August turned to her. "I know how important your twin is to you, my lady. If you wish to delay the wedding until Lord and Lady Hopewell have returned to England, I am more than willing to do so."

His words touched her deeply, moving Georgie to tears, and she cradled his cheek with her palm.

"That is a kind gesture on your part, my lord, but Pippa and Seth will be gone at least another year—if not longer. Pippa told me to follow my heart. My heart tells me to wed you as soon as possible."

He gave her one of his rare, sunny smiles, putting Georgie on top of the world.

"It is time for the supper dance, Lord Edgethorne," Mama said. "Perhaps you and my daughter would like to dance it together and then sit at the head table with us during supper."

August inclined his head. "I would be honored to do so, Your Grace."

James added, "We will make the announcement at the beginning of supper, then." Frowning at August, he added, "And you had better love my sister the way she loves you, my lord."

"I would give my life for Lady Georgina," August declared. "And I plan to love and cherish her each day more than I did the day before."

James nodded approvingly. "That is good enough for me. Come. Let us go to the center of the ballroom."

James offered his arm to Sophie, and she took it. August did the same for Georgie, and she placed her fingers lightly upon his sleeve as they followed them to the center of the room. She noticed how the ballroom buzzed with conversation and chuckled to herself.

"You find our situation amusing, Georgina?" August asked, mischief in his own emerald eye.

"I rather think I will enjoy being the topic of gossip. Just this once, though. For now, I merely want to dance with my betrothed."

The musicians struck up the waltz, and soon Georgie was being twirled about the ballroom by the man she adored. They did not talk while the music played, but their eyes spoke volumes to one another.

When the music ended, August escorted her to the supper room and the head table.

Mama was already there and said, "You make a striking couple on the dance floor. Georgina has always enjoyed dancing, my lord."

August smiled. "Then I will make certain we dance together every day, Your Grace."

James and Sophie joined them, and her brother said, "I have already asked Powell to see champagne distributed before others go through the buffet line."

She looked up and saw footmen bearing trays and guests accepting flutes.

When everyone had one in hand, James stepped forward and said, "Tonight's ball is in honor of my sister, Lady Georgina Strong, who is making her come-out this Season. I am pleased to announce that she has accepted an offer of marriage from the Marquess of Edgethorne. Lord Edgethorne is a good friend of the Strong family, and we thoroughly support this match."

Raising his flute high, James continued. "To Lady Georgina and Lord Edgethorne. May they live and love well."

"To Lady Georgina and Lord Edgethorne," their guests echoed, raising their flutes in a toast to the couple.

Georgie turned to August, who was now officially her fiancé, and tapped her flute lightly against his, saying, "To us—and our love."

They each sipped on their champagne as some guests seated themselves, while others headed to the buffet.

August turned to her and said, "I have never been happier in my entire life, and that happiness fills me now to the brim, spilling over."

She reached for his hand and clasped it. "I feel the same. Why don't we slip out for a few minutes? I am a bit overwhelmed, being scrutinized by so many."

They excused themselves and headed toward the buffet, veering off and leaving the supper room altogether. Georgie took August's hand, threading her fingers through his, pulling him along.

"You seem to have a destination in mind," he noted.

"You'll see soon enough," she told him, leading him to her bedchamber.

Opening the door, she pulled him inside and threw the lock, grabbing the lapels of his evening coat and pulling him down to her. Their mouths collided, and they kissed hungrily.

August finally broke the kiss. "We should not be here."

"Who would even think to look for us here?" Georgie challenged.

Her gaze met his and she said, "I want to be yours, August. No one but yours. Make me yours now."

"You realize what you are saying?" he asked, apparently stunned by her boldness.

"We will be wed in two days' time. I want to know all of you. Now. Do not make me wait."

A slow smile lit up his face, and he pulled her into his arms. "I will love you the best I can, Georgina. I will always be faithful to you. You saw who I was when so many others couldn't. You have made me want to live again. With you. A life which is long and full and incredibly satisfying."

Then his smile turned wicked. "Prepare to be kissed everywhere. And I mean *everywhere*."

A shiver of delight ran through her at his words. She knew what they now did together would bind them for all time. Physically. Emotionally. Spiritually.

"You will need to guide me, August. Show me the way into love. I know you have the experience which I lack."

Tenderly, he framed her face with his long fingers, his thumbs stroking her cheeks. "I have been with other women, Georgina. But I have never loved until now. Our coupling will be a new experience for me, as well."

Then he kissed her deeply, sending Georgie to the heavens.

They kissed as he removed her clothing, and then kissed even more. She would have thought, being reserved in nature, that she would feel shy standing bare before him. Instead, she stood proudly, knowing he would be the only man who ever saw her in this way.

She gazed at the perfection of his large body, placing a palm on the muscular chest, slowly gliding it back and forth, watching the muscles bunch. Her fingers moved to his nipple, one fingertip circling it. August groaned and took her hand in his.

"Do this lightly," he instructed, having Georgie rake her fingernail back and forth across his nipple.

He moaned, and Georgie felt feminine power swell within her. Suddenly, she had the urgent need to kiss him there.

And did so.

She boldly flicked her tongue across his nipple, and he clutched her shoulders, a deep sigh coming from him.

Raising her head, she asked, "Do you like that?"

"I would tell you yes, but you might not believe me, love. Let me do the same to you and see what you think."

His mouth moved to her breast, sucking on it hard, causing her core to tighten in response, filling her with desire. He then toyed with her nipple, using his tongue and teeth, grazing his teeth across it, while using his fingers to tweak the nipple of her other breast.

Georgie gasped. "Oh! That *is* rather delicious. May I try again on you?"

August smoothed her hair. "You do whatever you wish with me, love. Because I am—and always will be—yours."

Eventually, they moved to the bed, where he thoroughly explored every inch of her. His hands caressed her as his mouth kissed her soft flesh, and she felt a deep yearning build within her. She knew something magical was coming but still had no idea what it would be. Whatever happened, though, it would be wonderful. Because August was the one with her. The man who would always stand by her side.

His lips brushed against her belly, even as his fingers parted her. He slipped a finger inside her, and her hips rose. He caressed her intimately, deeply, causing that incredible tension from before to build inside her. She trembled in anticipation.

Then his mouth moved lower and suddenly, it was at her core, his tongue thrusting in and out of her. Georgie whimpered in need, her fingers pushing into his hair, holding on tightly as the sensations continued growing, pushing her to the edge. A moment came when she finally tumbled over that edge, the pleasure almost violent, rocking her body. She rode the wave of that sensual pleasure, crying out his name.

When it subsided, her fingers fell from his hair, her entire body going limp.

He rose, hovering over her, his hands cradling her face.

"I love you, Georgina Strong. I commit my body, heart, and soul to you."

She felt his manhood pressing against her slick core. He thrust inside her with one quick movement, and she drew in a sharp breath. A brief shot of pain had run through her, but it vanished as quick as it had appeared.

"Get used to me inside you, love. I know there was a flash of pain, but I promise it will never occur again. Tell me when you are ready to move."

Georgie clasped his shoulders and raised her hips instinctively.

"Ah, that felt good," August said, his voice low and rough.

"It did for me, as well," she replied. "Perhaps we should do it some more."

"What we do now is create our own dance, Georgina. A dance of love."

August kissed her tenderly and then thrust into her again several times, causing Georgie to meet each thrust.

He was right. It was like a dance. A new type of music she was eager to learn how to play.

And play, they did.

The feeling he had brought to her earlier returned and once more, Georgie took a leap of faith and tumbled over the edge of that cliff into delicious pleasure. August pumped away, his own cry of enthusiasm letting her know he enjoyed the experience as much as she had.

He collapsed atop her, kissing her thoroughly, before he rolled to his side and they faced one another.

"That is making love," he told her. "I already want more of you, Georgina. All of you. More of all of you."

She laughed in delight. "I think this will be something we do quite often," she said, smiling. "You told Mama we would dance together each day. I will tell you now, August, this is my preferred method of dancing with you."

He roared with laughter, covering her face in kisses.

Rising from the bed, he went to the table, returning with a basin of water he had poured and a cloth.

"I broke through your maidenhead, and there is a slight bit of blood. As I said before, that will never happen again."

Tenderly, he ministered to her and then helped her to redress in her ballroom finery before he slipped into his own evening clothes again.

Glancing in the mirror, she said, "Let me repair my hair. I do not want others to know we have been dancing in private," which caused him to laugh again.

August helped remove the pins which had remained in her hair, and then she twisted it again into a simple chignon, which she had worn earlier in the evening. Hopefully, none of their guests would be the wiser as to what had taken place upstairs during the supper hour.

They returned to the ballroom, seeing a few guests were

already drifting in from supper. Georgie suggested they step out onto the terrace to catch a bit of the evening breeze. They remained there until they heard the music begin, and August led her inside and danced a second time with her.

Once the dance ended, he said, "Dance with your other guests now—but save the last dance for me, love."

"I will always save the last—and best—dance for you, August."

CHAPTER TWENTY-FOUR

AUGUST WAS ON his way to Shadowcrest, the special license he'd bought yesterday tucked into his inner pocket.

Georgina had asked him to stay after the ball ended, and he had gone with her, her mother, and the duke and duchess to a small parlor. His new fiancée admitted that she was so eager to wed him, she had thought having the ceremony in town would be what she wanted, but she revealed that all Strongs wed in the chapel on Shadowcrest lands. That was her preference, and so August agreed wholeheartedly to the plan.

It did make things simpler for all. The duke and duchess had decided the ball they had hosted would be their final public event of the Season since the duchess was increasing. They had already planned to return to Shadowcrest the following day, where their first child would be born. It would also prevent Georgina's family from having to hurriedly pack and make a quick trip to London for the ceremony.

The Dowager Duchess had asked August if he would give them a day at Shadowcrest to make the wedding and breakfast preparations before he arrived. He agreed, seeing to the purchase of the special license yesterday and now driving down to Kent today. The wedding would take place tomorrow morning at ten o'clock.

It had been hard being away from his betrothed. Now that August was fully committed to a love match, he felt the need to be near Georgina. He told himself they would have a lifetime together, and a day apart shouldn't matter. It had, though. She had been constantly in his thoughts. When he had passed a bowl of roses his housekeeper had placed on a table, the scent triggered memories of being in her bed, that faint scent of roses always clinging to her skin.

He had instructed Pole to pack his things, and the valet now rode atop the carriage with the coachman. His London staff knew he would not be returning until next Season at the earliest, and the Reddings would have things well in hand during his absence. Redding had spoken up for the entire household, telling August how pleased the servants were that he was taking a bride.

The thought of soon becoming a married man made him smile. He planned for Georgina to be in his bed every night. He laughed aloud, thinking how he had thought he would be satisfied with a marriage of convenience, getting an heir in what would in effect be a business arrangement, and then retreating from the world. Now, he wanted to be alive in that world, soaking up every moment with a woman who knew him better than he knew himself.

The carriage slowed and made a turn, heading up a wide lane lined with trees. He was on Shadowcrest lands now, a place he hoped would become a second home to him and the children he and Georgina would have. The rich, green land reminded him of Edgefield. He couldn't wait to take his bride there.

And to Scotland. To Dalmara.

After some minutes, the vehicle came to stand in front of an enormous house, one befitting a duke. He saw Georgina standing in the drive, waiting for him, her beautiful face beaming as he exited the carriage. Convention be damned. He rushed to her and pulled her into his arms for a long kiss. Just the taste of her made everything right in his world.

Breaking the kiss, he gazed into those cornflower blue eyes

and said, "I have missed you, my lady."

"Not half as much as I missed you, my lord," she said pertly. "Come. The others are waiting for you. I did not want you to see so many new faces as you were besieged by questions. I told them I wanted to greet you myself first, and then they could have at you."

She linked her arm with his as his valet took charge of August's trunks.

"We are having tea on the terrace since it is such a lovely day," she said as they strolled through the impressive house.

"Tell me again whom I will see besides Their Graces and Lady Mirella."

"My youngest sister Effie. She is ten and six and a tomboy like Pippa. Aunt Matty, who is my father's sister. She never wed and had a hand in raising all of us. Then there are my cousins. Caleb is the steward at Shadowcrest. The twins are Allegra and Lyric."

"More twins?" he asked, wondering if twins might be in their future.

Georgina laughed. "They were born on the same day as Pippa and me. My aunt had given birth to two boys previously, but having twins was too much for her. My uncle wanted nothing to do with girls, and so he sent Lyric and Allegra to live with us."

"Your mother had *four* babes to raise?"

"Yes. She was a first-time mother, and the nursery held the four of us. We had one very stern and organized nanny, but Mama spent a great deal of time with us. Then she added Mirella and Effie to the nursery. It was quite full."

August stopped. "Do you hope we have a full nursery, Georgina?"

Her sunny smile warmed his heart. "Very much so. I have longed to be a mother."

"I am eager to be a father," he admitted. "It was only Peter and myself, but we were quite close. I think it would be wonderful to have a full, noisy nursery, though we might need two nannies instead of one."

They continued through the house, and Georgina said, "Miss Feathers might be present at tea. She is Effie's governess. Actually, she served as governess for all of us when she first arrived, but these days, Effie is her only pupil. She often takes tea with the family and even dines with us sometimes."

By now, they had reached a set of open French doors. Georgina stopped their forward progress.

"Just one more quick kiss, August," she said, her hands claiming his face, pulling him down to her, their lips meeting in a soft, sweet kiss.

She broke the kiss. "That's better."

They stepped through the doors, and he saw the large group gathered on the terrace, two teacarts nearby. Everyone rose, and he greeted the duke, duchess, and dowager duchess first.

Georgina's mother said, "Let me introduce you to everyone else, Lord Edgethorne," moving him toward an elderly woman with twinkling eyes.

"This is Lady Mathilda Strong, my husband's sister," the dowager duchess told August.

He took her hand and kissed it. "I am happy to make your acquaintance, my lady."

She nodded approvingly at him. "I knew Georgie would make a wise choice when she decided upon a husband. Welcome to the Strong family, Lord Edgethorne. And everyone calls me Aunt Matty. I expect you to do the same, young man."

"I am not one to upset the apple cart, Aunt Matty," he said teasingly, earning a smile from the old woman.

Next, the dowager duchess led him to two young women. He recognized Lady Mirella, with her auburn hair and Strong eyes. Lady Effie also had the same cornflower blue eyes which ran in the family, but her hair was golden.

"It is good to see you again, my lord," Lady Mirella said, the large plaster encasing much of her arm.

"I was sorry to hear of your accident, my lady," he told her. "The gentlemen of this Season could certainly have used your company. When might you be freed from your plaster?"

"The local doctor has told me another two weeks," she said, sighing. "It has been an inconvenience, and it is itching to the high heavens."

"I hope it has healed nicely," he replied.

"I am glad Georgie is marrying a military man," Lady Effie said. "I would love to hear stories of where you and your men fought, my lord. I long to travel as my sister Pippa is doing on her honeymoon now, though I doubt I will ever take a honeymoon."

He frowned. "Why not?"

"I have no wish to wed," Lady Effie declared.

"Euphemia!" the dowager duchess scolded. "Just because Lord Edgethorne is going to be family does not mean your tongue should run off with you."

"Sorry, my lord," the youngest Strong said. Then, with mischief gleaming in her eyes, she mouthed, "Not really," causing August to roar with laughter.

The dowager duchess guided him to what had to be her nieces, the twins Georgina had spoken of. Both young women had the same cornflower blue eyes, though up close he saw Miss Allegra had sable hair, while Miss Lyric's was a dark russet in color. Both twins favored one another, but August found he could easily tell them apart.

"And this is Mr. Caleb Strong, my nephew," the dowager duchess concluded.

August offered his hand to the steward, and the two men shook.

"I might have a few questions to ask you," he said. "I was in the military until recently and have now taken over my family's estate in Surrey. Actually, it isn't far from here, being on the border of Surrey and Kent."

Mr. Strong smiled affably. "I would be happy to answer whatever you ask, my lord. I have found my calling in being a steward."

"I couldn't do without Caleb," the duke said. "He keeps

Shadowcrest running like clockwork."

"Perhaps I might even come to your country estate and see it," Strong offered.

"Come and sit, everyone," the duchess said. "I have been pouring out as you have been introduced to Lord Edgethorne."

He took a seat next to Georgina and doctored his tea before saying, "It would be nice to have your opinion on a few matters, Mr. Strong. You would be welcomed at Edgefield any time."

"Please, my lord. Call me Caleb."

"I would be happy to do so, but only if you call me August." He looked around. "I hope all of you will call me by my Christian name. My family was small, and I always wanted to have many siblings. I thank you for the warm welcome you have given me today." He paused. "I know you were warned of my appearance. I hope I have not frightened any of you overmuch."

"Georgie would not have chosen to wed you unless you were a good man," Lady Effie said. "Who cares what you look like? We welcome you into our family."

He smiled at the young lady. "I appreciate that welcome, my lady."

"Effie," she prompted. "You cannot go around calling Caleb by his given name and Aunt Matty by hers and not do the same to us. Just make certain you never refer to me as Euphemia. I abhor it!" She looked to her mother. "I know it was your mama's name, Mama. I *am* happy I received her golden hair, but I am ever so glad you chose to call me Effie. Unless you are scolding me." She glanced back to August. "I am always Euphemia at those times."

The dowager duchess chuckled. "You are as outspoken as she was, my darling girl." She looked to August. "I agree with my family. At least when we are in private together, I would hope that you would call me Dinah. We enjoy the informality when we are alone."

"I am honored you would allow me to do so, Your Grace. That is, Dinah."

Teatime proved to be entertaining. August got to know his

betrothed's relatives better, even Daffodil, Effie's cat, who wandered up and jumped into August's lap. Effie assured him Daffy was quite particular regarding whom he made friends with, and she told August he had risen in esteem in all their eyes since he was so accepted by Daffy.

"What are your plans for after the wedding?" Sophie asked. "Will you return to Edgefield?"

He slipped his hand around Georgina's. "We have not really talked about our honeymoon. I would like us to go briefly to Edgefield because that is where we will spend the majority of our year."

"I cannot tell you how happy I am that Edgefield is so close to Shadowcrest," Dinah told him. "It has been terrible having Pippa half a world away from me for so many months, with so many more to come. At least this way, I can see Georgina every now and then."

"I do need to visit a property I have inherited in Scotland. It is from my mother's side of the family. It is in the Lowlands."

"Truly?" Georgina asked, anticipation lighting her face. "We could go to Scotland? Oh, I have never been anywhere. That would be wonderful, August."

"If we like Dalmara, we could visit it each year after the Season," he told her.

"I think Sophie and I are going to stick to what we did this year," James informed the group. "Attend the beginning of the Season and then when the heat arrives in June, return to Shadowcrest."

"We could do the same, August," Georgina said eagerly. "Go to the first of the Season so that we can spend time with family and friends, and then we can travel to Scotland each year." She sighed. "Dalmara just sounds like the most romantic place on earth."

"My mother always said Scotland was beautiful. I suppose we shall soon find out."

"Then let us go to Surrey and Edgefield after the wedding

tomorrow. We can stay for a few days, long enough for me to find my way around, and then journey to Scotland," Georgina suggested.

"Oh, you'll miss the house party," Lyric said.

"What house party?" Georgina asked.

"Aunt Dinah said since we did not wish to make our come-outs this year, she hoped we might compromise and allow her to hold a house party for us," Allegra said.

"When would this be, Mama?" Georgina asked.

"I was thinking of the last week in August. Most people are ready to leave the heat of London by then and escape to the country," the dowager duchess said. She turned her gaze to August. "But you will be newlyweds, August. Scotland is a good distance away. You should stay at Dalmara as long as you wish. I can always hold a house party next year, too, if James and Sophie do not mind."

"As long as you organize it, Dinah, we have no objections," James said, laughing. "Sophie will continue to work from Shadowcrest, with Mr. Barnes coming to Kent once a week to keep her apprised of business matters."

Georgina smiled at her cousins. "I am glad you two are allowing Mama to hold this house party in your honor. Who knows? Cupid's arrow might strike one—or both—of you."

CHAPTER TWENTY-FIVE

AUGUST ALLOWED POLE to bathe and dress him for his wedding day. He reflected on what his life had been like a year ago. He had still been an army officer, a captain leading his men into battle, still living a charmed life.

He had thought losing his eye and his commission was the end of his life. Instead, fate had led him along a road he never would have thought to have traveled, but it had given him a companion in life to make that journey for decades to come. August looked forward to the years ahead as he and Georgina shared a life together and created a family of their own.

Pole finished tying an elaborate knot for August's cravat and stepped back, looking pleased with his efforts. August glanced into the mirror and saw not a man marred by physical blemishes—but one who was in love.

Turning to his valet, he said, "You have done an excellent job, Pole."

"I have everything ready for the trip to Edgefield, my lord."

"Good. We will only stay there for a handful of days, and then we will make our way to Scotland, where we will remain throughout the summer."

"Scotland?" the valet asked. "Isn't it rather cold there, my lord?"

"My mother once told me the summers there are quite cool, but the beauty of the land made up for any chill you felt."

"Then I will see that we are ready to make the journey after our short stay at Edgefield," the valet promised.

A knock sounded at the door, and Pole answered it, briefly speaking with a servant before turning to August.

"My lord, if you wish, His Grace has invited you to have coffee with him before the ceremony."

"Then I shall make my way to the breakfast room," he said, tucking the tissue-wrapped brooch he had brought to Shadowcrest into his pocket.

August went to the breakfast room and found Seaton seated there, along with Silas.

His old friend leapt to his feet, coming to him, and slapping him on the back. "Are you ready for your wedding day, August?"

"What are you doing here?" he asked, his gaze turning to the duke.

Seaton merely shrugged. "I can take no credit for Lord Blankenship's presence. That is all my duchess' doing. She knew of your longstanding friendship, and she thought it would be a fine idea for Blankenship to attend the ceremony."

He smiled at his friend. "I am delighted you could come today, Silas."

"We went through a lot together as boys and young men. I hope our friendship will continue to flourish until we are old and gray, August."

The three of them sat and lingered over coffee until the butler came in and spoke to his employer.

Seaton said, "It is time for you to make your way to the chapel. A coach is available if you choose, but it is only a short walk there."

"I know exactly where the chapel is located. Georgina took me to it after tea yesterday," August said. "We will walk and leave the carriage for the ladies' use. But I do have one favor to ask of you, Your Grace."

"James," the duke prompted. "Remember, you are now family."

A warm feeling filled him as he removed the brooch from his pocket and handed it over to the duke.

"I assume you will see Georgina before the ceremony begins. If you would give this to her and ask her to wear it. It belonged to my mother."

"I will do so," the duke promised.

He and Silas left the house and walked the short way to the Shadowcrest chapel.

"It is a fine day for a wedding, August."

Looking about, he saw the blue skies with only a few scattered clouds in them. "I couldn't ask for a better day—or a better life, my friend. Will you stand with me when I make Georgina my wife?"

Silas grinned at him boyishly. "I would be happy to do so."

They entered the chapel. Georgina had not let him set foot inside it yesterday, telling him that Lyric wanted it to be a surprise for the both of them. And surprised, he was. Even Silas gasped.

"This looks like a wonderland in spring," his friend said. "Who spent all this time bringing it to life?"

"That would be Miss Lyric Strong, a cousin of Georgina's. She is known in the family for her talent with plants."

"I have a bit of an interest in gardening myself," Silas admitted. "I need to meet this cousin and talk blooms with her."

They wandered about the chapel, admiring the flowers, and then a voice called out, "Might you be Lord Edgethorne?"

He turned and saw a clergyman, accompanied by a woman whom August assumed was his wife. That proved to be the case, as the man introduced himself, telling August he would be performing today's ceremony.

The clergyman went through a few brief notes with him, and August told him that Lord Blankenship would be standing with him.

"The bride and her family should be arriving soon." The

clergyman paused and then said, "Thank you for your service to our country, Lord Edgethorne."

"I was happy to do what I could for Great Britain," he replied, recognizing for the first time that no bitterness sounded in his tone regarding his service.

"There you are," he heard.

Turning, he saw Georgina's sisters and cousins had arrived. He introduced Silas to the five, and then Mirella said, "We should go ahead and take our seats. Georgie will be here at any moment. Go stand at the altar, August. You, too, Lord Blankenship."

The two men did as Mirella asked, while Allegra sat at the pianoforte. He had learned that Mirella would have been the one to play for them, except for her injury, which kept her from practicing and playing.

Moments later, the doors opened. The duchess, the dowager duchess, and Aunt Matty entered the chapel. All three women smiled warmly at him as they took their seats. Again, August thought how much his life had changed in a year's time and how openly the Strongs had accepted him into their tightknit family.

Anticipation filled him as he gazed at the door, waiting for Georgina to make her appearance. When she did, on the arm of her brother, a rush of love for her swept through him, causing his throat to thicken with emotion.

Her gaze met his as Allegra began playing, and Georgina seemed to float down the aisle. She reached him, and her brother kissed her cheeks. The duke turned to August and offered him his hand.

"Take care of her, my friend," James said.

"I will," he promised, taking Georgina's hand, and slipping it into the crook of his arm.

Mirella had stepped forward, joining them at the altar, standing beside her sister as August and Georgina recited their vows to one another.

When the clergyman pronounced them man and wife, August turned and framed his bride's face in his hands, lowering his lips to hers for a tender, lingering kiss.

Applause sounded in the chapel, and August broke the kiss, beaming at his new marchioness.

"Thank you for the lovely brooch, August," she told him. "I felt your mother's presence as I pinned it to my gown. I am glad she was here with us today, and I am especially happy we will get to see her family's land at Dalmara."

"This is the first day of the rest of our lives together, Georgina. You loving me has made all the difference in my life."

August bent and kissed her again, hearing laughter from the others present.

"Take the carriage back to Shadowcrest," James told them. "We will all be there shortly."

Spontaneously, August swept his bride off her feet and into his arms, marching down the aisle to the cheers of her family. He reached the carriage and set Georgina onto her feet again, handing her up and then following her.

Inside the carriage, he lifted her into his lap, kissing her the entire way to Shadowcrest.

EPILOGUE

Dalmara—Scotland—July 1814

AUGUST CRADLED GEORGINA in his arms, kissing the tip of her nose.

"You always make me feel so safe and cherished, August," his wife of four years said, resting her cheek against his heart, the one which always beat for her.

He kissed her hair. "You have done the same for me, my love. Everywhere we go—Edgefield, town, or Dalmara—you create a home for us and our family."

She lifted her head, a hint of a smile playing about her lips. "Possibly our growing family."

"What?" he eagerly asked. "You are with child again?"

"I think so. I just missed my courses, but you know how regularly they come. That—and the tender breasts—are always the first sign that I am increasing."

"Yes!" he said enthusiastically. "Yes! Yes! Yes!"

August brushed his lips against hers tenderly, making love to her sweetly and gently, filled with wonder that she might be carrying another little Holt.

When she rested in his arms again, he said, "Perhaps it will be twins this time."

She sighed. "That would be lovely. We will have to wait and see, though."

"Will you tell Pippa and Seth while they are here with us?" he asked.

"I want to wait a bit. Until we know for certain. I should know before we all leave for England again." She chuckled. "Though Pippa will probably take one look at me and guess the news."

He kissed her, wanting her all over again, but knowing how she tired easily when she carried his babe.

"Why don't I have breakfast sent up to you?"

"Oh, that would be lovely," she said. "So decadent to loll about in bed. Remember, we are taking the children on a picnic at eleven o'clock this morning."

"I haven't forgotten." He kissed her again and climbed from the bed. "I will dress and have breakfast sent up to you soon. Go back to sleep, love."

Georgina burrowed into the pillow, pulling the bedclothes about her. August heard her soft snores before he finished donning his banyan, smiling to himself. His wife's snoring was one of many things that endeared her to him.

He rang for Pole and dressed, telling the valet to go to the kitchens and have Cook send breakfast up for Lady Edgethorne in an hour. He thought it wouldn't hurt to let her get a bit of extra sleep, especially since he had awakened her early for a morning dance.

After breakfasting with Seth, August excused himself, going to his study to write a final letter to Dr. Morrow, the battlefield physician who had saved his life five years earlier. After all, Morrow had seen the dejected state August was in and had told his patient to write of his life and progress after six months, a year, and even five years. He had done as Dr. Morrow had asked.

The first time he had written, he had been in mourning for Peter, having lost his brother and taken up the title of Marquess of Edgethorne. He had written from Edgefield, telling Dr.

Morrow about the country estate he had inherited and Peter's request for his brother to go to town and participate in the Season. The second letter to the physician had been sent a month after his wedding to Georgina. They had traveled to Scotland to visit Dalmara for the first time on their honeymoon, falling in love with the property, and vowing to come back to the Lowlands every summer.

Now, five years had passed. This would be the last time he wrote to Morrow. August took out parchment and dipped into the inkwell and began to compose his final letter.

Dear Doctor Morrow —

I am writing to you on what is the fifth anniversary of my darkest day, the one where I lost my eye and three fingers on the battlefield. The despair and pain I suffered that bleak day made me wish I were dead, knowing I no longer had a purpose in life, being told I was unfit to lead my men. And yet here I am a handful of years later, happier than I could possibly imagine, my purpose clear and certain.

When I wrote to you last, it was to tell you of my marriage to Georgina. She saw in me what I could not see myself, and she has been the shining light of my existence, lighting the way to a full, incredibly satisfying time as we journey down the path of life together.

We have been blessed with a girl, who is three, and a boy who will be two come the autumn. Spending time with them fills me with joy, Dr. Morrow. Pure, unadulterated joy. They are not afraid of me in the least. Their love for me is the same as their mother's—open, giving, and complete.

As I write to you, we are in Scotland, at a property we come to each summer. Scotland is a magical place, and Dalmara is a second home to us. Georgina's twin and her family come and stay with us during our summers here, and it is sheer delight to see their children and ours playing together, the cousins building shared memories.

I want to thank you, Dr. Morris. You saved my life. You kept the infection at bay. I walked away bitter and morose—but alive. You gave me the opportunity to find a new life for myself, and I count my blessings every day.

I will write no more, but I do hope now that Bonaparte has abdicated and Wellington has defeated Soult, you will finally return from your long years abroad. If you ever find yourself in London—or Kent or Scotland—my wife and I would be happy to welcome you for a long visit.

Thank God the war is finally over. I hope this reaches you and that you are well and in good spirits. Again, all my thanks.

Lord Edgeworth, formerly Captain Holt

August read through the letter and then sealed it, addressing it to Morrow. The physician had once told August that he was from Chilham, about five miles outside Canterbury. If the physician had made his way home there with Wellington's victory, August hoped this letter would find Morrow.

He left his study, giving the letter to a footman to post, and went to the drawing room, where he found Georgina, Pippa, and Seth in an animated discussion. Over the years, the couple had become not only family to August, but they both were close friends. They saw each other frequently during their time in the country, since their estates were not that far apart, and every day of the Season when in town. These trips when they all came to Dalmara, however, were quite special.

"There you are," Seth said as August crossed the room and kissed Georgina's cheek, taking a seat beside her. "It is almost time to collect the children and nannies and head to the lake for our picnic."

"I had a letter to write and post," he shared. "An important letter to a very special man. The one who saved me and convinced me I still had a good life ahead of me, despite my injuries."

He took his wife's hand and lifted it, brushing his lips tenderly against her fingers. "But it took meeting this exceptional, remarkable woman—who loved me unconditionally—to realize what is most important in life."

Tears misted in her eyes, and her palm touched his cheek. August leaned into it, savoring her light touch and scent of roses.

"We were meant to be, August," she told him. "Meant to love one another and create our family."

Gazing deeply into her Strong eyes, he said, "I love you, my sweetest, dearest love. Now and forever."

August moved to kiss his wife, knowing Seth would probably take the opportunity to kiss his own wife.

And as his mouth came down on Georgina's and he thought of the new life which grew within her, August was at peace.

About the Author

Award-winning and internationally bestselling author Alexa Aston's historical romances use history as a backdrop to place her characters in extraordinary circumstances, where their intense desire for one another grows into the treasured gift of love.

She is the author of Regency and Medieval romance, including: Dukes of Distinction; Soldiers & Soulmates; The St. Clairs; The King's Cousins; and The Knights of Honor.

A native Texan, Alexa lives with her husband in a Dallas suburb, where she eats her fair share of dark chocolate and plots out stories while she walks every morning. She enjoys a good Netflix binge; travel; seafood; and can't get enough of *Survivor* or *The Crown*.